"Presents Mexico in a darkly surrealist light: corrupt politicos, ~~...~~ dgar y' Mendieta o.. ~~.. e of . angels~~

BARRY FORSHAW, Independent on Silver Bullets

"Casts a wide net over modern Mexican life and an array of well-drawn characters, some powerful, some weak, some depraved . . . Mendoza's creation is nothing like standard pulp fiction"

JUSTIN WARSHAW, Times Literary Supplement on Silver Bullets

"A vivid glimpse into an ultraviolent world of macho posturing, unorthodox policing and ruthless criminality"

LAURA WILSON, Guardian on The Acid Test

"Essential reading"

JAKE KERRIDGE, Sunday Express on The Acid Test

"Mendoza's style is spare but fast-paced . . . As the plot moves along the reader is swept along with it. Lefty is a likeable character who has somehow managed to find a way to navigate through all the killing aided by a detachment which serves him well"

MATTHEW GEDDEN, Irish Examiner on Name of the Dog

"[Lefty is] cynical, witty and despairing, but never less than entertaining. Readers may have to occasionally check the useful cast list to remind themselves who's who. It's worth the effort"

MARCEL BERLINS, The Times on Name of the Dog

"Mendoza conveys a clear sense of life in Culiacán through the violence of the competing cartels and a simmering expectation and acceptance of corruption" Publishers Weekly

Also by Élmer Mendoza in English translation

Silver Bullets (2015)

The Acid Test (2016)

Name of the Dog (2018)

Élmer Mendoza

KISS THE DETECTIVE

Translated from the Spanish by
Mark Fried

MACLEHOSE PRESS
QUERCUS · LONDON

First published in the Spanish language as *Besar al detective*
by Literatura Random House, Barcelona, in 2016
First published in Great Britain in 2021 by MacLehose Press

MacLehose Press
An imprint of Quercus Editions Ltd
Carmelite House
50 Victoria Embankment
London EC4Y 0DZ

An Hachette UK company

A CIP catalogue record for this book is available
from the British Library

ISBN (MMP) 978 1 52940 399 2
ISBN (Ebook) 978 1 52940 400 5

2 4 6 8 10 9 7 5 3 1

Designed and typeset in Minion by Libanus Press
Printed and bound in Great Britain by Clays Ltd, Elcograf S.p.A

For Leonor

TRANSLATOR'S NOTE

Kiss the Detective is the fourth novel in a series set in Culiacán, a prosperous and sweltering city of nearly a million people and the capital of Mexico's Sinaloa state. Surrounded by desert and irrigated fields, it lies half an hour's drive from the Pacific, nine hundred kilometres south of the U.S. border, and far off the tourist track. The city's elite still thrives on commercial agriculture, but the trafficking of marijuana, cocaine and heroin has long outdistanced the sale of cucumbers and chilli peppers. This tale occurs in 2015, more than a year after Mexico's new president declared an end to his predecessor's war on drug trafficking.

CAST OF CHARACTERS

SINALOA STATE MINISTERIAL POLICE

Angelita, homicide department secretary

Briseño (Omar), commander of the Sinaloa State Ministerial Police, also known as the Commander

"The Camel", homicide department officer

"Gori" (Gorilla) Hortigosa, specialist in extracting confessions

"Lefty" (Edgar) Mendieta, homicide department chief detective

Montaño, homicide department forensic doctor

Ortega (Guillermo), head of the crime lab

Pineda (Moisés), chief of the narcotics division

Robles, homicide department officer

"Stevejobs", homicide department undercover officer

"Tecolote", police officer

"Terminator", homicide department officer

Zelda Toledo, homicide department detective, Lefty's partner

9

"*Chacaleña*", Pacific Cartel spy keeping an eye on Dr Jiménez

"*Chopper*" *Tarriba*, bodyguard and gunslinger for
Samantha Valdés

"*Crazy Mouse*", Pacific Cartel operative in Los Angeles

"*Devil*" (*Benito Urquídez*), former policeman, now bodyguard
and hitman for Samantha Valdés

Gordowski, Pacific Cartel operative in Los Angeles

"*Hyena*" *Wong*, head gunslinger for the Pacific Cartel affiliate
in Mexicali

"*Killihawk*" (*Rodrigo Méndez*), unaffiliated drug trafficker

Max Garcés, chief of security for Samantha Valdés

Minerva Valdés, mother of Samantha, widow of former
godfather Marcelo Valdés

Monge (*Frank*), Pacific Cartel point man in Tijuana

Osuna (*Víctor*), attorney, top negotiator for the Pacific Cartel

"*Pockmark*" *Long*, deceased gangster, father of young Long

Samantha Valdés, supreme leader of the Pacific Cartel, also
known as La Jefa

"*Shakes*", a deceased Tijuana-based trafficker, friend of the Flea

Wence, gunslinger and errand boy for the Pacific Cartel

Young Long, gunslinger and sidekick of Hyena Wong, son of
"Pockmark"

Dr Adame, physician in Tecate and friend of the artist Blancarte

Belascoarán Shayne (*Héctor*), Federal Police (Federales) intelligence officer based in Mexico City

"Bionic Chair" (*Jack Mahfuz*), movie extra and owner of a Los Angeles liquor-store, friend of Jason Mendieta

Blancarte (*Álvaro*), Tecate-based artist, originally from Culiacán

Bonilla, Army captain, head of the troops deployed to Virgen Purísima Hospital

"Charface", head of a network of professional assassins based in Mexico City

Chuck Beck, police academy schoolmate of Jason Mendieta

Cindy Ford, police academy schoolmate of Jason Mendieta

"Curlygirl", waiter at El Quijote, Lefty Mendieta's preferred watering hole

Edith Santos, wedding organiser, friend of Zelda Toledo

"The Elf ", professional assassin working for Charface

Enrique Mendieta, brother of Lefty Mendieta and former guerrilla living in Oakland, California

"The Flea" (*Ignacio Daut*), childhood friend of Lefty Mendieta, living in Los Angeles

Francelia Ugarte, daughter of secret agent Héctor Ugarte, caught by Lefty in *Name of the Dog*

Irene Dueñas, boutique owner, girlfriend of Leopoldo Gámez ("Polo")

Jackman, police academy instructor, retired Los Angeles policeman, also known as "Wolverine"

Jason Mendieta, son of Lefty Mendieta and Susana Luján

Jeter, F.B.I. agent based in Los Angeles

Dr Jiménez, expert surgeon at Virgen Purísima Hospital

Machado Torres (Octavio), petty thief

Mariana Kelly, deceased romantic partner of Samantha Valdés

Doña Mary de Luján, mother of Susana Luján and neighbour of Lefty's housekeeper Trudis

Señora Vicky de Meneses, member of elite Culiacán family and mother of wounded teenager

Oropeza, Army captain who directed the attack on Samantha Valdés

Dr Parra, Lefty Mendieta's psychiatrist

"Polo" (Leopoldo Gámez), fortune-teller found dead in Ecological Park

Quiroz (Daniel), star crime reporter for "Eyes on the Night" radio programme

Rodo, fiancé of Zelda Toledo

Rommel, friend of Tecate-based artist Blancarte

Rudy Jiménez, owner of Café Miró and friend of Lefty Mendieta

Sánchez, retired police detective, Lefty Mendieta's former mentor

The Secretary, a federal cabinet minister

Susana Luján, one-time girlfriend of Lefty Mendieta, mother of Jason, living in Los Angeles

12

"Trucks" Obregón, head of the Federal Police deployed to Virgen Purísima Hospital

Trudis, housekeeper and cook for Lefty Mendieta

Win Morrison, F.B.I. agent based in Los Angeles whom Lefty helped on a case in *The Acid Test*

Záizar (Enrique), professor and a regular at Café Miró

Zurita (Manlio), the new federal prosecutor for the state of Sinaloa, to whom the Federal Police in the state report

MEXICAN FOOD AND DRINK

Agua de cebada, a cold drink made from barley, sugar, cinnamon, evaporated milk and water.

Bistek ranchero, fried strips of beef with jalapeño chillies, onion, garlic and mushrooms

Café cortado, a single espresso shot with a touch of hot milk

Camarones rancheros, shrimp sautéed in olive oil with onion, garlic, serrano peppers, chopped tomato, cilantro and salt

Chamoy, a spicy savoury sauce made from pickled fruit, usually apricot or mango

Filete de res al burro negro, barbecued steak

Jícama, a sweet, starchy tuber eaten raw, usually with lime, salt and powdered chillies

Machaca, marinated beef or pork that has been rubbed with spices, pounded, dried and shredded

Pescado calabrese, fish filet broiled with onion, tomato, basil, oregano, lime juice, olive oil and white wine

Quesadillas, soft tortillas filled with melted cheese

Rajas, roasted poblano chiles sliced into strips, often simmered with cream and onions

Salsa bandera, a condiment in the colours of the Mexican flag, made from raw tomatoes, onions, jalapeño chillies and lime juice; also known as *pico de gallo*

Salsa de rosas, a sauce made from rose petals, sour cream, walnuts, rose extract, honey and salt

Tacos de vampiro, soft tortillas filled with marinated steak and melted cheese, and topped with mayonnaise, chipotles, lime juice, cilantro and salt

Tamales de elote, sweet dumplings made from young tender corn, steamed in a corn husk

Thus the door opens to other versions.
Luis Jorge Boone

Revenge is a dish best served cold.
Anonymous

One

No-one suggested it. She simply decided Tijuana would be the place to meet and she asked Max Garcés to make the arrangements. Only the guys from the North, Max; a few spots need shoring up and Tijuana is always so nice to visit. Garcés thought it strange, but he telephoned around, thinking maybe what she wanted was to cross the border to see her son, who would turn eleven around that time, or maybe she wanted to go shopping at places she liked. Hyena Wong was opposed from the get-go. Max, Tijuana's not to be trusted, it's a fucking pressure cooker, Mexicali would be better, here we've got everything under control. I'll tell her, but in the meantime get ready, you know what she's like. In Tijuana, Frank Monge paused before responding. Are you sure? in my opinion the place for her is right where she is, in Culiacán; if you remember, her dad never went any further than Bachigualato. These are other times, Frank, no way around it, besides, it's our territory, isn't it? are we that bad off we can't tie up the Boogeyman for a few hours while we have a quiet meeting? Yeah, but around here you never know, she should send people she trusts; as you like to say, bad times bring worse and better safe than sorry. The people in San Luis Río Colorado, Nogales, and Agua Prieta made no comment. Same story with the guys from San Francisco, Los Angeles, San Diego and Phoenix. The government's war against drug trafficking had been over for more than a year and business was moving like a hot knife through butter, though the body-count was holding steady.

Devil Urquídez, now the father of a small child, and Chopper Tarriba, who was dating the latest Miss Sinaloa, rode with the boss, who was wearing a tight red dress and a black silk scarf. Lovely. If she was worried, it did not show. Middle of the afternoon. A small plane was waiting for them on a clandestine runway near El Salado, just outside Culiacán. The idea was to fly towards the Gulf of Santa Clara on the Sea of Cortés, land on the highway that crosses the Great Altar Desert, and from there continue by car to Rosarito, where the cartel kept a house that attracted no attention. Someone, however, had other plans.

At the southern edge of the city, when Samantha Valdés's caravan reached the top of the bridge past Humaya Gardens Cemetery, where the Costerita Highway ends and you pick up the freeway to Mazatlán, a bazooka scored direct hit on the motor of the lead black Hummer, which was carrying the lady capo, stopping it cold. Flash fire. Squealing brakes. Can you see anything, Chopper? Devil at the wheel. Nothing, Devil my man, looks like somebody's having a party and we're invited. The front of the vehicle in flames. Gunfire on all sides. It's an ambush, Samantha shouted from the back seat, adrenaline at the max. Give me an iron, boys. Chopper handed her an A.K. while lowering the armoured window, then fired his own; she did the same. Señora, wait, Devil suggested, we'd better get out before the flames reach us. From an S.U.V. beside them that was under fire, but not on fire, Max Garcés shot a bazooka and sent one of the many vehicles blocking their way flying. Rat-a-tat-tat. Blam blam. More shooting all around the flaming Hummer. Blam blam. Boom. Drivers who had nothing to do with it, that is the ones who couldn't flee, got down on the floors of their cars, sweated and prayed. Chopper and Devil stepped onto the road without letting up their fire and took cover behind the armoured doors. The shooting accelerated to the point where the armour began to give way. Vamos, señora, Devil shouted as he opened the back door, we've got to make ourselves scarce. I'll cover you, Devil, you take the señora; Chopper was enjoying himself, spraying the wide enemy camp with bullets. Devil looked inside and saw Samantha Valdés choking on her own blood. Oh, fuck. Pallid and trembling. The boss is hit, Chopper buddy. Gone limp, face drained but serene, almost saintly. I'm taking her out of here. Dress stained. Do it, these guys are real fuckers.

He lifted her into his arms and ran back towards the

cemetery, using the S.U.V. as a shield. Max, who saw the movement, ordered sustained fire and then with his A.K. vomiting bullets set off after the young gunslinger. The cars they passed looked empty and some of them really were. Not until they came down off the bridge did they find one that could exit the jam. They pulled out the terrified driver and sped off. The gunfire continued apace. The boss, bleeding from the nose and mouth, started cursing; there was no time to lose. Max got hold of the number of Virgen Purísima Hospital and that's where they headed.

Two pickups pulled out of the cemetery and took off after them. By some good fortune the car they had commandeered was new and soon outdistanced their pursuers. They flew by two patrol cars from the Narcotics Division travelling full-tilt towards the battle scene, their occupants no doubt aware any gunfight this big was their baby.

A tall red-headed doctor was waiting at the entrance; he wheeled the wounded woman directly into the operating room. What do you make of it, doctor? Devil stared at him intently. Very serious, I can't guarantee she'll make it. Samantha had lost a lot of blood and had fainted, her dress was a mess, the scarf was gone. Devil felt like threatening him, but the doctor moved so quickly he did not have a chance. A nurse treated Max for a small shoulder wound. What's the redhead's name? Dr Jiménez, she said, he's the best. Max was worried for his men, and he clung to the hope they had escaped without serious losses. When he left only two had been killed. Of course three questions would not stop pestering him: Why hadn't he sent an advance party? Why hadn't he put his S.U.V. in front of the señora's? and Who was behind this? Samantha Valdés had better come out in one piece, her son was way too young to take over the business. Someone had sent them a warning that was going to be difficult to ignore.

In a little while he sent word to the whole cartel that La Jefa had a slight wound and was receiving medical attention, she was chatting calmly with her mother and the doctor. A nice story, but Max Garcés knew he had made a serious mistake and that the unknown enemy on the horizon, given what he attempted to pull off, was no small beer.

Leaning against an ambulance in the street, he brooded about it. Across from him a patrol car from the Ministerial Police rolled slowly by, its lights flashing but the siren off. He caressed his pistol and they drove on as if nothing were out of the ordinary. They're smart to get lost, since we still have no agreement with the new authorities, and that complicates things. Who could have dreamed up this mother? What a bastard, I'm going to hang him by the balls. Who could field enough people to block that bridge? Not many. Meanwhile, in the operating room Jiménez knew he had only one chance.

In Mexico City, in a well-appointed office overlooking

a garden lit by the late April sunset, a cellphone and a landline rang at the same time. A hand with three fingers chose one.

Two

Inside the yellow-taped perimeter, Lefty Mendieta and Zelda Toledo briefly examined the crumpled body of a young man. He had received a coup de grâce, his chest was filled with bullet-holes. Awful grimace. He must have gone down dancing like a fucking puppet, the detective reflected. Freshly shaved, wearing royal-blue designer clothes, shirt all bloody. The technicians were working the grass by a few young trees in the bit of Ecological Park next to the Sinaloa Science Centre. They were near a winding path popular with runners. It was 7.34 in the evening and at that time of year still fairly light. People of all ages were out walking or running, every one of them giving the police as wide a berth as possible. Why would a guy like him get killed? What mistake did he make? Who would have done him in? The murderer had made no effort to hide his crime, and when does that happen? Journalists took pictures, noted down the facts, and left to write their stories. All except for Daniel Quiroz, who enjoyed needling Lefty. Do you think this means the city is condemned to suffer violence in the years to come? Why don't you ask my balls? they're made of crystal and they've got all your answers,

Papa. O.K., give me your theory. Ink-shitter, I'm a badge, not a fortune-teller and I'm sure no politician. Zelda scrutinised the scene with her usual care, ruminating, taking pictures with her cellphone, and dictating into it: Thursday, April 28, small plants trampled, maybe he fought back or maybe just the murderer's footsteps. I'm sure you have some idea. That I do: given the style, so many bullets and all, I'm debating between Al Capone and Pablo Escobar. Fucking Lefty, if you weren't my buddy I'd tear you apart. And I'd toss you in the slammer, charge you with rape, and hand you over to the horniest cons we've got. The press would have a field day. And if you liked it, I'd set you up in a special cell so you could keep doing your nasty shit. They'd be all over you, you know how crazy we get when we pile onto a public servant. Ortega interrupted, exhaustion written all over his face: Lefty, we found a voter I.D. in his wallet, his name was Leopoldo Gámez, 36 years old, 1800 pesos in 200-peso bills, a lucky dollar, a credit card, a bank card, and a lottery stub; we found eight shells, they might be from a Sig Sauer 9mm. Are you sure? As sure as I am that our commander is the world's top cop. They smiled. Let me write down his address. The detective pulled out a small blue notebook. Those bros walking over there, could they have seen something? Hmm, I don't think so, and anyone who did for sure won't say a thing, people don't want trouble. He also wrote: no telephone. He's been dead two to three hours, said Montaño the forensic doctor as he walked over, the body's still pliable; one bullet went through his head and fourteen made a mess of his thorax. In other words the dude was lucky. He didn't suffer. You said you found eight shells? They might have put seven in him somewhere else and the rest here. I didn't know you knew how to count. And now dear friends, I've got to go, there's a little blossom waiting for me; as far as this one is concerned I told the boys to take him to the Unit, they'll do the autopsy, and if you have no objection and the family turns up, we'll give them the body in the morning. You're going to die on top of a woman, fucking Montaño. Until that day I plan to enjoy myself to the max, I've got about thirty-nine years of crazy pleasure left, after which I'll have to ration myself; Agent Toledo, as always it has been a pleasure seeing you. Same here, doctor. I admire the perfection of your body, your lovely hair. Cut the bullshit, and since you're finished, you can get lost. The forensic doctor went off smiling, thinking: You are going to fall, little dove, you'll see, and you'll like it so much you'll be sorry for all the time lost. Ortega gave final instructions to his team and departed, saying he needed a hug from his wife. Quiroz took several pictures and said goodbye; if he got hold of Pineda from Narcotics, who he had been chasing for three hours, ever since the gunfight at Humaya Gardens, he might get a headline. Listen, Lefty, do you know anything about a shoot-out on the bridge where the Costerita Highway ends? Nope. The body was carted off and three minutes later all that was left, besides Lefty and Zelda, was the yellow tape, a policeman to make sure no-one crossed it, and the officers Terminator and Camel, who stood and stared, clueless as to what they were supposed to do.

Zelda, here's the address, send Termi and Camel to notify the family, they can go to Forensic Services now to identify him, but they can't have the body until tomorrow. You really think we should send those two? To wake the bastards up; do you know why I prefer them to the others? Tell me. Because they're honest. That's true: people who think they're stupid just don't know them. Although, like people say, it's hard to know who's more dangerous: an honest man or a corrupt one. No doubt about assholes, though, right? Seems not.

Close by, the Science Centre was all lit up; in the other direction the Botanical Garden stretched out like a dark stain. Zelda gave the agents their orders, then took a taxi to the Forum, she wanted to buy a gift for Mother's Day and underwear for herself. Lefty got into his Jetta, turned on the stereo: "Have You Ever Seen the Rain?" Rod Stewart's version. He lowered the volume, looked over his notes, dialled Commander Briseño, who did not answer, and jacked the volume up again.

Twenty minutes later he was home. He sat in the car and eyed the gate to his driveway, listening to "Something Stupid" by Nicole Kidman and Robbie Williams, and thinking about getting an automatic gate-opener, and that a coat of paint would not hurt, but these were thoughts he had every night he did not feel like getting out to open the gate. Why would they kill a man so apparently upright as Leopoldo Gámez? To teach somebody a lesson, or to remind them of something? People do use bodies to send messages; we also have people who kill just to kill, but in such a grisly way? Murder is a statement, no doubt, but who would go that far? There must be some idiotic scheme behind it. He realised someone was approaching from his left, so he pulled the Walther P99 from the glove compartment and put it between his legs. His brother crossed his mind, the afternoon long ago when Enrique came into his room; Enrique was a teenager and he was a boy. What are you up to, kid? Nothing, listening to the Beatles. He had missed getting caught with the *Playboy* by a hair.

Hey, Lefty, remember me? Short, thin, baseball cap with the logo of the Culiacán Tomateros, dark T-shirt, baggy jeans, sneakers. Lefty looked him over in the weak light from the garage filtering through the bars of the gate. To tell the truth, no. I'm Ignacio Daut. Lefty examined him again tip to toe and nothing connected. Well, I still can't place you, what's up? You bastard, I'm the Flea, Doña Pina's son, from Seventh, the fucking street that isn't even called that anymore. Mendieta looked a third time and it all clicked. Fucking Flea, you look awful, how was I supposed to recognise you? you're disguised as somebody respectable. He switched off the ignition and got out. That's what I am now, my man Lefty, I pay my taxes,

I go to Mass on Sunday, and I celebrate Independence Day as a double-header: Fourth of July for where I live and Sixteenth of September for dear beloved Mexico. They hugged each other. That means miracles do happen. They do, my man Lefty, for sure. So? Foreman Castelo told me where to find you. That faggot? it's been more than a year since I last laid eyes on him. He's fine, he's respectable too, he says hello. Great. You lived around here when you were a kid, didn't you? Indeedy, I did, Flea buddy, it's been my neighbourhood all my life. Are you getting home from work? If you can call it that. Foreman told me you were a badge, but I already knew that, about four years ago I ran into your bro in Oakland and he told me. Enrique is a fucking gossip, so what's up with you? Anxiety was getting the better of Mendieta; the last time he had seen the Flea, the man was wearing ostrich-leather boots and a silk shirt. Lefty, can we have a little chat? As long as you aren't too hard on me. Of course not, want to talk here or could I buy you something at Meño's? That taco stand doesn't exist anymore, Flea. Too bad, the dog tacos were unbeatable, is there someplace else? Not like that one.

They drove to Tacos Sonora. Lefty ordered three with roast beef, Daut ordered four of the same, plus two vampire tacos and a quesadilla, plus a pitcher of agua de cebada for the two of them.

On the way over he let on that he had been in Culiacán for three days, that he had been living in Los Angeles for seventeen years and his family was there: wife and two children, a boy and a girl. The gringo lifestyle, my man Lefty. He asked if Lefty knew why he had disappeared from the neighbourhood. Mendieta did know, but he shook his head. He asked if Lefty remembered Pockmark Long. Lefty knew the man was dead, but claimed ignorance. What kind of badge are you, fucking Lefty? A really tough one with a lousy memory. Mendieta also knew that Daut had killed Pockmark after the guy raped his fourteen-year-old sister, and that was why he had made himself scarce. For the rest of the drive the Flea moved on to small talk.

I'm doing well over there, Lefty, we've got a tortilla factory, my children are grown, they didn't want to go to college so they came into the business. Lefty thought of his son Jason, it had been a week since they last talked. Mendieta knew the Flea had sought him out for some reason and he was tired of waiting. Are you on vacation? No, I'm back for good, and on my own; the family's staying in Los Angeles. I don't get it, if you're so happy over there, asshole, what are you doing here? your fling with Pamela Anderson didn't work out? Daut smiled, he finished chewing. I'm going to die soon, Lefty. That's news, thought the detective. He waited a moment, then asked, What have you got? Nothing, I'm healthy as could be. So? Somebody's going to whack me and I'd rather it happen here, where I belong. Ah, that's a bitch, and could I ask who? One of Pockmark's kids, they've grown up and I've got it

29

from a reliable source that since last year they've been going around settling accounts; you might have heard I brought the dude down before I took off for the other side. A minute went by. I don't understand why I should know about what's going to happen to you. Well, I've always liked you and I want you to know. Who's going to do it? Maybe his son, he's nineteen now and he looks as Chinese as his fucking father. Does he live here? No, but he'll come looking for me. Aren't you something, baring your breast. No, I just want him to know I'm not afraid and that it's a man he's going to kill. Well, good for you. Lefty thought he might mention it to Pineda, the head of Narcotics, although he was sure it would do no good. Defend yourself, if you can. My man Lefty, thank you for the permission, I expected no less of you. They smiled. Did Pockmark have several sons? Just the one, the others are chicks and until they get married they won't get involved, can you eat another two? No, I'm full, thanks. Daut paid, then asked Lefty to let him off at Santa Cruz Church, he wanted to take a stroll; they agreed to meet up another day. Mendieta still did not understand why he had confided in him about that Chinese guy Long, who was unscrupulous and cruel, or about the threat from his son. Seventeen years since they last saw each other and all he wanted was to chat, could that be it? He changed the C.D.: "Brown-Eyed Girl" by Van Morrison. Maybe, sometimes you need to hang out your dirty laundry to keep from going crazy.

At home he opened the gate without delay; one supper was enough. He dialled Jason, who answered sleepily. It's Edgar, how are you? Papa, hello, I'm fine, I was writing a paper all afternoon and I fell asleep. Angels have to sleep too, eh? A trip to Culiacán is what I need, to recharge my batteries. You can come for summer vacation, I want to see you; did you fix things with that teacher who was bothering you? Mister Salinger? he resigned and moved to Boston. Don't let him affect you and don't leave any loose threads hanging; if you're going to be a badge you need to learn that right away. I'm training to run the mile again, there's a police academies' meet in two months. Poor bastards, they're going to eat your dust for sure. I'm also listening to your music, it's not bad. Good taste makes for a good life, my son. Some aren't so cool, but they're still nice to listen to. The years may go by, but they still stand up to a critical ear as severe as yours. That Bob Dylan is something else. His singing is awful, but no question he is the best. They talked about singers until they said good-bye. Lefty revelled in a comforting glow: he had Jason and he would not trade that feeling for anything in the world. Fucking kid, he's tougher than he is pretty; he thought of dialling the mother, Susana Luján, but a slight shudder banished that idea. Fucking hag, I'm not going to fall into her clutches again, even if I die and get reborn. A year and a half before, Lefty had fallen in love and they had made a commitment to each other, but then she vanished without explanation. He drank his whisky in one gulp and poured another. That's right, no way: there are wounds that never heal. He lay down on the bed, turned on the television, "Notting Hill" with Hugh Grant and Julia Roberts, the scene in the bookstore when she tells him she is only a girl asking a boy to love her. What a beauty, he gazed at her. There were two minutes of commercials and then right at the end, when Grant goes into the press conference, his cellphone rang out the Seventh Cavalry Charge. No, please. He answered because it was Zelda Toledo. Tell me quickly or forever hold your peace. Boss, Leopoldo Gámez was a fortune-teller. So? The boys say when his mother and brother came to identify him, they told them that, then the mother let slip that the guy responsible was a small-time narco named Killyhawk. I'll call Pineda in the morning, right now he must be really busy with the gunfight in the South, did you hear anything about it? People say it was really gruesome. Maybe there were more survivors than victims; listen, you better relax, you sound kind of tense. Good night boss, dream about angels. On the television the credits rolled. He got up, brushed his teeth, drank another double whisky, and went to bed. "Back to the Future" was starting, but he fell asleep.

Three

Exhausted, Dr Jiménez lay back in a reclining chair. The operation on Samantha Valdés had lasted nine hours and he was still not sure it had been a success. That's what he told Minerva, the mother of the lady capo, who had stubbornly refused to leave the hospital. Outside, Max Garcés's people stood guard, making no attempt to hide who they were. They filled the waiting room, drank sodas in the store across the street, smoked, and kept two Hummers double parked, blocking traffic.

Víctor Osuna, a lawyer hired by Samantha to obtain deeds to some land, walked into the waiting room bright and early. He looked worried. He went straight to Max. Señor Garcés, good morning, how is the boss? The bastard who can put an end to Samantha Valdés has yet to be born. That's good news, it was on television last night and today it's in the headlines. Of course, she's an important person, what can I do for you? Max did not quite trust Osuna, who wore plaid suits, shirts in shrieking colours, and orange ties. Could we speak in private? The gunslinger stood up and they went to a far corner. There is a rumour, Señor Garcés, that the Army is going to occupy the hospital. Who told you? One of my colleagues who is very close to them. O.K., don't leave until I tell you. Osuna took a seat, Garcés retreated a few feet and called on his cell. He listened closely, said thank you, and hung up. He went into the private room where the surgeon was still stretched out with his eyes closed: Doctor. Jiménez sat up drowsily. We've got a problem, in half an hour the Army is taking over the hospital. Are you sure? Yeah, I just confirmed it. They can't come inside; they'll have to stay in the street or on the roof, it wouldn't be the first time it's happened. I cannot leave the señora unprotected. I'll take charge of that. Sure, you do what you can, but, as you must understand, I cannot abandon her. Pick two men, dress them in white, and tell them to keep their weapons out of view; the hospital routine has to continue as usual. How is she doing? Her status is still critical and we're not sure she's going to make it, let's put our trust in God; her mother is with her now. You're not at all confident? No. The chief bodyguard felt a stiletto in his heart. If she dies I will never forgive myself, my God, why was I so stupid? could it have been the Zeta guys? we blame everything on them these days; it was probably some new group, they're always popping up, and they always want to grandstand; when I get hold of those bastards they're going to wish they were never born.

Twenty minutes later the street was empty. In the doctor's office, Devil Urquídez and Chopper Tarriba, dressed in nurses' uniforms provided by the lawyer, were trying to hide their pistols and stash two Kalashnikovs into long cardboard boxes. What had them most worried was that they would not be able to chain-smoke.

A squadron of soldiers soon laid siege to the building. They closed off the emergency exits, took up positions in the street, on the roof, and in the adjacent parking lot. Captain Bonilla notified the head of the hospital, Dr Avilés, who brought Jiménez onto the call so everything would be clear. His patient was under arrest and as soon as she was well enough to travel she would be transferred to a military hospital in Mexico City. Jiménez filled them in on the case, that they had taken out half a lung and she had not yet awakened from the anaesthesia; he added that if she pulled through her recovery would be very slow and any sudden movement could be fatal. Bonilla said as far as they were concerned there was no hurry, and if she died the country would come out ahead.

The atmosphere was tense. Staff and all the other patients felt cornered. The soldiers seemed pretty nervous, too. Only the presence of pretty nurses allowed them to think they were just doing their jobs; they fantasised that those beauties in white had no connection to their celebrity prisoner, the bloody boss of the Pacific Cartel, somebody named Valdés. Soon they noticed two male nurses who kept stepping outside into a tiny patch of green next to a staircase to smoke like chimneys. No bullets needed to do in those nitwits, cancer will fuck them, concluded Sergeant Bazúa, who later on would die in circumstances to be revealed. Chopper spotted the sergeant on the roof, but chose to pay him no heed, though he warned Devil not to look up while they were smoking. There's an asshole up there uglier than spit in God's face, he won't take his eyes off us.

The triggermen remained calm. Devil called home and his wife offered to bring him breakfast. Chopper joked around with his girl and did not dare mention where he was; she might show up and that would be enough to draw the entire squadron like flies to honey. Dr Jiménez managed to sleep until Patty, the nurse on duty, woke him with the news that the patient had not come around and that her mother was getting nervous. The doctor went over to intensive care and, sure enough, Samantha was still sleeping, but on the instrument displays her vital signs looked normal. Every so often her heart stops, the nurse said; after ten or fifteen seconds it starts up again. Please don't leave her, that means she's still in a coma. Oh, doctor, what a cruel blow, lamented Minerva. Trust in God, señora, and wait; if you like, go lie down for a while, Patty will be here. Not a chance, I'm not moving from this chair until she wakes up, then I'll call my grandson. Very well, and if you two get to chatting, don't forget to keep an eye on the instruments. Jiménez withdrew, thinking: She's going to survive, I can feel it, I only hope she doesn't have a relapse when she finds out she's under arrest.

At sundown, Captain Bonilla strode into the room next to the patient's without knocking. The hired guns glanced over, while Jiménez, who had been dozing in the recliner, leaped up and blocked his way. Captain, you cannot come in here. Of course I can, we have a dangerous criminal under arrest and I need to know her condition. Uh-uh, the street and the roof are yours, but you cannot come in here and upset my patients, this is a hospital. He gave the officer a light but firm shove: So do me the favour of leaving. Don't you push me. The news on the patient is the same that I reported this morning in the presence of the director. I could charge you with harbouring a dangerous criminal. And I could charge you with violating the human rights of a dying woman. The gunslingers did not bat an eye, kept their hands in view of the officer, and continued with their tasks, one reviewing a clinical report, the other rolling cotton balls. You are going to regret this. The doctor did not answer and neither did he stop pushing, until he managed to get the intruder out. We'll set him straight, doctor, he heard as he was bolting the door. Devil stood up: If that sonofabitch sets foot in here again I'll blow him away. You aren't going to shoot anybody, don't forget, this is a hospital and the patients come first, including the one we have next door; nobody wants to die and from what I've heard neither do you, so cool it and let's hope the señora's condition improves. Yeah, take it easy, Devil my man, there's more time than life to give buddy out there his due. I'm going for a smoke. Better not, they might be planning to catch us out, watching from the roof. That's likely, Jiménez agreed, you better just bear up. Now I'm really pissed off. Don't give a flying fart about it, Devil my man, you could bear up under a piano.

So it was: not far above them, three soldiers and Bonilla were squatting on the roof, waiting for one of them to step into the tiny garden they had turned into a smoking area.

In his pickup, Max Garcés was on the telephone, sticking to his story, though each time with less conviction. All the bosses calling in had heard interpretations very close to the truth. Don't anybody go nuts, La Jefa is getting a check-up, I'm telling you, and that's that.

Yup, there are days when you're ready to trade everything for a fucking truck and just scram, don't deny it.

Four

Charface was short, heavyset, with a thick moustache; the sweat that constantly bathed his dark-brown face only added to his fierce appearance. He was dressed, as usual, in an immaculate black suit. He made a call on a cellphone, but not the one lying next to the landline. Those two were only for receiving calls about jobs completed or hiring people for special cases. He was the favoured connection of many powerful people ever since his cold-blooded murder of a journalist investigating the string of women killed in Ciudad Juárez. That very year he carried out twenty-seven other assignments and proved he was infallible.

Señor Secretary, I'm calling just to confirm that you have no need to worry, everything is under control.

Everything under control, you say? fucking mother, Charface, how dare you talk to me like that? the fucking bitch is still alive and the guys in the group are squeezing my balls, what are you waiting for? you better apply yourself the way God wants it, understand? and no more bullshit; one mistake and I'll fuck the fingers you have left.

Take it easy, señor. My man is already in Culiacán, as that woman will learn soon enough.

We want her dead, is that clear?

Clear as can be.

And make it fast, if the gringos get her first, she's going to sing and I don't want to think about how the big boss will react.

That won't happen.

You know what to do with the loser who fucked up, right?

Precisely what one does with losers who fuck up.

Well, make sure everybody knows, I want noise.

The Secretary hung up. Charface let some of his dark rage show.

Fucking geezer, he thinks he's a big shit; as if I didn't know power comes and goes. Doesn't he remember how he went from being ambassador to Japan to being nobody? He only got rehabilitated five minutes ago.

He looked at his eight fat, ugly fingers.

The only all-powerful is money and as long as that ass-licker keeps giving it to me I'll put up with him, the moment he stops he'll just be one more dead politician. I know who he owes and how much they'll pay for his hide; and good thing he's so old, otherwise instead of wanting to cut off my fingers he'd threaten to kill me, like they all do now.

He let his attention wander to the stupendous garden, which was a riot of colour in the spring sunshine. The yellow tulips, his dearest passion, captivated him. Then he reached for the two telephones with his three-fingered hand. In some professions a single minute can be decisive. He picked up the landline and dialled.

Five

He called Zelda first thing to ask her to go to Forensic Services
and bring Leopoldo Gámez's relatives to Headquarters before
letting them have the body. Then he drove to Ecological
Park, which was crowded with the usual runners and walkers.
The policeman on guard duty was calmly drinking a supermarket coffee. They said hello. Any news? Nothing, boss, it
was a peaceful night. For sure, you must have had a great
sleep. Actually no, I suffer from insomnia, I've been twenty-
two years on the Force and they're always assigning me these
jobs, you never met me before because I was with Commander Pineda, but I know you; I also take care of hanging
the yellow tape, I trained with Pablo Faraón González from
Ciudad Juárez. Any thoughts on what might have happened?
For me, sir, it was a whim; the victim was well-fed, wearing
brand-name clothes, and the killer said to himself: today, it's
the cream's turn and pow, how do you like that?; then he
brought him here, because I don't think the guy got knocked
off in the park, too many people around, can you imagine
what a scene that would be?

Lefty looked the site over without finding anything of

42

note. He remembered they found eight shells: would they have shot him eight times after he was dead? plus they gave him a *coup de grâce*, here or somewhere else? let's see: Gámez was feeling calm, he went out for a stroll along the Diego Valadés Parkway thinking about what to give his mother on the tenth of May; no, he lives far from here and the parkway isn't close by either, more likely he went to a talk at the Science Centre, something about black holes, and when he came out they murdered him; the shooter stepped right in front of him: Hi, how long has it been since you've been killed? And pow, he or she put seven bullets in his chest and then in the park the other seven, along with one in the head. Why? since the guy died instantly. To lighten the heart of fifteen slugs, like that writer César Güemes says? It could be the work of a narco or a crime of passion. Or maybe it was that guy Killyhawk the mother pointed us to. An accomplice must have helped carry him to the park. What murderer would do that in the light of day? A real bastard, that's who; what, are there other kinds of murderers? Maybe he wanted to take him alive, he resisted, and they did him in not meaning to. It was somebody desperate, maybe somebody whose fortune he got wrong. It's strange. If they'd left him in a vacant lot, I'd understand, but here where so many people come by, especially in the afternoon? If it was a message, who was it for? Maybe they asked him here for a chat and then took him down, that'd be easier; but suppose the guard is right?

It was a dapper fellow's turn and this guy won the lottery. We learned about it from somebody out for a walk who did not want to identify himself. If he was murdered somewhere else, why bring him all the way here? Fucking murderers, every day they get wilier. I think they must have brought him here, because no-one heard any shots, not even the eight, did they bring the shells along too? That could be, or they might have used a silencer. Around him runners were zipping by dressed in all sorts of bright colours. Why is running so popular? People from Sinaloa aren't known for athletics. He studied the weeds that had not been trampled, or had they? He looked closer, nothing unusual. Why would they leave him his voter I.D.? Was that meant as a challenge? To whom? He looked over at the policeman: What's your name? Tecolote, boss, Teco to my friends. Great, tell the guy who relieves you to make sure nobody walks on the area; last night, did anyone come by? No-one, but I've never seen a murderer return to the scene of the crime; it might happen in the movies, or I suppose when there aren't so many murders. That makes sense, Mendieta thought, but is this the scene of the crime?

He wandered along the park perimeter looking for an abandoned car, but found nothing, did he use taxis? A Culichi doesn't take a taxi to go running, if that's what he came to do, but he wasn't dressed for that either. A friend gave him a lift, the same guy who whacked him in front of the Science

Centre and then left him where we found him. Mendieta drove towards the Café Miró, which was on the other side of the park. No question about it, every dead body is a multi-faceted universe with plenty of fucking mysteries, as if I didn't have anything better to do. Heading down Las Américas Boulevard, which separates the park from Sinaloa Autonomous University, he grooved to "You've Got Your Troubles" by The Fortunes. He called Ortega, but got no answer. Fucking bastard, who does he think he is, why doesn't he pick up? He walked into the café with an image of Leopoldo Gámez in his mind. Hey, Rudy, have you been behaving yourself? As I should, how about you? Whatever I can get away with. Would you like machaca and eggs? And coffee, please, don't put any salt in my eggs, you must have heard about the silent killer, oh, and make it half an order. Would you mind sharing a table? Why not? Enrique Záizar was an outgoing fellow about Lefty's age, and he was drinking a café cortado. So you're a detective. What about you? A lawyer. You don't say, and do you practise? Well, once in a while; I teach Roman law, which is my real passion. Aha, the Romans were crazy, weren't they? Not at all, they were an admirable people, they always thought big: their architecture, their military, their politicians, and of course their poets; they never thought small, listen to Horace: "For Jupiter, when slighted, often joins a good man in the same fate with a bad one. Seldom hath punishment, though lame of foot, failed to

45

overtake the wicked." Sheesh, who is this bro, thought Lefty. You in your profession can appreciate how right the great lyric poet was, though it's not that unusual for a villain to get away. I can see you're deep into it, Rudy said, serving Lefty his breakfast. Evidently, the best things in life are inevitable, he added, and he took a seat with the two of them, who then moved on from Horace to corridos, to the importance of obeying the law, and finally to the dead man who took up a quarter of the crime page in that day's *El Debate de Culiacán*. Záizar ordered his third coffee. Last night, Quiroz, the reporter from "Eyes on the Night", gave an amazingly precise description of the crime scene, that young man will end up a novelist. Do you think? That's my impression. Well, we left an officer there with milk and bread in case the murderer showed up, but he didn't. I guess he didn't like the menu. That journalist mentioned you, you can tell he admires you. Lefty felt like saying something, but kept his mouth shut. Is the investigation getting anywhere? It's a curious case, we found eight shells, but he had fourteen holes in his chest and one in the head; the body might have been dumped in Ecological Park. Interesting. Rudy my man, the guy lived close by, maybe he came here for coffee or a beer. The restaurateur looked at the picture. It could be, I'll show the girls, they always see more than I do. The cavalry charge rang out, Mendieta answered. Boss, when are you coming in? because I've got Gámez's brother here and he's anxious to get going. Give him a tranquilliser and tell him to cool it. He's already been to Forensic Services to sign out the body, and the funeral home picked it up. I'll be there in twenty minutes. Got it, you know the gunfight you mentioned last night? Tell me. No report yet, rumour has it they tried to kill or kidnap Samantha Valdés. It couldn't be a kidnapping, Zelda, those people don't get kidnapped. Kill her then; they say she was taken in critical condition to the Virgen Purísima. God must have caught her confessing. She's your friend, isn't she? Not exactly, we live in the same city and among the same people, and we have coincided in meaningful ways, but nothing more. Well, now you know, in case you want to visit her. Agent Toledo, stop supposing things that are not in either my interest or yours: we have no friends who are narcos, nor do we work in Narcotics, is that clear? Sorry, boss, I'll be waiting for you after you interrogate Gámez's brother, I need to tell you something. He hung up. What do you think of this, detective? Záizar showed him the front-page photograph of the ruins of Samantha Valdés's Hummer. Demons are on the loose, attorney. They smiled, Lefty said goodbye; in his car: Marianne Faithfull singing "As Tears Go By".

Before interrogating Gámez's brother, he dropped by the office of Commander Briseño, who was in a foul mood. Nothing but bullshit, Mendieta, it's always the same story, we never solve the real problems, don't you read the newspapers? Uh-uh, I only listen to Daniel Quiroz. Well, he's the worst, he's always shovelling shit at us, nothing will satisfy that bastard. But Commander, you used to be great friends, what happened? You should see what he writes about us, the nicest thing he calls us is incompetent. Send him a present and you'll see how he turns around. Will you take it to him? Why not? Because he's attacking you, too. That's just to get at you, you know what journalists are like. He handed Lefty a manila envelope. I hope this will satisfy him, there's enough there for a couple of weeks' vacation; so, what have you got on the body in Ecological Park? He was a fortune-teller. The ones you see on television? Hmm, I don't think so, we've got a brother of his in the interrogation room right now, we'll see what he has to say. Don't leave him in Gori's hands, I don't want Human Rights all over us again. They killed him with a 9mm, which, as you know, is a calibre that spells revenge, fourteen bullets in the chest and one in the head. This society doesn't deserve us, Edgar, we serve in an epoch when every-one has gone crazy, acting on their worst instincts; in any case, make sure everything comes out right, there's a new guy in charge at the federal prosecutor's office and we ought to play up to him; at least until we find out where he's aiming. Does Pineda know? Of course, as a matter of fact he's all tied up now dealing with a gun battle that included Samantha Valdés, someone I'm sure you've heard of. More or less. Well, get to work and keep me in the loop. What do you know about Killyhawk? He's a small-time narco without a cartel, dangerous, a hothead, a bit unhinged. Leopoldo Gámez's mother thinks he's the one who killed her son. Do you want me to tell you what to do or have you got some idea? He left the office regretting he had asked.

Should I go see Samantha Valdés? Fucking dame, let her rot. Go see her for something worthwhile, not to pick a fight – that was his body talking, which loved pleasure as much as it loved itself, and which had not forgotten the lady capo's sensual silhouette. No-one asked your opinion. Yes, but who is the one who suffers because you're shy? When I want your opinion, I'll ask, fucking body, for now you shut your trap, which is the best thing you've got going. Don't threaten me, Lefty Mendieta, or you'll find out who I really am. I know what you are and stop messing with me. Silence.

He stepped into the office and Angelita, typing at top speed on her computer, handed him the telephone: You've got a call, chief. Mendieta, said the detective, and he heard a click. Angelita, who was it? Wouldn't say. Man, woman, or thing? Thing, because I couldn't tell if it was male or female. Did the people from Telcel stop calling? Yes, now the one who won't let up is Banamex, they want to know when you'll pay the balance on your card. Aren't they a delicate bunch, the bums; well, I'll be in with Zelda.

Alfonso Gámez, civil engineer, site manager at Sinaloa Concrete, forty years old, married, three children. My brother had a job with the Health Ministry, he was a nurse, but he resigned six years ago to focus on fortune-telling; that brought in a lot more, the guy was a born entrepreneur. Was he on television? He didn't get that far. Where did he meet with his clients? In cafés or in their cars. I thought he'd have a home base. Well, now you know he didn't. The killers were extra cruel with him, what relations did he have with narcos? My mother thinks Killyhawk was involved. What do you think? Honestly, I don't know; four years ago he told me most of his clients were hustlers, ladies of pleasure, and the occasional decent sort. It's curious how people want to know what's to come, Zelda intervened. My brother lived from that, they say he was really good at it, and I guess he had all sorts of adventures. Why does your mother think it was Killyhawk? Yesterday she told me he threatened my brother several times, he even sent someone to tell her that if he didn't show his face and stop hiding he was going to regret it. Have you ever met Killyhawk? When Mama told me about him yesterday, it was the first I'd ever heard of him. Did Leopoldo tell you about anything or anyone he feared? Never, he always seemed confident, but we didn't talk that often, the last we saw of each other was two months ago; his life was really wild and I'm just a work-a-day guy. Was he married? Divorced for nearly eight years, no children. Do you know where his ex lives? No, only that she moved to Mexico City after the separation; listen, detectives, I'd like to finish up, they'll be delivering the body to the funeral home in a little while and my mother won't be able to keep it together. Tell me the names and addresses of your other siblings. I don't have any, we were the only two. Did you meet any women he went out with? One day he introduced me to Irene Dueñas, I think she's the owner of Bou Tik, that chi-chi clothing store; he seemed pretty excited about her. Zelda punched the store name into her cell: It's in Cinépolis Plaza, and it sets the standard for women's fashion. Did your brother and you fight a lot? A little, Mama used to worry about his lifestyle and we argued about that, but it never went any further. Who's going to inherit? Maybe Mama, he lived with her; we still have to look into that. One last question, who was your brother's best friend? No idea, I never knew he had one.

It was an utterly pointless interrogation and they let him go without further ado. Listen, boss, that bit about ladies of pleasure pissed me off, what are we? women of woe? Woeful is something you women will never be, that's why no man can live up to your expectations. In his little cubicle, Lefty dialled Pineda, certain that he would know whatever ought to be known about Killyhawk, but he did not pick up.

Six

At a sidewalk stall across from the Virgen Purísima, the Flea
Daut was using a plastic fork to nibble at a fruit salad
sprinkled with lime juice, salt and powdered chillies from the
plastic cup he held in one hand. He observed the commotion
and chewed on a slice of jícama: Trucks Obregón, head of
the Federal Police contingent, talking on his cell; soldiers
waving away flies; Captain Bonilla reading the newspaper;
the arriving patients looking surprised by the siege; the
doctors used to it all. He spied Max Garcés getting into a
pickup and smoking robotically. From his looks, Daut figured
he was important and guessed his line of work. His stint
as a criminal was good training for sniffing out bad guys. He
watched two men in white coming down the sidewalk towards
the hospital, one of them young, thin and short, both of
them Chinese; he stopped chewing, pulled his cap down over
his forehead, and froze, cup in hand. The young one could
not be anyone else but the son of Pockmark Long, and the
other had to be Hyena Wong, a bit taller and wearing cowboy
boots, no doubt recently arrived from Mexicali. Here we go,
pair of bastards, who would have thought? He had heard of

Wong, but never had any problems with him. A terrifying killer-for-hire. They went up to Max, shook hands, and all of them went into the hospital. Ten minutes ticked calmly by. So the kid grew up, now he's ready to kill or die, will he dare? Well, I'm afraid so, they made a mess of Shakes in Tijuana, same story with Indira in Sacramento, two people who lost Pockmark a lot of dough, though I don't know if it was young Long who did the deed or Hyena; in any case that was the alarm bell for me. The Flea got to his feet and wandered off towards Sepúlveda Street, the black market for dollars. He looked relaxed, his expression bemused. He stabbed a slice of papaya, chewed quickly, and threw the half-full cup into a garbage can.

He passed a group of Federales, knowing full well what he ought to do.

Seven

Some people thought the war against the narcos was over, but bodies kept piling up. At lunchtime that day, Lefty and Zelda went to El Quijote for a few cold ones. Curlygirl welcomed them: I'm so glad you're here, I've got a request from the gay community and some news. Before you start in on your complaints, bring us two half-litres and whatever you have for snacks. Zelda, how do you put up with this lout? he's got no class, but don't think it's his lineage, I knew his parents well and they were beyond reproach; this guy has no trace of them and even less of his brother, who was a gentleman; listen to me, Edgar: we're not happy with what people are saying about the violence, it's not true that it's on the wane; drop into any bar, dearie, and you'll hear all about it, dudes go to dance halls toting huge pistols and nobody calls them on it, they carry girls off by force and no-one lifts a finger; just because dead bodies aren't all over the newspapers doesn't mean they aren't everywhere else. Curlygirl, bring the beers and stop haranguing us, I'm pleased you're a card-carrying homosexual, but don't make us die of thirst. I'm telling you, Edgar, don't make a joke of this, it could get you into a lot of trouble. Don't pay Lefty any mind, Curlygirl, we're just having a bad day. Well, I won't give him the good whipping he deserves, but only because he's over forty, otherwise I would. Please, Curlygirl, if you don't have any beer, bring water, anything, but something at least, so later on people don't go around saying we did nothing to keep ourselves alive.

He served them two Pacíficos and a plate of shrimp with octopus. First of all, boss, allow me to say something, she paused to sip, for a month I haven't been able to tell you. Confused, Lefty stared at his partner, whose expression had grown serious. I'm getting married. That's not news. Next week. Aha, no shit, am I going to be an uncle? Not yet, but, well, look, if we don't do it now, who knows when we'll get married; it's not that I'm in a hurry, but Rodo is; besides, he just got a promotion to head of licences, he's getting a desk job and we think it's time to start our family. Is that the thing you said you wanted to tell me yesterday? Precisely, and I need some time off. As of when do you plan to leave? Right now, I have to arrange everything and it's not simple; a girlfriend is lending me a hand, but she can't do it all, I've got to be there. You look kind of thin. Every girl getting married loses weight, didn't you know that? Well, I never got married. Don't lose hope, would you like to be the godfather? If there's no way around it.

They raised their beers. Salud. Zelda relaxed, gave the news to Curlygirl, who wanted to toast with them and in passing he scolded Mendieta for not having taken that step.

Boss, have you heard anything about your friend in the hospital? No, and as I already told you, we are not friends. Well, it's just that she's always there, like part of our life, always on top of everything we do. Criminals are our counterparts, it's thanks to them that we exist and even if it destroys our livers, they always know what we're up to. Why do I see her as more connected to you than to Pineda? Because you like to be annoying, and even if she's been involved in some of our recent cases, her direct relationship is with Pineda, who as a matter of fact must be very busy, word is he's getting nowhere on the case of the bridge to the Costerita, eleven people killed and all those S.U.V.s and pickups burned to a crisp.

A fourth round of beers came their way, along with a pair of grilled groupers with fresh salsa bandera. I'm going to take two weeks, I hope you don't replace me, suppose they find somebody you like more. You are irreplaceable, Zelda, so don't even think about that, you take charge of organising your wedding and I'm sure it'll be great. Think of the money I'm going to save, you can't imagine how much people charge for running a party. Well, now you can relax, don't worry; tell Angelita to draw up the request, I'll sign it, and off you go. I've already got it; from her bag she pulled a folded paper with the official seal, which Lefty signed, chuckling. As of today? you really are taking off early, that's why people don't trust us. Oh, boss, between organising the bash, picking up the dress they still haven't finished, and booking a place for the honeymoon, I'm barely going to have time; and don't forget, it's Friday next week and you'll be the godfather. In the whole get-up and all? Absolutely. Seventh Cavalry Charge from Lefty's telephone. Robles.

Chief Mendieta, we've got a body in the parking lot of Cinépolis, Ortega's people and the forensic doctor are on the way. Me too; he cut the line. Zelda, our workmates are inviting me to join them in activities appropriate to my gender, so you go off and do your thing and we'll see each other at the wedding. Don't stand me up, remember, you are my godfather. I won't forget, and if there's anything else I can do give me a buzz. He put the cost of the meal on the table plus a generous tip and out they went. Zelda took a taxi. In the Jetta: The Kinks' "All Day and All of the Night".

A man about forty years old, shaved head, clothing nothing special, lay on the ground next to a pillar in the covered parking lot of Cinépolis Plaza, closer to the casino than to the movies or the café on the corner. He had a woman's black handbag clutched in his right hand. One of the technicians greeted Lefty: We found the shell and it's a .22, he's got a bullet-hole in his head, we found no identification, and now we're going to pry this thing loose. Lefty put on surgeon's gloves and helped pull on the dead man's fingers to free the bag. He opened it, saw an amazing quantity of objects inside, pulled out a change purse with money and credit cards. The voter I.D. showed it belonged to Margarita

Bournet, a resident of Valley Gardens in the northern end of the city. The photograph showed a white middle-aged woman with short hair. An intern told him the man had been dead for about four hours from the gunshot wound to his head. He imagined the scene: the guy grabbed the handbag from the señora, she pulled a pistol out from somewhere and fired, then she got scared and ran off without her bag. Good thing we know where she lives. Bring me the guy in charge of the parking lot. Camel returned with a portly man in a baseball cap bearing the logo of the Mazatlán Venados. The name he went by was Catfish: The truth is I didn't see or hear a thing. Of course, you're blind and deaf. Vehicles are always coming and going, they make a lot of noise. Is there a security camera taping all that? Fat chance, we had to fight like hell to get a gate installed so people would have to take a ticket and pay. The woman who ran away, how was she dressed? That's something I didn't catch, people come and go too, some are going to the movies, others to the casino, and most of them walk fast on their way in and slow as molasses once their pockets have been plucked. When did you notice the body? About two hours ago, when a señora pointed it out and called you on her cell. You didn't call? Well, I was going to, but the lady got there first. How many years did you do? What's that about, I've never been in prison. Mendieta liked Catfish's frank smile and decided that the man had lit no candle for this funeral.

He ordered Terminator and Camel to arrest the woman on the I.D. and bring her to Headquarters. An hour and a half later he received a call from the agents: We're on the way, sir, with the prisoner in custody.

At Headquarters he went to see Ortega. Listen, you bastard, before you go home to chug beers with French fries and watch T.V., I need a hand. Don't fuck with me, fucking Lefty, we're doing just fine, if you miss seeing bodies in the newspapers that's not my problem, let's enjoy the fact we're not so overwhelmed right now; besides, today we're playing Honduras. Don't be a fucking masochist, whenever the national team plays you come in the next day spitting nails. Today we're going to win three–nil. Sure, do you remember yesterday's body? More or less. Four hours ago somebody else got capped in Cinépolis. Poor bastards, they didn't get to see the match. Stop whining, enough with your fucking match. Let me take another look at the report and tomorrow I'll tell you what's what. According to his mother, yesterday's was whacked by a narco they call Killyhawk, give me whatever you've got on him. Fucking Lefty, you think I have nothing to do? Come on, look in your files or ask one of your slaves to do it, and the pics might help, I need to know who Leopoldo Gámez really was; listen, what are you doing next Friday? It's Zelda's wedding, I'll be there. You know about it? My old lady already stuck me for the dress, aren't you going? Sure am, I'm the godfather. Now it's all turned to shit, I'll tell my wife to go as she is. Don't be a fucking crybaby; listen, give me a hand with this, I need to know what's what. You sure are a pain in the ass, lucky Zelda, getting a few days' break from you, and if you want to know, I hate the fucking archives, damn the day somebody thought of giving them to me. I hope the team wins, crybaby.

Angelita had two messages for him: one from the Commander who was expecting him in his office, the other from Edith Santos. And who is that? A friend of Zelda's, she's helping her with the wedding. You know about the wedding? For two months, don't forget I wrote up her leave request; boss, don't be mad at Zelda, she just couldn't figure out how to tell you. So, everybody knew except for me.

Briseño was still in a foul mood. At your service, chief. How do you make raviolis? Sir, I never cook, I simply can't. But you must know something, you live alone and a man who lives alone can at least fry a couple of eggs. Not in my case, besides, if I set foot in the kitchen Trudis might kill me, can I help you out with anything? Yeah, I can't seem to make my wife understand that what we ate a little while ago wasn't up to snuff, it needed to cook for another minute at least and the sauce was too thin, besides, that squash filling doesn't do it for me. Oh boy, that is serious. Don't mock me, you bastard, who do you think you are? a moron who doesn't know how to fry eggs has no right to comment on anything. Sorry, chief, I didn't mean to make fun of you. Shut up and report in, you just found another body, right? At Cinépolis, he was clutching a woman's handbag and the owner should be here any minute. He must be a thief. The other was a fortune-teller. Silence. Lefty tried to deduce what the Commander was driving at, since he was always more interested in politics and cooking than in police matters. What's your theory? the Commander barked. Well, it might be a pattern. I figured, you don't have a clue; make sure you stay on these two cases until they're solved; Attorney Manlio Zurita, the new federal prosecutor for the state, congratulated me and I don't want you to ruin it; he even suggested that one of his experts, a guy from Mexico City, could help out if needed, what do you think of that? so, I've practically solved your case. Thank you, chief, I expected no less from you, but the Gámez case falls outside my purview, his mother says he was done in by Killyhawk, that narco about whom you gave me such valuable information. It is fully within your purview, it should keep you occupied until Zelda gets back. Are you going to the party? To the party and the Mass, my wife is so excited, you'd think she was Zelda's mother, they even found out they have a friend in common who knows about organising weddings and we're paying for her to lend a hand. No kidding, I've been treated like the cuckolded husband, Zelda's going to hear about this when she gets back. Here's the expert's telephone number, remember he's a Chilango, meet with him and try to learn something; now I'm going to show my wife just how risky it is to contradict a man who is right. Lefty walked out feeling discouraged, all his prior experience with expert advisers had been appalling.

In his office, Angelita was on the phone: He just came back, I'll put him on. To Mendieta, covering the mouthpiece: Boss, Señora Edith Santos, should I send it to your extension? Lefty took the call right there: Yes? Good afternoon Señor Mendieta, how are you? Fine, but so it goes, how about you? Losing my mind, thank you for asking; I know you are going to be Zelda's godfather and I would like to know if you have a black suit. Too bad, I only have white ones. Then if it isn't inconvenient, I would be delighted to show you a few, could I see you now? Right now? Forgive me, I know you are a very busy man, but I am at Liverpool and you don't know how grateful I would be if you would come and try on a few possibilities in black, the wedding is only a week away and we have no time to lose. Is it that complicated? No, Señor Mendieta, this is so it won't become complicated. Well, if there's no way around it. Perfect, I love people who cooperate, I'll be in the men's department and I'll have a few suits ready so you can choose which to try, it won't take long.

In the interrogation room a middle-aged woman was waiting for him. Before stepping in, one of his subordinates briefed him: She says her handbag was stolen this morning and that she didn't kill him. Let her grandmother believe that one, Camel piped in, that old bag has murderer written all over her face. Did she resist? Yup, she kicked and punched, but her daughter, who is in the other room, convinced her to come along, that nothing would happen to her. I gather she's a tough broad.

I'm Detective Mendieta, how are you? Very frightened, never in my life have I set foot inside a police station, but I did not kill anyone, although I certainly wanted to when that vile hooligan attacked me; I have an outstanding balance with Coppel, this morning about eleven, I was taking in the monthly payment when that bald wretch grabbed my bag and ran; I screamed but no-one came. Where did it happen? At the Coppel store in Fiesta Plaza, there weren't many people around. Did you tell the police? No, I told the security guard at Coppel; look, I'm from a decent family, my husband used to be the local mayor, but nobody liked him because he never took anything that didn't belong to him; besides, in my life I've never held a gun. What calibre pistol do you prefer? What would I know? she bristled, never have I fired a gun, I'm telling you, don't you understand? No worries, we'll do a test and it'll show how many times you pulled the trigger. Then go right ahead; what times we live in, my God, nobody believes decent people, you have to prove you're honest again and again. Lefty stepped outside a moment, asked the agents to go to the scene of the robbery and question the guard about her, he might still be on duty.

What did the thief look like? Shaved head, I already told

you, about fifty years old, dark skin; an ugly man. Is this him? he held up his cellphone to show her a photograph of the dead man. That's something like him, I'm not sure, I was so scared I didn't get a good look, but he was practically bald; oh, detective, don't complicate matters, you might accuse me of many things, but not of murder. Of what, for example? Of letting my husband drink more than he should and smoke until he's hoarse, of going off on a cruise and leaving him with one of his sisters, of spoiling my granddaughters. Why didn't you report the robbery? Don't be offended, detective, but I don't trust the police, I've heard of many cases where reporting something is counterproductive. Is this your handbag? Another photograph. Yes, will you give it back to me? A few minutes later Camel called. Boss, the guard identified the señora in the photo on my cell as the one. Good work, come back here; how many times had you seen the robber before? In my life I'd never seen him, how could you think that? in my friendships I'm very particular. Very well, you can go home. Thank you, detective, I never imagined there were any well-behaved policemen and now, look, what a surprise. Thank you, we'll get your bag to you in a few days, we've got to check for fingerprints.

He remembered that he had an appointment.

Waiting for him was a woman of about forty, not pretty, but with a sculpted body and a delicate smile. Whew, the great unwashed are in luck, said his body, reacting to the sight of Edith Santos, who was wearing a tight-fitting dress. You calm down, said Lefty, who always felt a bit nervous around attractive women, we've got nothing to do with this one. I know she's ugly, but she's got that lovely behind, Mama, it'll drive us wild. Calm down, I said.

Señor Mendieta, what a pleasure.

Same here, Edith.

Me too, Lefty's body was taking the lead.

I didn't think you would be this young.

Edgar, that poodle wants a bone.

Thank you, I never thought Zelda had such good-looking friends.

Shall we call each other *tú*?

I'd be delighted.

They looked at six suits. He was impressed, he'd never done anything like this before; he was the sort to go into a store, point at jeans or jerseys in black, tell the salesman his size, how many he wanted, and never worry whether they fit. He tried them all on and had no clue how to choose.

Edith, I think I will rely on your good taste.

Zelda warned me: the boss will seek your advice. Alright, this is the one that looks best on you, how did it feel?

Well, that's the one.

Lefty, take her to Sanborns, at least, did you see her tits? just right for us to finish nursing at last, buy her a beer.

Don't mess with me, fucking body, she's a decent woman

and we aren't going to put our foot in it.

Of course not, we'll put something else in, the beer is just to test the waters.

I'm seeing Zelda at eight-thirty and it's still early, would you like to go out for coffee?

Her voice was velvety, her lips revealing, and her hair reached her shoulders.

See what I mean, you bastard? this chick knows what she wants.

They sat at a booth in Sanborns and asked for Tecates, a red-label and a light. She made her living organising weddings, she had been divorced three times and was hoping to marry again as soon as possible.

Although I suffered horribly, I think the pain of love makes you stronger and gives you more insight into life; in the end there's nothing unusual about two people who love each other doing each other so much damage, or is there? in any case it happens, and like I tell you, it makes you stronger for whatever's coming next.

It's like loving your enemies.

Sure, at least I appreciate them.

Lefty, you've got to move in on this babe, lasso her, remember I've been on the bench for a while.

You've got a pretty face.

I'm ugly, I know it, but there's something about me that makes men look twice.

I could tell you just what, little girl.

They drank a second beer and his body was getting antsy.

Would you like to have supper here or somewhere else?

I would love to, but I have to see Zelda, who is at last free of you; tomorrow we get everything ready and Sunday we begin to set up; how about Monday?

It's my favourite day.

Come by for me at eight, I live in Las Quintas.

She gave him the address.

Listen, you really are lovely; you look like a character from a bolero.

Really? You're much better than I expected.

On the way home, listening to The Grass Roots' "Midnight Confessions", he felt his heart thrumming. His body was happy. He heard his cellphone ring, but did not even look to see who was calling.

Eight

They call me the Elf and not long ago I got the contract to eliminate Samantha Valdés. The man who made the connection for me knows I never fail. The power Valdés wields keeps a lot of people awake at night, and now it does me too. For her I'll be one more coincidence and here's hoping that will suffice. I just got a Face message, let's see from whom. Hmm, as I was saying, I'll be a simple coincidence in her life. She just suffered an assassination attempt, but she survived, a whole commando couldn't put her away. One of her men betrayed her and revealed where she could be ambushed. What will happen when she finds out who, will she throw a fit or go to the beach? Coincidences, I tell you, it's nothing more, and to make good on my contract I'll be one of them. That woman is getting in the way of too many people. A detective from Mexico City is here, what for? what sort of coincidence is he cooking up? Samantha Valdés will soon fall into my clutches; if she dies in that hospital I'll lose half my honorarium, and if I don't get her I don't know what happens next. The people behind the attack are the same ones now paying me to correct the error that she's still alive; a change in strategy and I'm king of the dodgers. I'll do the deed, period. I'm stuck in this horrible city where you hear nothing but boasting: that the women are the most beautiful in Mexico, that the farmers are on the cutting edge in agriculture, that the symphony orchestra is world-class. Foolishness. If all that were true, you'd see it in the architecture of the city, and the crooks would have less influence; for sure they invest millions upon millions, and they only manage to make it more grotesque. You'd see it in the bookstores, too, in the cathedral, in the cleanliness of the streets. Well, the Botanical Garden may be a jewel, but I don't think the narcos have anything to do with that. I've studied the circle around Samantha and except for two suicidal gunslingers who look like idiots there is nothing there; the guy in charge of her security is a blubbery jerk who only knows how to shoot, same as the killers keeping him company. It'll be a cinch to pull it off; that hospital is vulnerable even if the Army and the Federales are occupying it. I'll move fast because this hotel is a disgrace, the lights are too glaring for my taste and there's an awful lot of hoopla, could it be they don't even think about their guests' privacy? This is what you have to put up with in my line of work, but either I do it well or I'll have to stop calling myself the Elf.

On Sunday morning, Charface's three-fingered hand turned the page of the newspaper. The photograph of a bullet-ridden body took up a quarter of a page. We see his gesture of satisfaction. Next to the telephones, the same photograph, the original, lay on top of others. The headline: "Dangerous Assassin Linked to Gulf Cartel Killed."

In the garden the tulips glowed.

Nine

At seven a.m. on Monday he walked into the hospital. What the hell am I doing here? You're being nosey, fucking Lefty, why pretend? it's not as if you were Padre Jeringas going ward to ward splashing holy water on the sick with disposable needles. Maybe I appreciate her helping me pay for my son's education. Sure, but you gave her a man you'd arrested and he wasn't the first. He was going to ask for Samantha Valdés, but Max Garcés, dressed to look like a janitor, stood blocking his way. Outside, soldiers yawned. The Federales, same story, except for tall, no-nonsense Trucks Obregón, who was talking on his cellphone. What's the story, Max, did you change jobs? Yup, I've gone straight, Lefty Mendieta, you came to see her, right? No way, I'm here to see a cousin. She came around the day before yesterday, but she has a hard time talking; the doctor's not sure, but he thinks the worst is over. Then she's made it through, doctors always say that just in case. That's what we all hope. Can you pee without them watching? Barely, but we don't lose sleep over that, what counts now is her getting better. Is she under arrest? That's what the soldiers keep saying. Who's that talking on his cell? It's Trucks

Obregón, just in from Sonora. Hmm, so what's going to happen to her? Once she's better we'll figure it out, for now everything stays as it is. Give her my best, tell her as soon as she's back to a hundred per cent I'll take her to a movie. I'll be sure to tell her. But now that I'm here, I want to ask you a question. You don't take a step without your boots on, do you, you bastard? They smiled. A fortune-teller got killed, they put fourteen bullets in his chest, seems with the same pistol. I know who that is, I saw his picture in *El Debate*, he was a dude who got around, so if he got fucked he must have deserved it. The mother thinks it was Killyhawk. That bastard fell off the burro a long time ago and he's the type who's capable of anything. Is he part of your group? No, he's a freelancer, he traffics opium paste, brings it down from the mountains; we let him because he doesn't mess with anybody and that stuff isn't our thing anyway, but who knows about the future, since the gringos are getting into heroin. Do you know where I might find him? He's a violent bastard, you'd be better off leaving him to Pineda, maybe he's got some agreement with him. Two doctors walked by chatting, they said good morning. So, anybody could have killed the fortune-teller. Plenty of people, if there is one thing the bros can't stand it's something turning to shit when they've been told it's going to smell like roses. But why blame that loser? You'll have to ask Killyhawk, or whoever it was took him down. Listen, if you lived someplace else, would you come back to

72

Culiacán so somebody would knock you off? Crazy I'm not. So it seems. Time to get to work, Lefty Mendieta, no way around it. I hope you're not implicated in this business. They can frisk me, and the señora too; I can't speak for anybody else. Who was it? Soon I'll know, once she's well enough to have a conversation. O.K. Max, we'll be seeing each other, behave yourself. And if I behave badly I'll invite you along. Sounds like a deal.

He went home. Trudis was sweeping out the garage, as soon as she spotted him she went in to put on the kettle for Nescafé. Lefty parked his car in the street and walked in. How are you this morning, Lefty? Like a new man, what about you? Poor but happy, as you already know, are you ready for breakfast? Coffee will do. Again? how many times do I have to tell you you have to eat properly? Agreed, whip up something quick. No way, here we eat like people, I brought some tamales de elote that will make you lick your fingers. That'll do. By the way, we've got to pay the bills: lights, water and telephone, I left them on your table, but you didn't notice. How much is it? Two thousand pesos. What! that's highway robbery. And you're telling me? tell the bandits who govern us, they love to boast they're on the side of the people and you can see it's nothing but pineapple juice. That's outrageous, go right now to the Consumer Protection Bureau and tell them how much two plus two is. A perfect plan, except they only take complaints from the person involved and your name is on the bills, right now I'm going to fry up those tamales with some rajas and beans, you polish them off, then zip over to Consumer Protection and take on those people, who in my experience are good for only two things: for nothing and for nothing. The scoundrels. Lefty went to get his pistol from the Jetta, removed the bullets, oiled it, and left it on the table in the centre of the room where it stained the bills. Trudis served him. Lefty, don't do anything rash even if they deserve it, it isn't worth soiling your hands with those louses, then she went about the house dancing to "Oh, Denny's" by Botellita de Jerez. Amused, Mendieta watched her.

Before leaving, he dialled the new federal prosecutor's expert adviser. Should we meet up at the prosecutor's office? Crazy I'm not. Mendieta said nothing, then: I thought you worked there. I work for them, but not there. O.K., how about my office at the Ministerial Police? Even worse, isn't there a single fucking coffee shop in this town?

At the Miró, Lefty ordered an Americano, the other guy asked for a regular Coke and lit a cigarette. Let's see if he turns out to be a fag, each of them thought. I'm Héctor Belascoarán Shayne, he introduced himself. He was not very tall, not especially heavyset, and had only one eye, which bore into you and made him look a bit roguish. Edgar Mendieta, Lefty said in turn. They did not shake hands. Rudy came along with a hello and the beverages, and left the menu. A waitress came to tell the man he could not smoke, but neither of them paid her any heed. In one corner Attorney Záizar was reading the newspaper. First time visiting Culiacán? Not much to see here. Belascoarán was a Chilango through and through; he missed his beloved D.F., the Distrito Federal, as Mexico City is known. O.K., let's get down to it, my commander says your boss at the federal prosecutor's office suggested we coordinate, did your boss tell you anything? Nothing, do you know what it's about? Maybe they want us to look into the assassination of Madero, it's only been a hundred years. No shit, they turned to their drinks. Lefty wondered if the new federal prosecutor for Sinaloa was also from Mexico City and asked. Belascoarán smiled: What about it? he finished his Coke and ordered another. Lefty thought about Gámez and about Samantha. It could be a coincidence, or maybe proof of how organised the government is. These fucking Cokes aren't bad. Mendieta sipped his coffee and fixed his gaze on a señora walking by, imagining she was Edith Santos. The visitor lit another cigarette. In general, he said, I think we've come into the world to be worth shit, you get upset about how much they charge you for the electricity or the water and before you know it you're rotting away even though you're still alive. Better than rotting over a woman, don't you think? For most of the day I couldn't give a shit. They fell silent. They turned to watch another señora in tight pants enjoy sashaying by. Their table was on the way to the women's washroom. They smiled at each other, pleased at her flirting. Any more women like her around, we'll all be slackers. Belascoarán drank the rest of his second Coke and knocked his ashes into the can. Listen, colleague, about 25 per cent of all Mexicans were born in the D.F. like me, so, anything you happen to find out by some coincidence is irrelevant; I on the other hand have a tidbit that's juicy as fuck-all: this government is going to throw everything they've got at Samantha Valdés, and they've got you down as one of her men. Mendieta was stunned. Don't fuck with me, I've got nothing to do with that woman. You've been fingered, pal, so get cracking and stop speculating on stupid shit. That's fucking slander. There's a word that doesn't exist at the federal prosecutor's office. How come you're their adviser? That's none of your business, and keep your eyes peeled or you're going to get fucked. Lefty looked into his only eye and knew he was not lying; what mess had he fallen into? He had better find out. Listen, is it true that the federal prosecutor's advisers are all faggots? Only the ones from Culiacán.

They agreed to meet again. Each went his separate way. Mendieta got into his car, turned on the stereo, The Association playing "Never My Love", and he drove slowly to Cinépolis Plaza; it was time for a conversation with Irene Dueñas, the fortune-teller's fiancée. He had to acknowledge that this new development would keep him from getting bored and that his colleague, Héctor Belascoarán Shayne, was tougher than he was pretty.

Fine features, carefully made up, shoulder-length hair with highlights and a youthful body. At least 45, thought Lefty, who preferred not to guess a woman's age because he was always wrong. She showed him into an office packed to overflowing with boxes of women's clothing and mannequins still to be dressed; one was quite eye-catching. Computer on a glass-topped desk, plus two state-of-the-art cellphones. We buried him on Saturday, she said and she dabbed at her teary eyes; it's awful, Señor Mendieta, impossible to believe, a man with so many plans. To lose a loved one takes a lot out of us, Señora Dueñas, and it often makes us feel horrible, however, I have to ask you a few routine questions. Nothing and nobody will bring him back, señor, and that's the worst part. Yes, but we still have to put the guilty party behind bars, did he confess to any particular worries or tell you he was afraid of anyone? Never, he was a brave man, he knew the risks of his line of work. Did you ever consult him? That's how I first met him, later on he'd tell me things about the future without me asking, and he was always right. She fell into a fit of sobbing. Waiting for her to calm down, the detective looked the place over, especially the mannequin that had drawn his attention. Did he mention any enemies in particular? Someone named Wence had him worried, I think he's a narco; I guess he didn't like what Leopoldo foresaw and he threatened him. Anyone else? Not that I remember, maybe that was the only one. Mendieta focused his attention on the mannequin, which featured a round protruding behind. She smiled a little. He liked that one too, it was his favourite; we keep it because anything we show on it sells right away. Did women consult Leopoldo too? More than he had time for, but ever since I came into his life his only interest in them was professional. With a beauty like you I don't imagine he looked twice at anyone else. I'm pleased that besides being a policeman you are a sensitive man. You're really hot, baby, anybody'd fall for you, said his body, a discerning observer. How much did Gámez earn in a month? He never told me, but enough not to worry about money; by the way, he made a sizable donation to the city zoo for feeding the animals, he figured they never get enough to eat and very few people care enough to help out; of course I'll follow his example. Why didn't he have an office? He said his work was more effective in the places his clients found intimate; when he met with me, she sobbed again, wiped her tears with a Kleenex, we took a walk in Ecological Park; but he liked cafés and restaurants too. Silence. Did he tell you if Samantha Valdés ever consulted him? They had an appointment for next week. Was that going to be the first time? Yes, and he was really excited; having certain customers gives my business credibility, it's the same with a fortune-teller. Do you know Leopoldo's mother? Of course. She thinks Killyhawk did it. She took a second to respond. I don't know, the only guy he told me he was afraid of was Wence; I thought he and Killyhawk were childhood friends.

Does Killyhawk live here in the city? That I do not know, I've never met him. Señora Dueñas, forgive me for having bothered you, I hope you feel better soon. Catch the guilty party, Señor Mendieta, society will thank you. That I promise you; was your relationship a long one? The happiest six months of my life. Did he go often to Ecological Park? No, just that one time.

He dialled Pineda again. Lefty-piece-of-shit, what a miracle. The sarcasm of the head of Narcotics struck Lefty as about as funny as getting kicked by a mule. Have you got a minute? As many as you like. What's up with Leopoldo Gámez? He was a fortune-teller, mixed up with narcos and swindlers. And with the streetwalkers too. Why did they give the case to you? it's closer to Narcotics than to Homicide. Because I'm so good. You don't say; well, here's your notice: I'm going to talk to the Commander and have him hand it over to us, we don't like outsiders muscling in on our turf. Well, you'll have to stuff it, I'm investigating the case and it's full of narcos, a big cheese might even be involved, and I'm the one to solve it. You're fucked, Lefty, I want you to drop it and you'd better respect my rank. The only rank I acknowledge is my balls. Fucking mother, and he hung up, evidently enraged. Lefty smiled derisively.

In the evening he took Edith to her choice, the Apostolis at Club Chapultepec, a restaurant with a short menu and a relaxing view. The music was soft, the beer cold, and the wine list tempting. They were served tequila and whisky as aperitifs. His body was ready to spring.

This is one of my favourite places.

She smelled like a woman, something from Yves Saint Laurent, maybe Manifesto.

I've never been before.

Zelda told me you don't go anywhere but El Quijote, I'd be delighted if you would take me there one day.

We shall take you there, my love, but first you have to earn your merit badge.

Your health, they said. Lefty was nervous, what is this? am I going to start all over again? what a drag, before you know it the world will fall apart on me. He did not want to complicate his life, so he left everything to his body, which was overjoyed and did not hesitate to make contact under the table. They were seated face to face. Without any apparent justification, Mendieta slid over to the seat beside her.

To be closer.

Are you nervous? Zelda never told me you were like that.

Sorry, would you like me to go back to the other chair?

I like decisive men, the kind who don't see the abyss until they're already falling in. But if we are going to have some action, let's have a quiet supper first, as if nothing is going to happen, how does that sound?

Fucking hag, for sure she was going to be a nun.

Forgive me, sometimes I trip over everything.

Then he railed at his body: You see, you son of a fucking whore? now you made me look ridiculous, all because of your fucking fever. Don't worry about it, Lefty, she's flirting with you, I bet you she's horny as hell. Well, let me enjoy this party in peace, none of your bad manners. Don't insult me, you fucking bastard, if you get prickly I'll make you go a few days without taking a shit, then you'll know what it is to love God in Indian country. Mendieta understood the gravity of the threat and backed off. Alright, but leave me in charge.

How come you've never married?

Because he's an idiot.

Don't think I don't ask myself the same question; maybe so I wouldn't get divorced.

You don't say.

It's because he fell out of bed when he was small.

Well, one time I was hopeful, but she ran off and I never saw her again.

I can't understand that, you've got a very nice way about you; I think maybe you're making this up.

Take off your panties and you'll see he's telling the truth. Enough, fucking body, please.

At first I wished I'd made it up, now it's all the same to me; it just didn't happen and that's that.

Aha, what happened to you was like in that movie with Julia Roberts and Richard Gere.

"Runaway Bride", I saw it on T.V. about a month ago.

They ate hungrily, she pescado calabrese fragrant with basil and lime, he filete de res al burro negro, both suggested by Ileana, the owner. And it was César, her husband, who proposed an exquisite Mexican wine. Then to watch their waists they shared a dessert. Once they had their coffee, she asked: Your house or mine?

Oh, Papa, forget everything I said, she is the most intelligent girl we've ever met.

Mendieta smiled, she gave him a soft kiss to encourage him.

In the Jetta they listened to Cher and Rod Stewart sing "Bewitched, Bothered & Bewildered". Edith sang along with "after one whole quart of brandy" in a good voice. No shit, his body exclaimed, thrilled, if she's singing now, imagine what she'll be doing tomorrow.

Her apartment on the river near Niños Héroes Parkway gave off a faint aroma of sun-ripened apples, and was lit by a floor lamp in one corner. The empty walls showed marks that paintings had once hung there and Lefty saw nothing else, all he sensed were her parted lips and the velvety murmurs of kissery. And then green shadows and everything was waterwillies, wild ambony, exasperating jitternals. Moonspurs glittered and they went at it skinploding, doublessing in a transpuntled volcano of sweatlicked kisses. Then it was the convulctive bedfury of matrissals, the pantpanting pluvimouthing of orgamocurdle, the vorticello of velcaresses which snared them, juxtapoled them, and paramoved them.

Aahh. Dark leather sofa. Soon she was navigating the crest of the murmspel, lovebirdling rummaglios and strewing naglesty fondillies, joyously squeezing her fragrantoblio. Aahh. Overpowering pinnaclice. Aggh. Handslung, she closed her eyes and again erupted, aahh, aahh, until, aggh, her face dripping sweat, she was fire, black rose, featherfloat. Four times. Then suddenly wildbursting, she taught the astonished man three of her secrets and the four-hundred thousand names of pleasure. Aggh.

Thus they grappled for eighteen minutes, during which time Lefty lost touch with himself and had to acknowledge that the female realm is the only domain without end. They lay quietly, pearly and kneaded, until they began to suffer from the tight confines of the sofa, which barely fit two people seated.

This is what saves civilisation. Tell me it ain't so.

Ten

The Flea Daut was sitting on the kerb across from Lefty's house, waiting for him. He smoked, chewed gum, and thought about his old life in the Col Pop. Every Saturday there was a party in one house or another, but he never dared dance. It wasn't that girls didn't like him, he would simply freeze, and no human power could help him overcome his inhibitions. The stereo would be playing a number by the Bee Gees or Dave MacLean, good for bringing bodies and cheeks close together, and he would sit on the sidelines, watching, cornered by a familiar throbbing in his temples. A few years later, by the time he was a crew chief serving the Tierra Blanca Cartel, he could not find any explanation for those moments, especially once he became cold and inured, the kind that always manages to survive. That steeliness proved essential when he had to hurry along the fate of Pockmark Long, who had taken advantage of his sister Blanca – Blanca, who was now living happily in Anaheim and delivering tortillas for him. Pockmark liked to eat supper at the Oriental and that's where he found him one night, looking very full of himself and trusting in the weight his name carried, and he put six bullets in his chest. The woman who was with him raised her hands and dropped her eyes to signal that he was not her concern, and he let her be. What times those were. The city has changed so, especially the rules for getting by; it's more dangerous now, more unpredictable. He remembered Mendieta not doing very well either at those get-togethers; he saw him dance only once, with one of Doña Mary's daughters, to a tune called "Je t'aime moi non plus", and the dude looked like a statue in shock. Ah, fucking Lefty was a mystery and just look where he ended up; that said, I've seen how well-connected he is, he gets plenty of respect and he can live as he damn well pleases. The Flea had heard about how the detective miraculously survived an attempt on his life when they were young, his car had been blown sky high and people started calling him the Cat. He wouldn't bring that up today; only the people who suffer such calamities have the right to recall them, that's how it is, no way around it. He was waiting for Lefty because he was going to risk everything and he wanted Lefty to know about it. After all, he didn't want to feel guilty for having got him involved; well, to be frank, the dead fortune-teller had told him something. He also felt like some tacos. Fucking Meño, why did he close?

He gave up and departed at the very moment Lefty became aware of the dimensions of the sofa.

Eleven

Early that day, Monday, a woman in her sixties had turned up to claim the body of Octavio Machado Torres, the handbag-snatcher at Cinépolis. She had seen his picture in the newspaper. She answered every question with "I don't know". She did admit he was her son, that she knew little about his life, that he never had held a stable job. He was single, she did not know his friends, and neither did she know he was a thief. Mendieta interrogated the woman, whose blue-grey eyes shed no tear and whose voice did not waver. Had he become a crook himself, he thought, he would have liked to have had a mother like that: cold and categorical. It had been a year since she last saw him, she said, now I want to bury him. Lefty, who did not expect to catch the guilty party, helped with the paperwork and in a couple of hours the señora had the body. It must have been some other punk who couldn't get the handbag off him.

On Tuesday, Mendieta arrived at Headquarters at the usual time. He looked for the Commander, but his secretary told him he would not be in until eleven. He went to see Ortega, but he was off with Pineda on a case of three people riddled with bullets in San Pedro, fifteen kilometres from Culiacán. In his own office Angelita was speaking with Zelda on the telephone. She connected him. How are you, boss? Fine, but so it goes, do you need anything? They called from Liverpool, you can pick up your suit. They called you? No, they called Edith, but she's busy getting everything set up at the hall and she forgot her cell; she really likes you, did you give her a present or what? She's a very nice girl. She's special, and she has only one defect; did you find a replacement for me? Sure, the Academy sent over a young woman who was carnival queen in Guamúchil. You don't say, Angelita told me they haven't sent anyone. She didn't want to worry you and she's right, you should only be thinking about the wedding, how's my man Rodo doing? He surprised me, he's more nervous than I am, how is our case coming along? It looks promising, Pineda wants it and I've nearly managed to get it turned over to him. Boss, don't get too involved, we don't want to get burned; and protect my job, don't be bad. How about I put the new girl to cleaning toilets? That sounds perfect; I'll talk to you later, you're the godfather on Friday, don't forget. I won't, see you then. Click. Angelita, if I forget I'm the godfather at that wedding, there will be a premature retirement from this office.

He was remembering Edith's sweet caresses when a call came through. It was Belascoarán. What's up? Not much, colleague, I'm heading back to the D.F., no need for me here;

if there's anything I can do for you, you know how to find me. Among the twenty-six million people who live there? you make it tough. If they found Cuauhtémoc's treasure, why shouldn't you find me? come on, I'm in the phone book. What's the problem, didn't you like the Cokes here? The water they make them with is fucking bad, I'm better off crawling back into my cave. O.K., any suggestions for making raviolis my boss might find useful? Let him ask Zurita; just one thing, colleague, and this might mess up your life a bit, watch out for a jerk they call Charface. Who? A bastard who is going to be on the lookout for you or more likely is going to send somebody to break you. Why? Look, I already told you, you're considered to be close to Valdés, but I'm sure you'll find it entertaining. It'll be a breeze, you're saying. Like in some lives, there won't be a happy ending. Aha, so I'll be a conceited corpse. And then a lovesick ghost. Click.

Are we menstruating or what? it's true that nothing is turning out remarkably well, but things are not that bad; why is Belascoarán taking off? who is Charface? who is he going to send? why did my boss take such an interest in the new federal prosecutor? Maybe the bastard came home to die like the Flea; that would mean it's not true that one place is as good as another for dying, we should ask an elephant. Fucking elephants, right? they've really fallen off the burro. Machado's mother didn't want to lay charges, she said her son was already judged by God. Well, yeah, if you look at it that way we're all judged by God and there's no salvation because the dude sees everything. Rudy's friend Záizar said something like that, though he was referring to another god. Angelita appeared in the doorway. Boss, the Commander wants you. Before going to see him, he called his agents: Termi, you're the skinnier of the two, dress up in something sporty and hang around Ecological Park, I need you there until nightfall, take in everything you see and hear, now give me the Camel; Camel, you're going to sit cross-legged in the Cinépolis parking lot, see if the card sharps can tell you anything, there's always somebody who'll give up information for a few pesos so he can go on gambling, especially the señoras; find the guy in charge of the lot and push him around, he must know more; if anything comes up, give me a call.

How's the case coming? So far we have nothing, chief, except that Gámez is buried and the other one we handed over to his mother. You don't say. Even the expert from Mexico City is headed back, I guess he didn't find our city so hot. Were you looking for me? Did you manage to fix those raviolis? How could I? my wife is deaf and blind when she ought to be dumb; however, yesterday she cooked a bistek ranchero that was unbeatable, what about you? oh, by the way, watch out for Edith Santos, she's a man-eater, she's been divorced three times and not only did she leave her husbands penniless, they're skinny and hollow-eyed from pining for her. What more can you tell me? Just that, she's a friend of my wife's and she told her that you were a fascinating man, that's why I'm warning you; Edgar, the world is full of dames, and even if they don't know how to cook I can assure you they're worth it; before I forget, they're sending someone over from the Academy to replace Zelda and get some experience. If you tell her, she may never get married, she just asked me about it. I know, don't worry; the girl will be here next week. I interrogated Señora Dueñas from that store Bou Tik, and she said Gámez was afraid of Wence. Believe her, that gunslinger is an animal; go get him and don't let down your guard, not even Pineda's been able to handle him. He left the office feeling rattled.

Angelita told Lefty that Ortega was looking for him. In the man's office: Fucking Lefty, where have you been hiding? Whoah, did you wake up on the wrong side of bed or what; viagra, you bastard, viagra is the answer for somebody your age, pay no attention to people who say it'll give you a heart attack and constipation, that's just counter-advertising. Shut up, fucking Lefty, what do you know, you get laid once a year and the broads leave you a mess; but sometimes I think your life must be pretty wild since you're free of the idiotic obligations of matrimony. I, on the other hand, think you people with families live better, three square meals and getting laid every night. Well, it has its good points, but sometimes you end up having a fit over stupid shit. Don't frighten me. You've got your son, you should consider just enjoying that; he hasn't been back, has he? He's in college. So what? tell him to come for a vacation. I'll do that, listen, what's up with the things I asked you to check out for me? That's why I wanted to see you, we haven't got much on Killyhawk, seems like he's never been fingered and he doesn't make a lot of noise. Don't be a faggot, that can't be, you mean everybody knows who he is except us? oh, by the way, who won the match? Don't ask stupid questions, fucking Lefty, we're on the job. Sardonic smile. Mendieta muttered: the only one who seems to steer clear of trouble is Montaño. What does the doc have to do with this? Well, as far as women are concerned he never complains. Why would he? he spends all day riding some young doll. He does get one every day, the weasel. He's a bastard with luck, money and influence, you want more? alright you jerk, I'll do some more digging, though I think you're crazier than the goat that discovered coffee. Thank you. I'll see you later on, maybe something will turn up, but like I told you we don't have much. Gámez was a fortune-teller, he had trouble with Killyhawk according to his mother, and with Wence according to his girlfriend. We've got everything on Wence. Well, go there, maybe the stuff on Killyhawk is nearby. When Pineda finds out he'll be pissed. That faggot already knows. So? Let him go ahead and make a fuss. You bastard, you miss Zelda, don't you? Why would I say no, when it's a fact?

That afternoon he stopped by the Cinépolis parking lot. The Camel was sleeping placidly in his car. People going into the casino looked pretty anxious and those going into the movies looked calm as could be. Maybe they don't even know what happened here. Mendieta leaned on his Jetta and wondered: Why kill a handbag-snatcher and leave the handbag? Who uses a .22 calibre these days? The guy was a lowlife who ran into another lowlife and they fought over the bag. No, that wasn't it, a gun went off and the guy in charge didn't hear it, is that possible? Maybe he saw the fight. Lefty did not have enough elements to think it through. And that mother with the glacial gaze; he must have been a handful. He opened the car door and pulled the Camel out – eh, who? boss, boss – and threw him to the ground. Get to work, asshole, unless you want a month in the slammer besides the week you've already earned. Forgive me, boss, forgive me, it's that—. Get going and stop doing stupid shit, you lazy bastard.

He found Terminator at Ecological Park stuffed into a pair of blue pants and a red T-shirt with "Aeropostale" across the front. He was chatting with a willowy girl, very close to where the crime occurred. She took her leave when Lefty was a few metres away. Any news? About Leopoldo Gámez, nothing, but I ran into Queta Basilio, a girl I went to high school with who's an athlete, and she saw the body, but nothing else. Can I speak with her? She just left. Is she that girl doing callisthenics next to the nursery? One and the same. Go over there, tell her I want to say hello and keep her occupied until I get there. Are you going for a run? Yes, but in another life, hurry up, don't let her get away.

How exciting, I've never spoken with two policemen in the same day, are you also a commander? Well, I'm not half as brave as this fellow, who by the way told me you were around when they killed somebody over there; where were you when you saw it happen? No, I didn't see it happen, I saw him on the ground, I thought he'd fallen, but then I realised he was covered in blood and all crumpled up. Which way did the killer run? With all that blood on his chest no way could he have been alive, I'm a nurse, and I didn't see anyone run away. She looked agile and strong. So what did you do? No-one wants to be connected to a corpse in any fashion, so I took off. Don't think that way, the police are more respectful every day, how many people came over to gawk at the body? None, everyone gave it a wide berth. But you called the police. That wasn't me. Did you see the photograph in the news-paper? Yes, poor man, and so young. Had you seen him before? he was a fortune-teller. No, why would I? You might have seen him running on the track, chatting with a pretty woman. If I saw him I don't remember, tons of people run here. Well, leave your telephone number with the commander in case someday we need something from you. I already gave it to him. Terminator smiled. Lefty sauntered off through the crowd of exercisers.

In the Jetta, listening to "I'll Never Find Another You" by

The Seekers, he thought about Edith, should I look her up or not? What a thing it is to meet someone, a few days ago I was unaware she even existed and now here she is influencing what I might do over the next few hours, and she isn't even pretty. To keep temptation from taking over, he turned off his cell and went home. He ate a bit of what Trudis had left him, cooled his throat with three whiskies, began to read *One Out of Two* by Daniel Sada, and fell asleep.

At that very moment, in the Lucerna, the Elf picked up the telephone that had been ringing for two minutes straight.

Twelve

I killed an undesirable in a parking lot, do you want to know why? I'll tell you, but don't breathe a word to anyone, especially that rotten-faced policeman who turned up to investigate it, he thinks he's so good, so educated; an idiot, he never even looked over to where I was sitting on the running board of a Cheyenne watching him. It was a coincidence. I was offered the job of doing Samantha Valdés, you already know that. That's what I was working on: who her people are, how much real power she has, how she organises her life, what time she goes out to buy bread; I checked the list of her collaborators they gave me in the D.F. They'd already deposited the downpayment so I had to act quickly. I don't know how to stand still, I'm hyperactive and some days I have to do somebody in just to keep my hand warm. I like the movies so I went to Cinépolis. The coincidence. You want to know who called me, right? The one who wants her six feet under, but I won't tell you; fact is, I don't know, and if I did know I still wouldn't let on; a pretty nasty-looking guy contacted me, an intermediary who I only saw once in my life, and here I am shadowing the victim. I went into that parking lot looking for some lucky guy I could wipe off the face of the earth. A scrawny old bat was fighting to keep a skinhead from taking her handbag. How pathetic. An unexpected set-up. I plugged him without thinking twice. She ran off after she heard the shot and saw him fall. A .22 messes with expectations. No-one would think of a professional hitman using that calibre to knock off some scumbag. Maybe I should have done the old bat too, but taking him out was enough: one day women will rule the world and they're so special they'd probably take revenge on my great-grandchildren's grandchildren. I'm the Elf, and an elf can turn up anywhere and at any hour of the day. On Face I got word that the moment to get Samantha Valdés is now, no more waiting, and that makes me happy. I couldn't stand another day in this horrible city. Maybe I'll dispatch someone close to her too, I'll see; or that policeman who has surely lived far too long.

Thirteen

Samantha Valdés was awake and lucid. Her strong constitution and the surgeon's expert care combined to pull her back from the brink relatively quickly. Dr Jiménez was pleased, although he worried about the growing presence of the Army and the Federal Police, which had everyone on edge, staff and patients alike, including the lady capo herself. By now she was well aware of what awaited her once the hospital released her. The soldiers even ventured into the operating room, heedless of the procedures underway. Another inconvenience for the staff was the woman's bodyguards, the original two had become many and the tension had escalated rapidly.

That morning, Max gave her some news that would not reach the media: Frank Monge was under arrest and according to Hyena Wong had cut a deal. Max was convinced the plan was to arrest Samantha Valdés no matter what, and when the time came the man from Tijuana would testify against her as a protected witness. It's clearer than water: some people want her dead, others want her behind bars. Samantha turned towards the window and remained silent. Even if she did not trust Monge completely, she had never expected this;

now she saw why her father never moved from his mansion in Lomas de San Miguel and did everything by telephone or by insisting people come to him. She also knew that some ways of working would be better left unchanged, but that could wait. As they say, revenge is best served cold. The previous evening, she learned from Dr Jiménez that she was under arrest and not exactly alone. She had made a face, but said nothing. Now she understood the extent of the plan to bring her down. According to her people, the perpetrator of the attack in which she nearly lost her life was dead, but the story did not add up: no active military officer gets shot in the street and pictures taken of the crime; that is, unless his superiors acquiesce and are killing two birds with one stone. What bastards, that message is not only for me, who was behind it? Who are they trying to put in my place? Soon enough I'll find out and they'll be royally fucked, I swear it by Malverde, by Saint Jude the Apostle, and by the Virgin of Guadalupe, don't abandon me. Her men were prepared to die to keep her from being captured, but whoever that guy was, he was singing from a different songbook. For the moment she saw two options; first, hold tight where she was, in her room, until she could slip away; second, escape right now, which despite her critical condition was what appealed to her more. She said nothing while Silvia the nurse took her blood pressure.

So the news about Monge did not come out on television.

Nor in the newspapers, señora. Has his wife called? She hasn't called me. How did he react when you told him about the meeting? He said it was dangerous, that you should send trusted lieutenants instead. The scoundrel, we've got to see who's behind that guy they took down in the D.F., Captain Oropeza, don't come to me with the story that it was the president, from what I can see the only adviser he has who's worth anything is his image consultant, he must have the best make-up artist in the world; we need to be absolutely certain who it is we have to kick in the crotch, I don't want things to get out of hand or bodies turning up all over the place, we'll make sure those assholes never forget this country is mine too and that even if they want more killing, I don't. Understood, señora. She thought for a minute. For now, everybody stays put, as if nothing happened; we need to use our heads as well as our balls, at least until I get out of here; but tell our spies to earn their keep, I want to know how they operate, the people who want to crush me.

Carmen, the nurse on the next shift, came in. Good morning, señora, you look much better than yesterday, congratulations. Thank you, dear. She checked the monitors, put a yellow liquid in her I.V. and left the room. Can these girls be trusted? The doctor says they can; Minerva walked in bright-eyed, she had slept four hours and felt refreshed. Max went out. Dr Jiménez says you've been born again, but you've got to save your strength because the worst is yet to come. I'll do that, Mama, I'll make the effort, you'll see, how's my boy? Fine, we told him last night, he wanted to come see you, but when we said it was just a routine check-up he agreed to stay in school. He's a little man. He is so much like his grandfather; daughter, you ought to eat something, look what I brought you. I have no appetite, I will eat, just not that, Mama, the doctor said only liquids. What a shame, I'll have to eat this sweetcorn-and-goat's-cheese omelette all by myself. Don't tempt me, you know it wouldn't be good for me. You're right, forgive me; by the way, Devil told me the other day that policeman came by to ask about your health. What policeman? The one who helped you out once. Ah, Max said something about that, but I didn't understand. Maybe he's a good man. I can't be sure, there's no policeman who is not a son-of-a-bitch, and that one has a past. Well, maybe you should give him the benefit of the doubt; I've never liked Pineda; as your father used to say, he's a thug from seventh hell.

Another nurse came in. Señora, how are you this morning? Wishing I were dead, she winced. Come on, the young woman chided her, none of that, everything will be alright, you're in the hands of one of the best surgeons not only in the country but in the world, follow his instructions to the letter and you'll see how quickly you'll be back on your feet. Samantha nodded: You don't have to stay. The nurse left the room and the lady capo went back to ruminating about who might be behind the attempt on her life. It couldn't be a narco, there were too many on that bridge and an officer in uniform was right there giving orders; could they really have such a big grudge against me? People are right when they say ambition makes you blind. If Monge turned himself in and they executed Oropeza, it means the order to kill me came from above, but how far above? Well, I'll find out soon enough and those assholes will pay big time; I've got to get better no matter what.

Outside, the guard was changing.

Fourteen

Wednesday night in Ortega's office, a long-haired kid they called Stevejobs told Mendieta and Ortega what he had learned: Leopoldo Gámez was a nurse and a fortune-teller; he had no direct connection to the narcos, though he might have treated some badly wounded capo or relatives of one at the Virgen Purísima, where he worked nights, but nothing more. He was clean. Octavio Machado Torres was a small-time crook, some time back he did two years in Aguaruto, but as usual he did not mend his ways. Killyhawk traffics in heroin, he's not affiliated with any cartel, and he keeps a low profile; he lives in Libertad neighbourhood, he's a hothead and likes to pick fights. He got his start early on with Pockmark Long, a narco who died seventeen years ago. He's never been arrested. Wence is an errand boy for the Pacific Cartel, he lives in Lomas Soleadas and is one of the most dangerous gunslingers they have. So dangerous not even Pineda will touch him. Never arrested. A fucking gangster.

Stevejobs laid out the facts and departed.

What do you make of it? like I told you we don't have much on them. Because you're a loser. What, wasn't that helpful? Of course it was, I didn't know Gámez was a nurse at the Virgen Purísima. So shut your trap, do you think we only work for you? Well, yeah, don't forget that I'm the one who signs your pay cheques. Fuck your mother, fucking Lefty. Don't get offended, fucking Ortega, it's not my fault the team lost, I just want to know which way the water's flowing. Then stop hassling me and do your own work. Mendieta smiled and nodded, but said nothing more. If I were you, I'd hand it over to Pineda. The Commander doesn't want me to and I can't figure why. Because he doesn't trust him and he thinks having you do it will put him in good stead with the new federal prosecutor; the chief likes the political fray, but he makes sure he hangs on to his job. So don't be surprised if we find out he's been named federal prosecutor next time. And you'll be his personal secretary, Lefty. There you go.

Ortega asked him to turn off the equipment before leaving and he departed.

Mendieta noted that neither the father nor the brother appeared in the file on Gámez, would the federal prosecutor's office know anything? According to Belascoarán they couldn't care less. Maybe the Commander doesn't want it solved and wants to keep it quiet. The guy was a Culichi, born here, and everything else coincides with his brother's statement.

I'll go find Killyhawk first.

Should I really bother trying to solve these cases? Probably not, most likely they'll bury the files and put them side by side so they can chat. Maybe I should wait a bit; Pineda is going to talk to the Commander and for sure he'll give him the case; why should I risk seeing Killyhawk? The narcos are real bastards, I don't want anything to do with them, as soon as they lay eyes on you they want to buy you, and if you won't be bought they kill you. Now, according to the Chilango, this guy Charface is looking for me. What's the story with Samantha? People say she was ambushed at the bridge just past Humaya Gardens, by a really well-armed commando, and she escaped by the skin of her fucking teeth. I bet you now Hyena Wong is calling her the Pussy.

He phoned Jason but got no answer. Then Enrique, same story. Pair of bastards, they're probably out having dinner with the governor of California and toasting world peace.

Since Angelita was not in the office he answered the telephone, which would not stop ringing. Mendieta. He listened to a long, loud smooch. Who is it? Click. What was that about? I know people hand out hugs, but kisses too? Hmmm, could it be Edith? Anything coming from her mouth I adore.

Finding the home of Rodrigo Méndez, better known as Killyhawk, was a cinch. A young gunslinger opened the door in the street wall and took his own sweet time to enquire whether the man would see him. He made him wait twelve minutes only to come back and say his boss would not, because he did not feel like it. Lefty, who by then was in a bad mood, put his Walther to the kid's forehead. Take me to him and don't be fucking stupid, asshole. The kid did not flinch and they walked across a neglected garden to the house. Killyhawk was watching a Pedro Infante movie. Eh, what the fuck, let the bro go, fucking badge, or I'll whack you. Lefty did so. I don't doubt balls are aplenty here, Killyhawk, but at the Ministerial Police we have them too; I came by so you could clear something up for me. And that can't wait until the fucking film is over? it's Pedro Infante, asshole, not just any jerk. The room was painted an ugly brown. I don't have as much fucking time as you. A few landscapes on the walls. I already know what you're gonna ask; even though lately I couldn't stand Polo I wouldn't kill him. I didn't come to ask if you killed Leopoldo Gámez, I want to know if you think Wence fucked him. That bastard has the balls to do anything, and he's got backing; but all the same, fucking Polo was real uppity, he even snatched a piece of ass from Wence. Can I ask who? Don't be a fucking gossip, badge. They smiled. They put fourteen bullets in his chest. So few? me, I would have stitched the son of a bitch with twice as many, he really was godawful, he'd spin you a tale of gold and it'd turn out to be nothing but fucking drool. So what did he do to you? That's my business, now let me watch my movie, I gave you your answer; and next time you pull your heater on the kid, even from afar, I'll fuck you. Aren't you the touchy type, don't they call you Killyhawk? weren't you one of Pockmark Long's men? Don't talk to me about my buddy Pockmark, asshole, that was a man, not a piece of shit; you're a fucking badge and he hated every one of you. He was a creep, even we wouldn't go near him. You don't know shit, asshole, so get lost, Killyhawk pulled his gun and so did the young gunslinger. I know why you didn't kill Polo, faggot. Like I said, you don't know shit, fucking badge, and you don't know why I didn't fuck him. You didn't kill him because you don't have the balls, and you're teaching this here kid that any day of the week he might meet the dawn ass-up because of you. I've got more than enough balls, idiot. Killyhawk fired. Lefty felt the bullet breeze by his head and froze. If you don't get lost, the next is going between your eyes, you fucking blockhead. Gulp. By the way, did anybody finally give Pineda his goodbye bullet? No way, as a matter of fact he says hello, he'll drop by soon to visit. Let the bastard come, I don't eat from his hand. I'm just telling you. Get going then, and stop digging, when a bastard gets killed he deserved it, nobody's guilty.

Driving away, listening to "Always" by Bon Jovi, he decided to see if Edith was around.

His body responded in the part that need not be named.

He knocked at the woman's apartment, but no-one answered. He called her cell and same story. He felt the kind of cruel let-down you get when you try to surprise someone and nobody realises it. Could she have gone off with one of her exes? That's a stupid thought. And if she has, so what? it's not as if she has any commitment to me. Well, yeah she does, not a big one, but it's there. Could the Commander be right? He said she was difficult, that her ex-husbands are in a really bad way thanks to her. He dialled Zelda. What's up, is Rodo feeling any better? No chance, he's worse than ever, what about you, how are you doing? Managing, where is the party going to be? At the Salón Jazmín, near the parkway, I was there all afternoon with Edith, it's looking spectacular. Just what you deserve, is she still with you? No, she must be at home, she said she was headed there. He did not want to know more. Days before, both Zelda and the Commander had said she had one defect, but he couldn't see any: she was a perfect woman. Disappointed, he drove to the hospital to see Max Garcés; he hoped Wence wasn't one of his favourites.

Wence was plastered, drinking with two friends, when Devil turned up later that night at his two-storey house to tell him Lefty Mendieta wanted to see him. Wha'for. He'll tell you. Not interested. You aren't, but he is. Wence and his pals were wearing jeans, plaid cowboy shirts, and sneakers. How d'you know? If he wasn't interested, why would he want to see you? it's logical. Well, tell him to g'fuck his mother, and you too; I jus' remembered you two're big buddies. Hey, hey, take it easy, faggot, you don't want to toy with me; since you know who he is, just talk to him and get it over with. I don' fucking feel like it. Well the bro is outside. Seriously? Smiling, he got to his feet.

Lefty was waiting in the Jetta with the door open, leaning back and listening to "Sweet Home Alabama" by Lynyrd Skynyrd. He was smoking, meditating, why did Gámez never want to have a place to see his clients? was he afraid of something? of course, afraid a customer whose future did not turn out the way he predicted would walk in and pickle him; did Irene Dueñas used to be Wence's girl? An hour earlier, Max Garcés had given in: he's yours, bro, but you've got to go get him, none of us gets involved; if Devil wants, he can take you over there, but that's his business. He thought about Edith, about how captivating she was and about the passion with which they celebrated having met, it was unforgettable. He did not brush off Commander Briseño's words about the brutal dependence she triggered in the men she divorced, but neither was he worried about it. In fact, despite her having said she could not see him until after Zelda's wedding, he was going to drop by her place again that night. He was learning not to be afraid of caresses that get you hooked. So fucking what? I'll be there tonight. Blam blam blam, he heard and he threw himself to the ground beside the car. What's going on?

Gunshots were coming from the garage and the bullets were zipping by him. What's this about, am I a moving target? He heard laughter. Two pickups were parked in the front yard, one of them on the lawn. Lefty took cover behind that one, about ten metres from the door to the house, pistol in hand; he waited. Protected by the armoured door of his

Hummer, Wence waved Devil into view, his hands up, held at gunpoint by the other revellers. So you wanted to see me, Lefty Mendieta? well, here I am, laughter. If you don't scram I'm going to drill your little buddy's noggin. Don't do what he says, Lefty, Devil yelled, I couldn't give a shit, this jerk can suck my dick. Just tell me why you killed Polo. Wence laughed again: The bullet slipped. That was some fucking bullet, it multiplied like crazy. Mendieta moved towards the truck's cabin, which he figured was armoured, but it was not; Wence shot five times, the windshield fell in and a bullet perforated the mudguard. Didn't you like what he said about your future? Another gunshot, a flat tyre. He stole a dame off me, a whore I'd set up with a boutique, and she went and let herself get seduced by that asshole. One of the friends emptied his pistol into the chassis and Lefty took cover behind the back wheel. Are you talking about Irene? Mendieta tried to peek out at his enemy. The jerk had to die just like you, fucking badge; Wence took two steps forward shooting like crazy: Fuck you, badge bastard. Lefty straightened up as far as necessary and put three slugs in his belly. The narco dropped to his haunches, then slowly fell over; his friends were stunned, a moment Devil took advantage of to grab the pistol of the closest one and give him and then the other a bullet between the eyes. Wence stopped moving once he got the same medicine. Let's go, my man Lefty, this rice is cooked. The neighbours, hidden as far inside as possible, cowered.

Right then they were ready to believe in Superman, Spider-man and divine intervention.

What do we do? Put the pistol in the hand of the guy you took it from after you clean off the prints. The old trick. You'll see how well it works. You've still got your eye, eh, my man Lefty? It's a good thing the bro was nice and wide. They smiled. People say Wence took Gámez down in the Science Centre parking lot, these friends of his here were the ones who dumped him in Ecological Park and made sure he was dead. Aren't they organised, the bastards.

An hour later the place was cordoned off, the technicians were at work, and Montaño's team was on the scene. After the ambulance picked up the bodies, Lefty called Edith. How are you? Exhausted, I just got back from the hall; Zelda is thrilled. I really want to see you. Yes, his body seconded. Let's make it another time, Lefty, I'm all worn out. They said good-bye. Mendieta was unnerved. No shit, you aren't even that good-looking. He was certain she was not home when he had stopped by earlier, and Zelda told him they had left the hall early. What was up? What game did I just start to lose? Why would she lie?

He got deep into "Heart of Gold" by Neil Young and let sadness take over.

Fifteen

Zelda Toledo looked lovely at the wedding ceremony. La Lomita church was chock-a-block with people from the Col Five, which is what people call Colonia Cinco de Mayo. Rodo was dressed elegantly and when he answered the required questions his white skin grew whiter still. Most of Commander Omar Briseño's team were in attendance, as were a dozen officers from the Transit Department, where Rodo worked. Boughs of white flowers adorned the prie-dieux. Mendieta, freshly shaved, his hair trimmed, and wearing the black suit, was unrecognisable, something his co-workers pointed out before the Mass, when they threatened to shower him with beer so he would look more like himself. Briseño's arrival saved him. He had even put on some of the Mont Blanc Presence Edith had given him that afternoon. Edgar, you don't use cologne? that I can't believe. Lefty did not feel like explaining that it would impair his ability to detect faint aromas, which had proven so useful in certain cases. The only thing he did not change was his Toscana boots, which after a good polishing did not look too grotesque. He felt fairly nervous until Zelda offered her nosegay to the Most Holy

Virgin and the organist struck up the wedding march. His former shrink, Dr Parra, crossed his mind several times, though it had been nearly a year since he had last seen him: He's probably drunk as a skunk at some conference to save the world. When the couple reached the door, Lefty pulled off his bowtie and steeled himself to face his co-workers, but by then they were chatting with their dates and thankfully left him alone. Edith went ahead with the Commander's wife, while everyone else waited to follow the newlyweds to the hall, where Banda Limón was to play the usual wedding repertoire in addition to their hit songs. Twenty minutes later, Montaño and Lefty were the only ones still in the nave. Are you going to the party, doctor? Do I ever wish I could, Lefty, but no, I'm killing time until I pick up a little girl who's about to get off work at Ángeles Hospital; listen, I saw the lady in red giving you a rather romantic goodbye, she's very attractive. She's a soprano who's been hitting on me. Well, hang on to her, don't forget that in bed all women are pretty; if you'd let me know I'd have lent you my little love-nest, but not now, no way. No worries, where to go is the least of it. You're right, well, I'll see you tomorrow, and I hope you wake up happy. Is your nest far away? Not from here; he handed him a card with the address. Warn me ahead of time and I'd be delighted to lend it to you. One question: doesn't it bother you that every day you're with a different girl? Not much, in the end they're almost the same, we talk about the same things and they're all named Karen. Do they just want to have a good time? Actually no, they want to be happy and they're quick to admit they don't know how to find happiness. Even so, there must be something, some key that makes women seek out certain men. Some are looking for love, others for an orgasm, lots just want to live the moment, maybe they go for men who know how to make that happen without demanding a commitment or somehow putting them in a tight spot; well, I'll see you later, listen, didn't Toledo look beautiful. She looked like a queen. Enjoy the party.

Lefty walked to the Jetta. Are you in a big hurry, Lefty Mendieta? He turned, from the shadows Max Garcés emerged, followed by Hyena Wong. Sort of, what's up? You don't look like yourself, all dressed up. That's right, sucker, for those of us born to be tamales the wrapping leaves are a gift from heaven. They used to call you the Cat, badge buddy, and we can still call you that all these years later, Devil told us how you fixed things with Wence. Like I told you, Max joined in with a smile, that won't be a problem; besides, his own pals fucked him. Something is going to happen, Lefty thought quickly, or something is already happening, these bastards are not a good omen. Is Mexicali still on the border? It hasn't moved a hair, badge buddy, and it's prettier every day. La Jefa wants to ask you a favour, Lefty Mendieta. Don't fuck with me, I'm the godfather of this mother, I have to be at the party. You can come willingly or we'll take you. Couldn't it be later on? My man Lefty, we're decent people, we waited until the ceremony was over, don't ask for more; besides, the señora is not well. And it's going to be quick and painless, Cat my friend. The detective understood that he had no choice. He took off his jacket, placed it in the back seat and got into the Jetta. Max occupied the passenger seat. Hyena Wong would follow them in a black Tundra. Lefty started the car, Badfinger rang out: "Day After Day", a little tune he liked for the guitar riffs. So, am I a victim plain and simple or am I just growing old? this stinks.

Good thing you got that over with. I suppose, the best is still to come; hmm, so what fucking instrument do I play in her orchestra? Would you mind changing the C.D.? You don't like music? Yeah, but I don't get that kind, norteña's my thing. You bet, he turned it off. Look, do you know what's up? No idea, you know what she's like, she probably wants you to take her to a movie, didn't you tell her something like that? Does she know she's surrounded by Army goons? She knows and she can't stand it, after you left they came on even uglier, and do they ever fuck with you. I didn't know. The situation's really tense and the señora's recovery is very slow. The good thing is she's getting better. When she's well enough to be moved they're going to take her to Mexico City, she found out from the doctor. So what's the story with you, haven't they fingered you? Sure, but La Jefa is news, she's a good trophy for the politicians, I'm just a fucking nobody. I hope you know who to watch out for. For the moment, everybody. Even if you knew you wouldn't tell me, right? That's correct, and how's the Killyhawk case coming? What Killyhawk? They laughed. In the rear-view mirror, he saw Hyena Wong tailing them.

Hospital. Garcés put on doctor's garb and went in through emergency. Trucks Obregón had his cellphone to his ear and Captain Bonilla was chatting up a nurse. Mendieta followed five minutes later. Thanks to Devil, he reached the lady capo without much trouble. Pale, under a sheet, in intensive care. The gadgets measuring her vital signs beeped in rhythm. Thank you for coming, Lefty Mendieta, have a seat, please. There was a chair beside her bed. Minerva left without a word and Max Garcés also slipped out. I sent for you to ask a favour, her voice was smooth, muted. That's your style. Who told you to earn my respect, I used to tell everyone you were a loser and now I find myself saying you're a tough bastard, imagine that! Thank you for the flowers, I'll come back tomorrow for the vase. She smiled weakly without taking her eyes off his face. I swear when I decide I want a man in my life I'll look you up, but you'll have to dress nicely the way you are now; oh yes, give my congratulations to your sidekick, getting married is more significant than most people suppose. Mendieta nodded, he was enjoying himself. I'm not well and I tire quickly, so I'll get right to it: in twenty-two hours I'll be leaving here, give or take a few minutes;

115

I want you to persuade the police to pull back for fifteen minutes, we'll take care of the soldiers. These badges are ugly, I have no clout with the narcotics people here, much less with the Federales. I know, that's why you can do it without arousing suspicion; they're under Trucks Obregón's command, he's from Sonora and he won't turn his nose up at fifty thousand pesos. That doesn't sound like much, the Federales are expensive. Sure, they come to Sinaloa and they think they're in tough-guy paradise, but you'll set them straight. Silence. Couldn't you ask for something simple? There are no simple favours, Lefty Mendieta, my men do the easy stuff; now I'm tired. Are you sure you can escape just like that? No way around it, if I don't I'll end up at Military Base Number One in Mexico City and who knows if you'll ever see me again. O.K., tomorrow at eight o'clock I'll take them out for ice cream. At seven-thirty if it isn't too much bother, the money's in that bag. Silence, nothing could be heard. Who's Charface? The lady capo opened her eyes and turned towards him. He's the asshole they paid to kill me, but I don't know who he is; we know he was involved in the attack and he's sent an assassin they call the Elf, who must be in Culiacán by now. I gather his mission is to do away with you and every-one around you, and they tell me I'm one of them. Pause. You should be proud to be on that list, how did you find out? From a Chilango colleague. Well, keep your eyes peeled because it's true, and now go keep your promise to Toledo, she's a good girl; take that envelope from the dresser, the one under the bag, and give it to her. Do I say it's from you? What do you think? of course, she won't trust a gift with no name attached.

Max and Hyena were outside the room. He contemplated them for a few seconds, observed Trucks Obregón, a light-skinned, powerfully built officer about a metre ninety, talking on his cell. See you tomorrow, he mumbled; Max was not sure if he was talking to them or to the Federales.

He arrived at the party at ten, when it was at its peak. Edith Santos in her tight red dress found him and led him to the table where she was celebrating with Commander Briseño and his wife and another couple, who turned out to be the new regional representative of the Federal Prosecutor's Office, Attorney Manlio Zurita, and his wife. The two were conspicuously plump. Right then the newlyweds, who were making the rounds of the tables, walked over. Exultant. Here, someone sent you something, Lefty murmured in his partner's ear as he handed over the envelope. With a gesture she asked who from. Lefty gave her a hug and whispered the name in her ear. Then Zelda said out loud: I hope you follow my example, Chief Mendieta. The detective smiled, his eyes wide, but said nothing. They kidded around, told the "up with the groom, up with the bride" joke, and they all raised their glasses. The supper began with a chilled soup from a recipe Briseño's wife concocted that everyone praised, especially the Zuritas; then mashed potatoes and pork filets cooked in tequila, something the Commander came up with, which also featured salsa de rosas. They drank beer and whisky. Then they danced.

I never imagined you had such good rhythm.

I was in the Delfos company for a couple of years, until two ballerinas tried to rape me.

You don't say, that's the first time I've ever heard that a woman could rape a man.

The prettier the abuser, the more violent the aggression.

That bit about Delfos, when was that?

Back when the hurricane hit; you're an incredible dancer.

Uh-huh, I manage to keep the rhythm and I like dancing. Look, Edgar, I don't want to pry, but I want you to know I was worried when you didn't turn up. I didn't know what to think, I imagined the worst.

You weren't wrong, the worst is part of my life.

Your duty comes first.

The woman glued her body to his.

How about we get going? This penis wants action.

Tell him to wait.

Well, hurry up, see what an exhibitionist she is?

Ortega and his wife were dancing beside them. The head of the technical team winked at him knowingly. Nearby, Commander Briseño was dancing slowly, holding his wife close, they clearly loved each other. The Zuritas were dancing apart, which is the style in the D.F., and they worked at it gracefully.

Mendieta did not want to tell Edith about dropping by her house and not finding her when she said she would be home. For sure she lied. Neither did he think about the defect that both Zelda and the Commander had alluded to. The loud smooch on the telephone flooded his memory. He only had eyes for one thing, and he kept them closed.

At a table near the door, Camel said to Terminator: People say Chief Mendieta offed Wence and his henchmen. Cammy my man, I've heard that where he puts his bullet he puts his eye. Their gazes were glassy and their conversation included many a long pause. As far as I'm concerned, he must have made a pact with the devil; Wence was a bloodthirsty savage, and he had scary aim. Well, this time he got fucked. There's more, the dames really like him, you see the hugger he's got? Their conversation drifted drunkenly on like that until each passed out, face-down on the table.

They did not see the thin man, about a metre seventy tall, armed with a Beretta, surveying the party, and especially Lefty, for two minutes, nor how two guards made for him and he quickly made himself scarce.

Sixteen

The Elf burst into his room at the Hotel Lucerna, placed the pistol in his suitcase beside the .22 flipped open a cellphone on the desk and studied six photographs taken inside the Virgen Purísima Hospital: two of Max Garcés in disguise and four of the security team, featuring Devil and Chopper Tarriba prominently. Three others were of Lefty Mendieta: one outside the church with Max and two in the Jetta. Then he logged on to Facebook. A friend with the face of a doll sent one word: hurry.

He poured himself a beer from the minibar and turned on the television. Nadal vs. Federer. He watched a few volleys and switched it off. He strapped on the Beretta and decided to return to the wedding. If he wanted to do the job, he had to seize the opportunity: eliminating Samantha Valdés entailed a number of difficulties, so he would start with the policeman. He had no orders to do him in, but the man was on the list; besides, he hated all badges and Mendieta offered a good chance to scratch that itch, to keep his hand warm, and to make a down payment on the job. Since a badge was no ordinary mark, he did not opt for the .22.

He took a taxi to Pablo de Villavicencio Theatre, where a large banner announced: "SAS-ISIC Season: Javier Camarena, star of the Met, in Culiacán." Just what I was saying, so damned full of themselves, they think all the best comes to them. He walked the block down Niños Héroes Parkway to the function hall. He knew by this time everyone would be drunk and he would have no problem plugging the detective. I'm here to complete your coincidence, he thought as he strode through the doorway; the band was playing "El sauce y la palma", the guests were stirring up the dust to that irrepressible danza, and no guard blocked his way.

He looked for Mendieta and Edith among the dancers: not there. Neither did he see them among those seated. He recognised Zurita, who was chatting with Briseño. He made his way around the room slowly, paying close attention, to make sure the fingered man had indeed vanished. It's understandable, with that curvaceous babe I would have too; that said, nobody beats death, especially when I'm the messenger.

He spied a couple of drunks sleeping at the table by the entrance and felt a wave of disgust. He resisted a powerful urge to eliminate them and he went on his way. It's an awful thing to acknowledge, but a high percentage of human beings are simply a waste of space.

Back watching the same tennis players, he decided he would take care of Samantha after seven on Saturday, so he would have darkness as a partner. Seventeen hours to go.

Seventeen

The Flea Daut arrived at the Virgen Purísima at dusk, convinced the hour would bring him luck. He believed he became shrewder, his instinct more precise. Years ago, when he was a fearsome triggerman, he always worked his jobs at that time of day, when his cruelty became an article of faith. Wearing a Tomateros baseball cap and the loose clothing favoured by gang members, and with a bit of alcohol to oil his spirit, he waited for young Long to appear, which he did at about seven o'clock, accompanied by Hyena Wong, who of course was the boy's mentor and protector. A pair of bastards. The Hyena was very good at his trade, he had made some pact with Satan and did not fear death. Sorry, the Flea concluded, I'm going to have to fuck the two of you, and it'll be practically the same time of day I whacked your father, that fucking shit of a rapist. As if he had heard the thought, the young man turned to face the very spot where the Flea was keeping watch; he was extremely thin and short, his face so smooth and clear it intimated tenderness, something Daut perceived instantly.

He spied three young men coming towards him along

the sidewalk where he was sitting on the bumper of a pickup parked next to a white car, eating fries with chamoy sauce. At the same time, across the street two men approached the hospital from opposite sides; all wore colourful shirts untucked. Those bastards are packing heaters, the Flea reflected, they don't fool me, they're up to something. At the clinic door Trucks Obregón was talking on his cellphone and chatting with two subordinates who smiled, amused. The former gunslinger spotted two men with backpacks some twenty metres from the hospital entrance, sitting, like him, cautiously between two vehicles. No kidding, scalps are going to fly, there are A.K.s in those packs; oh-oh, Lefty Mendieta, what is that bastard doing here? He watched him walk out of the parking lot facing the hospital, cross the street, and slip right by the chief of the uglies without saying hello. O.K., so those guys don't know each other, what's next? is this a plan? He hesitated a moment. I don't think I'm going to be able to do this bit today, and if the shit is going to fly, it's not my fight, so, see you later, alligator, if I saw you I don't remember. Fucking Lefty, what's he got himself into? It's a little after seven, I'm going to stick around for a few minutes to see if I can catch him leaving, he's probably going back to the neighbourhood, he can give me a lift. The Flea observed an older man hanging around near the entrance to the parking lot. That guy is awfully skinny and besides he's really short; I don't think he's a badge or a narco, but the bastard is looking for something, it's written all over his crafty face. I think the fortune-teller was right when he told me I was headed for chaos, that I should be careful, that my life depended on it.

Is Lefty really a friend of Hyena Wong's? Maybe I should use him to get close to the kid and take apart his pretty face; easy now, something is going to happen here and it's a bitch not knowing what.

Eighteen

There is something funny about Saturday evenings all over the world. People relax, cheeks recover their healthy glow, and the prettiest women decide – why not? – that Saturday must be their favourite day.

It was just such a day that Samantha Valdés chose to escape from the hospital. At the agreed hour, 7.30 p.m., Trucks Obregón received a telephone call informing him that by order of his commander, Attorney Zurita, he was to assemble all of his men urgently at the locale of the Federal Prosecutor's Office. Lefty, wearing a black T-shirt that said Policía Federal across the chest underneath his unbuttoned shirt, and a black cap with the same, hung up the telephone in Emergency as soon as Obregón asked who was calling. Though surprised and uncertain, the officer ordered all his people to the office downtown. As best he could, he resisted the temptation to call Zurita to see if the order could be lifted or if he could at least leave a contingent behind to stand guard. Hyena Wong and his men were ready. Mendieta buttoned up his shirt and kept his eyes on Obregón. So did Max Garcés, who was waiting for the uglies to depart so he could lead the boss out. When Lefty saw Trucks put away his cell, he relaxed. He put the cap on the head of an old man waiting for a doctor and went out into the street. Obregón explained to Captain Bonilla that he would be back soon; then two trucks filled with federal agents pulled out. Lefty had planned to meet with Trucks that morning to negotiate, but he could not find the money. It had vanished from the back seat of the Jetta, bag and all, and he could not fathom how. He saw it there when they left the party and neither doors nor windows had been forced. Fucking crooks, they get smarter every day. He touched his nose like Paul Newman in "The Sting" to let Garcés know he had done his part. He thought of Edith, he had agreed to pick her up and go eat tapas at the Miró, and he went to get his car from the lot across the street. He saw the soldiers at ease, some of them napping, as well as a few jittery young men, whom he presumed were with the cartel, keeping watch on the entranceway. Among them was a Chinese boy who wouldn't leave Hyena Wong's side. Why did I let myself get dragged into this? he wondered. Truly, what is it about her that keeps me from saying no? Is it because of that business with Wence or have I fallen into her clutches? If Pineda finds out, I'm fucked; same story Zelda, how could I possibly explain this to her? The fact is he had crossed a line; a passing collaboration was one thing, but this was an operation that could have fatal consequences. He had better keep it together. Look, it's not like I'm sucking my thumb.

Where did I lose that money? I didn't take it with me when we went into Edith's house – or did I? No, I put the bag on the floor of the car; she told me she hadn't seen it. He noticed a weather-beaten man, about a metre seventy tall, strolling along the edge of the parking lot. Fucking crooks, they think they're so hot. He did not see the Flea, who was sitting stock-still in his refuge, keenly attentive to everything around him. What would he tell Samantha, that because he was horny somebody stole Obregón's fifty thousand? What a beach, as they say; but now she'll manage to break free and she won't even find out about my mess-up. The things I get caught up in for being a jerk.

As soon as the police took off, the lady capo, unplugged and bedecked in doctor's garb, came out the front door, her short steps matched by Garcés at her side and, a few metres back, Devil and Chopper in their regular attire. Hyena Wong and three men, among them young Long, put themselves in the lead. Minerva had left earlier to get the bedroom ready. Samantha made her way slowly across the street and climbed into an armoured compact waiting for her in front of an Army truck; Garcés got in to drive. Mendieta had by then pulled out of the parking lot and, without intending to, they ended up behind him, followed in turn by a Hummer carrying Chopper and Devil ready for anything. At that moment three Federal Police trucks blocked off both ends of the street. We're worth shit. In his rear-view mirror Mendieta watched

Trucks Obregón trot from the corner towards the hospital, his finger on the trigger of the ram's horn in his hands; several officers in the same pose were on his heels. The fucking bastard managed to get in touch with his boss. At the other end of the block, a dozen soldiers with arms at the ready poured out of two vehicles. Led by Bonilla, they looked to be on maximum alert. All this in thirty-four seconds. In the next thirty-eight, Chopper Tarriba kicked off the fiesta with a bazooka blast that destroyed one of the trucks blocking the street ahead of Mendieta and wounded several officers. Since everyone's trigger finger was hot, not even God in heaven was going to keep that gunfight from happening. Rat-a-tat-tat. Blam. Blak-blak-blak-blak. Blam. Ratt. Narcos, badges and grunts were having their fifteen minutes of fame and they were loving it. Rat-a-tat. The medical staff, the patients, the kid minding the parking lot, the Flea, the Elf and a few passers-by all threw themselves to the pavement. Bang-bang-bang, Blam. Ratt. Blak-blak-blak. The police and the narcos hit the ground too, without letting up their fire. Hyena Wong, from under an archway, showed off his aim and his nerve; young Long, clearly terrified, echoed him but managed not to hit a thing. From their armoured cars soldiers fired machine-guns every which way like demons. Chopper let loose another bazooka blast; this time rocking an olive-green truck.

Samantha, ashen-faced, felt awful. She lay back in her seat and waited for whatever God willed. That fucking badge had betrayed her, why else would the Federales have come back so soon? She should never have trusted him. A loser is always a loser. He tricked me, played me for a sucker. I want to kill him, he deserves it, cut his head off, the traitor. Take me back in, she said to Garcés, I don't want to die here like a dog. The gunslinger did not know what to do, if the soldiers grabbed her they would take her straight to the D.F., if the Federales got her it would be just as bad. If we hang in a little longer with any luck we'll get through. The cars were hemmed in. Lefty opened the passenger door of the Jetta and waved to Max for them to climb in. We're getting you out of here, señora, the chief bodyguard said as he struggled to climb over her, since she was sitting in the seat beside him. He managed to get himself out the passenger door, then he picked her up and, hunched over, made his way to Lefty's car, where he deposited her in the back seat, while the bang-bang proceeded full steam. Several bullets perforated the Jetta, whose rear window had already been shattered. Boom, Chopper Tarriba, seeing what was afoot, sent another bazooka blast at the truck he had already hit once. Thanks to Hyena Wong, who never stopped shooting, the gunfight had swung towards the other end of the block; in fact the police who had piled out ahead of Lefty's Jetta could no longer be seen. Several of them had taken cover behind parked cars and others had joined the battle at the hospital door. Hyena and two of his men were now using a burning car as a shield.

The Elf, who had picked Samantha out, understood the invaluable opportunity before him; in a crouch, he ran towards the Jetta, the Beretta in his right hand. In full view of an astonished Max, who had no gun on him, he took aim at the lady capo, but suddenly crumpled, shooting wildly; his bullets struck the chassis and one of them landed in the head of a sergeant named Bazúa, who collapsed behind an armoured truck by the hospital door. Lefty recognised Ignacio Daut, who had his pistol in view and who nodded at him before scurrying away from the battle scene. Fucking Flea, you just won the right to a few more years of life. Lefty drove up over the kerb, got past the abandoned car in front of him, and somehow managed to squeeze between the burning truck blocking the road and the corner house. They were out, even if the car was tattooed with bullet-holes. What happened, why did that bastard come back? Because I lost the money and I didn't fix things with him. What? Just what you're hearing, a few minutes ago I telephoned pretending to be his boss's assistant, but it didn't work. What a bastard you turned out to be, fucking Lefty Mendieta, another hair and we would have been worth shit; what do you mean you lost the fifty thousand? Last night I didn't sleep at home; this morning the money was gone from my car. Well, we'll see about that later, now we've got to get out of here; the guy who killed the assassin wasn't one of my men, but you knew him, I saw you smile. I'll tell you later.

Devil and Chopper had seen the commotion and since they were the ones in charge of protecting the boss they tried to follow as closely as they could, while the rest of the gang kept up their fire on the soldiers and police. In the process, Chopper gave in to his worst instincts, emptying full magazines from his A.K.-47 on anything that moved. At the corner their vehicle knocked over what was left of the Federales' truck and took off in pursuit of the Jetta, which was ambling peacefully towards Madero Boulevard.

Before the Jetta had travelled even three hundred metres, it rolled slowly past four patrol cars. Cavalry charge from Mendieta's cell, it was Edith, but he did not answer. Samantha had fainted. They called the doctor. You did what? you're off your rocker, you don't play with death. Doctors don't, but we do; in fact that's what we do every day; get ready, I'm going to send for you, the señora is unconscious, where are you? At home, but I'm leaving now for the hospital to see my patients; listen to me, señor, if anything happens to her don't you dare think of blaming me, you should never have moved her. We won't, but we need you, when you finish with us you can go do whatever you have to, how's that sound? No, I am going to the hospital and I'll stop in later on if I can. Until then, what should we do? Put her to bed, she needs rest, did you take along the medicines she had in her room? Yeah, I've got them. Let her sniff the one in the green box; that should wake her up, then have her take one pill from the purple box and another from the blue, understood? Sure, I'm already opening the green one. Put her where she can rest easy; I have to go, see you later. I'll call you in a little while, doctor, thank you. They hung up.

They headed over to what had once been Mariana Kelly's apartment on Valadés Boulevard. Mendieta was feeling low. In the parking lot of the building: Lefty, take the señora up, I'm going to tell the boys to drive on in case they followed us. The detective, who wanted out of there immediately, was obliged to take the boss of the Pacific Cartel in his arms; she was limp, lighter than he could have ever imagined; once they were in the elevator, without opening her eyes, she scolded him in a voice that was barely audible: I don't understand you, Lefty Mendieta, first you betray me and then you pull me out of hell, what game are you playing? That was fun, wasn't it? You bastard, haven't you noticed what a state I'm in? They say a bad weed never dies. False, death will take us all. Samantha Valdés, I don't know why I helped you in this mother, but I do know one thing: I do not want any dealings with you, I will never be one of your people, and I couldn't give a fuck what you do. Don't exaggerate, Lefty Mendieta, neither your life nor mine travels in a straight line; we move to the beat of whatever comes at us, tell me it isn't so. Though I don't like it, I'll admit that once in a while we dance to the same tune. I'd say that's always the case, even though it's not on the same dance floor; fucking mother, I'm really screwed.

You'll get better, and if I happened to be where I was, it wasn't so they would fuck you, let me make that clear. Well, it sure seemed like it. What is true is that I lost the money you gave me for Trucks. You—? Maybe I got robbed while I was at Zelda's wedding. There's no fixing you, the harder I try to think you're really something, you contradict me right away, she smiled weakly. Max appeared on the stairwell, panting, they opened the door and went into the apartment, which looked to be exactly as it had been when Lefty once spent a night there.* The detective blocked the memory of that sweet disappointment by biting down on one ball. They put the señora, clearly much the worse for wear, to bed. I called the doctor and he didn't pick up, we have to wait. Good luck, Max, I've got to go do a few things appropriate to my gender. Lefty Mendieta, the lady capo whispered, thank you, and it had better be like you say. When you're all recovered we'll have breakfast at the Miró, they do eggs with machaca that can't be beat. She did not respond; they tucked her in and went to the living room.

Mendieta was trying hard not to remember the last time he had been in that apartment, but there are things that will not leave your brain even after you die. He wanted out. What was he doing there of all places after everything that had gone down? Are we closer to our enemies than we think?

* In the first book of the series, *Silver Bullets*.

What a fucking drag. He had to go to Edith's, for sure she was waiting for him. Is she the type who worries and starts calling half the world? Frankly, I'd rather she keep sending me those sweet smooches, they're unforgettable. Garcés interrupted his thoughts. Who fucked the guy who tried to take down the señora? The Flea Daut. I don't get it. He was the one who whacked Pockmark Long; after that he left town, but since he learned the son is settling accounts he came back to Culichi to die here, that is, if we can't do something to fix things. What was he doing at the hospital? Use your imagination. O.K., we'll take that up with Hyena Wong before anything happens. Do that for me, and I'll see what's up with the Flea, what about the assassin, do you know who he was? No idea, we got word from Mexico City that some dude was coming for the señora, maybe that was him. Could it be Charface? Probably, who knows? They lit up.

A car horn is worth a thousand words.

Lefty, I need another favour, but this time it's between men. Don't fuck with me, what I just did was between faggots? That wasn't bad, but hang on, tell me what you think: I want you to arrest Dr Jiménez and bring him here. Don't pull my dick, Mendieta's mouth was hanging open, he knew immediately what this was about; he tried to evaluate the situation, but there was no way. Fucking Max, I give you my hand to shake and you take me by the foot. If you don't do it, the señora is going to die on us, you saw her, she's sweating non-stop and I know it'll be a long time before her condition gets out of critical; if you were fond of your centavos I'd make you an offer, but I know that's not your thing, and I don't doubt you really did lose what we gave you, so I'm asking it as a favour, in fact I could give you a few of my men, like I did with Wence, so your boss will make you hero-for-a-day in the papers. No shit, Max, you've really fallen off the burro. I know, Lefty Mendieta, but if you think about it I've got no alternative, and if you don't already know, Jiménez is the only specialist in Sinaloa who can deal with damaged lungs. But, do you realise what you're asking me? you've got the Army and the Federales there, no less, and after the escape do you have any idea what they'll be like? a caged fucking tiger would be nothing compared to those bastards, for sure they're already interrogating him, can you imagine how much clout a State Ministerial Police officer has? they'll laugh at me. I have faith in you, Lefty Mendieta, an idiotic faith if you like, but I've got it. Sure, I show up, I identify myself, slap the cuffs on the doc, take him out in full view of everyone, bring him here, and then I can take him to Gori Hortigosa so he'll confess who killed Palomino Molero. Sounds like a plan, why not? let's do it, otherwise the señora is going to die and you know how the shit will hit the fan and spread all over us, just picture the gangs trying to get us out of the way. Max remembered the smoke and led Lefty to the stairwell. Don't forget that when it's the Army goons an interrogation can last for days, I bet you they're already into it and keep in mind he was her doctor, the detective smoked avidly; that guy Charface, is he from the D.F.? That's right, maybe the order to take us out came from there. In other words, from above, as they say. That's what we believe. From fucking Popocatépetl Volcano. More likely from the Nevado de Toluca. Devil and Chopper were coming up the stairs, at ease, as if they had been out for a drink. Should we take these bastards along? Don't even think about it; boys, wait here, one of you stay in the bedroom with the señora, if she wakes up tell her we went to pick up the doctor. Lefty my man, don't you look good! No better than you, Devil buddy. Have you seen my father-in-law? No, say hello to the fucking beer-belly. Next to the ruined Jetta stood Hyena Wong. What's up? We're going to get the doctor. I'll go with you. Follow us in the Tundra, we're going to the hospital and let's hope it doesn't get grim; wait for us a block away, on Carranza, don't take anyone else. Cavalry charge, Lefty saw on the screen it was Jason, he stepped away and answered: My son, how are you? But the call got cut off.

As soon as Lefty and Max took off in a white Volvo, Hyena called his own people to tell them to gather at the spot where he would wait; he pulled a small envelope from his pocket, with two fingers he picked up a bit of powder and sniffed.

His eyes had a shine that seemed not quite human.

Nineteen

The Army did not allow the police to pick up any of the bodies outside the hospital. The soldiers set three of their own apart and piled the rest in the back of a truck, including that of the Elf, already dispossessed of his cellphone by a crafty soldier. It soon lay under three cadavers in checkered cowboy shirts. The vehicle departed quickly, destination unknown. The media managed to get a few hurried pics, which during the next few hours filled screens across the country. Fourteen dead and six wounded, none critically. Bonilla and Obregón each made statements, neither of which mentioned the fact that Samantha Valdés had escaped.

An hour later in the Elf's hotel room, the telephone rang endlessly.

In Mexico City Charface let the landline ring and ignored his second cellphone, which vibrated for an entire minute. He turned it off. His face was sweating more than usual. The shoot-out in Culiacán at the Virgen Purísima Hospital was on the television and he had a premonition of the Elf's calamitous failure. He did not imagine how his henchman had been killed because assassins do not imagine. For several

137

hours, while rumours of the lady capo's escape mushroomed, the telephones continued ringing and still he did not answer. If the caller was the Secretary, he was done for; he knew they would not bother cutting off his fingers before turning him into cold meat. Politicians are quick to pick up certain habits. The good part is that hundreds of them get killed every year and no-one protests. Politicians are cursed, not lamented.

He stood up, strapped on a 9mm pistol. He contemplated the tulips, lovely under the garden lights, and closed the window. Needless to say, he would have to take over; he did not like Culiacán, but there was no way around it.

Twenty

Hospital. Mendieta took his time walking down the block ravaged by the gunfight. How do I get the sawbones out? Are they holding him here or at the base? What would work? No doubt he's a clever guy: probably he went to them first, so they wouldn't finger him as an accomplice. Maybe he's used to it. Belated journalists were snapping photographs and filming videos and chatting among themselves. For sure they're interrogating him and they're probably torturing him too. The goons do it in style, whenever they give us courses they always have new and very effective tricks. Ever heard of Military Camp Number One? They wear it like a gold star on their foreheads, it's the cathedral of evil. What could I possibly say? Señores, Edgar Mendieta of the State Ministerial Police, I've come for the suspect, that fellow who fixes lungs; what, I can't take him? you're out of line, this is my jurisdiction and you can't simply come in here and push us aside; of course I know what I'm talking about; oh, yeah? you don't say, you and who else? that's all? you people don't even add up to an appetiser; what happened here anyway, why so much commotion? there was a big gunfight? who was it? did you catch them? the only thing missing is someone having escaped, I mean, people might suspect some funny business, so I'd better take the doctor with me, just in case the worst happens and he escapes from you too; I don't know anything, I just suppose; you understand me, right? so give me the sawbones and if you want him for anything come to Headquarters and ask for the head of public relations, Gori Hortigosa, he'll be happy to help you.

Outside, the place was infested with Federal Police. He looked for Zurita, but no luck. Trucks Obregón was giving precise orders and answering questions posed by Daniel Quiroz, who had him cornered. Emergency was in a tremendous uproar, so he went in that way. The girl who had lent him her telephone was caught up admitting someone seriously wounded. Dr Salazar will be here in a moment, señora, please be patient. Nothing doing, responded a middle-aged woman, a bit overweight, but perfectly made up, I want Jiménez to see my son and I want him now. Dr Jiménez is in a meeting, Dr Salazar is his top assistant. A pallid young man was stretched out on a gurney. No-one but Jiménez will lay a hand on my son, so you tell him we're here. But. What is it you don't understand, girl? go and tell him that Señora Vicky de Meneses is here with her son who's been shot in the chest, and that he is the only one who will attend to him. Señora, he's with Captain Bonilla of the Army. A captain? And we have orders not to interrupt. You don't say, where are they?

They remained silent for a moment, the nurse glanced over at a door. Lefty saw it all. The matron knocked loudly. A soldier opened the door pointing his rifle. Stand aside, she pushed him coldly and stepped into the room. Jiménez got to his feet. Doña Vicky, what's wrong? Nothing at all, they shot my kid again, I've got him outside. In the thorax? Something like that, in the chest and belly. The doctor is not available, Bonilla said rudely, and you should not have barged in here, leave immediately. You don't say, the woman pulled out a pink cellphone with gold inlay. If you don't clear out, I will have to throw you out, do you understand? And she dialled. You and how many more? Bonilla's face turned red. General, so sorry to bother you again, I brought my son to the hospital, but there is a dog here barking at me and he does not want to release the doctor who is going to treat him, she handed the cell to Bonilla. Yes, sir, of course, sir, I agree, sir. After three seconds of silence, the officer returned the telephone to its owner. We'll continue when you finish with the young man, doctor; Señora de Meneses, forgive me. Jiménez followed the woman out the door. Lefty approached, took him by the arm, and whispered in his ear: I've come for you for Samantha Valdés. I can't go with you, I have to take care of this lady's son, did you see how influential she is? You come with me or I take you in handcuffs. You are not going to take me anywhere, what's wrong with you? do you think the world belongs to you? if I go, I will do so of my own free will and after taking a look at this boy, who is badly wounded; meanwhile you can go to the pharmacy on the corner to fill this prescription and wait for me there. He wrote it quickly. While you're there get an oxygen tank, tell them I sent you, and make sure no-one sees you put it in the car. Lefty liked the healer's pluck. I'll give you fifteen minutes, the señora is unconscious and we don't know what to do. I'll be with you before then, you'll see, go get the medicine.

As he left the clinic, Daniel Quiroz intercepted him. Lefty, don't start telling me the city has gone to hell and you're doing all you can, what is really going on? Ink-shitter, for a while now this country has been a tumour about to burst, I'd love to keep you company shedding bitter tears, go on your programme and whine, but I won't, that's somebody else's job. What happened here, what is a Ministerial policeman doing here where I only see Federales and Army goons? Well, I came to say hello to my friends, Trucks Obregón and I went to kindergarten together; excuse me, I've got to go. Forced disappearances are on the increase, as are threats to journalists. It's hard to protect people like you, you know that. We have to get together, Lefty, we've got plenty to talk about. How about we meet in hell? you'll see, we'll end up burning at the same stake.

He rushed off. Eighteen minutes later Jiménez appeared.

Let's go, quickly, and may this be the last time anything like this occurs. Bonilla wants to send me to prison thanks to you people.

Nothing will happen to you; if Meneses fails, Valdés won't. Trailing the Volvo, Hyena's Tundra guaranteed safe passage.

He hooked her up, connected the oxygen tank, injected her, promised that she would get better, and asked them to call him a taxi.

By then, ten o'clock at night, news of the escape was finally divulged on television. Trucks Obregón was quoted declaring they were pursuing three lines of investigation, but he could reveal no more so as not to disrupt the work of the police. They showed three photographs of a young Samantha – for sure they had no recent ones – plus a short video taken with a cellphone of the Jetta rolling down the sidewalk. We should be able to share more details soon, Trucks added. You are in deep doo-doo, Lefty murmured. Bonilla declared with a straight face that they had repelled the attack without suffering any losses and that organised crime will never defeat the Army.

We'll give you a lift. Don't be offended, but I insist: I'll take a taxi. I can take you, Mendieta suggested, recalling that Edith was waiting for him at her house. He did it in Valdés's white Volvo, which was elegant and silent. First they covered the Jetta with a tarp, after Lefty removed his C.D.s and the envelope with the money for Quiroz. It was nearly eleven o'clock at night when he knocked on Edith's door; no-one answered. He called her on his cell; the message said she was

143

out of range. What's this about? Is she trying to give me the slip or what? Fucking broad, I'm dying for your kisses and your firm flesh.

He went home upset. He had lived through an afternoon not even a dog deserves and now no sign of Edith. What should I do? Maybe I better drop that girl, mysterious relationships are not my thing. His body protested, but he paid it no heed. "Because" by The Dave Clark Five purred softly from the stereo. The Seventh Cavalry Charge rang out, he saw it was the Commander and he let it ring. Settling in after a difficult day accords you certain privileges and he decided to avail himself of them.

Twenty-One

He did not know what time it was when someone knocked softly on his door. Edith? how I love that woman, she's going to have to repeat that loud smooch she sent me over the telephone live and well-salivated. He went to the door filled with hope. Who's there? My man Lefty, it's Ignacio Daut, the Flea. He stifled his yearnings and opened the door. What's up, Flea buddy? come on in to where's it's been swept clean. I won't take much of your time, Lefty, I just want to clarify a couple of things, he had not changed clothes since the afternoon. I've got whisky and whisky, which would you like? Well, if there's nothing else, whisky, although I would have preferred whisky. Lefty brought out a bottle of Macallan and two glasses. He poured. Fucking Flea, O.K., what do you want to clear up? Your health, my man Lefty, they toasted. First things first: I was watching you on the move this afternoon, you're with those bros, aren't you? And I was watching you, my man Flea, I witnessed how you pickled the nutcase who came at my car. We're buddies and I was not about to let him send you to Saint Peter, no matter the reason. Thank you, pal, did you see anyone with me? Hmm, I saw something,

145

but not enough to tell who was who, they were like shadows, of course it was fucking ballistic, bullets flying everywhere. The hell everyone is afraid of. The other thing I saw was the kid, Long, shitting his pants, I watched him suffer like you wouldn't believe, so I'm thinking his plan for vengeance isn't going far; I figure Hyena Wong won't put up with him much longer; so probably he won't be looking for me anytime soon; I'm going back to Los Angeles. Good point, I don't think he'll do anything either, so you're going to live for a fuck of a long time, let's drink to that. They finished their drinks and poured again. So you're with them. With whom? With the Pacific people. Not really, sometimes we coincide in work matters, but I still haven't fallen into their net. That guy was after you, did you spot him when you left the parking lot? Sort of, but I didn't see he was up to anything. Well, I did, and I did not let him out of my sight, because when you left the hospital he was following you. No kidding, thank you. So what was that big fat fart all about? Silence while Lefty weighed how to respond. Samantha Valdés was in that hospital. Was? During the shitstorm, she escaped, that even came out on television. Silence while the Flea smiled. No kidding, which means that you . . . you helped her? Something like that. He got to his feet. I understand; well, if there is anything I can do for you in Los Angeles, don't hesitate to look me up. What the fuck could you do for me over there, fucking Flea? here is where I am, stuck in the very same city and with the very same people, just the way Juan Gabriel puts it. Anything at all, even if you feel like a night with Pamela, I'll lend her to you. Forget it, the women of my friends are sacrosanct. Thank you, my man Lefty, it was fucking great to see you again. Iguanas faunas, my man Flea, same here and long life. What a hot car you've got, Daut commented as he departed. At your service, it has the most expensive deodorant in the world. He closed the door. Suppose I go look up Edith? Take it easy, fucking Lefty, I need some rest. Rest, what for? some bodies can't withstand a thing. He turned out the light and went back to his bedroom. He read a page of *One Out of Two* and fell asleep.

Utterly unaware of the tremor that began to shake the city.

Twenty-Two

The ringing of the cellphone awakened him. Edith! The vixen, she remembered me at last. He had left it on hoping she would call. Hi, he answered. Still asleep? wow I can scarcely believe it, you, a public servant and essential part of the social fabric, lying about? do you know what time it is? You bastard, you don't even say hello, since when did you become one of those people who loves to make demands? You're really hung over, aren't you? No, I don't think so, more like I'm still drunk, how've you been? On top of the world, a couple of weeks ago I saw Jason, he's really stuck on this badge thing, what do you make of it? He does have that in mind. He's going to be good, that kid, you'll see. Well, of course, you bastard, what did you expect? he's my son. Don't start acting fucking conceited. He's also your nephew. He's a Mendieta, I ran into him that day by accident before heading back to Oakland, the babes were all over him; don't try to claim that one, in that way the two of you couldn't be less alike. Not like you either, if memory serves me well. There's no cure for us old men, but how about that new generation? They are heavy. Why aren't you asking about Susana? What for? Haven't you seen her? Not even a selfie. Have you called her? No, I only talk to Jason and actually it's been a few days. Give him a buzz, don't be a scumbag. As soon as we hang up. Listen, so why did you get drunk this time? Because I had no reason to. That's pretty. Now that you mention it, Jason told me you really hit the beer. He told you that? He was mortified to say so and he also told me you don't watch what you eat. A gossip like his fucking father, but listen, besides waking you up I called so you wouldn't forget to go to the cemetery to take flowers to Mama, today is Mother's Day. Don't worry, I'll take care of it, and thank you for waking me up. What else, some new girl? Not until I finish with the old ones, last night I had two of them here with me. They must have been nurses. Fucking Enrique. We'll be seeing you, flesh of my flesh, take care. Say hello to your wife and to my nieces. The same to Jason. He turned off the cell.

I've got to call my son, I'm so glad everything seems to be going well. Soon he'll be a rookie policeman and then, fasten your seat belts, criminals of California, you'll never hear the end of that kid. It's great, isn't it? Being a dad, I mean. It's so easy to find words to praise your kids, even if you'd rather not say them out loud; my son, for example, is much better than me. He got to his feet, went into the shower; when he came out he heard Trudis rustling around in the kitchen and singing that little number by Café Tacuba that goes "*Ya chole chango chilango, que chafa chamba te chutas...*"

Mendieta smiled, there's no fixing Trudis, she's got rock'n'roll in her blood.

Ready, Lefty? Come have some breakfast, I made you a liver and onions you'll never forget and the water's ready for your Nescafé. Liver? isn't that high in cholesterol? Only for weak people, it has no effect on healthy people, when you get sick it's because you're going to die and you've got a long way to go before that; you're from good stock, my mother told me your father was a snappy dresser, very handsome, do you remember him? Of course, now tell me, what are you doing here on Sunday? To remind you about your sainted mother, don't forget to take flowers to her grave, today is the tenth of May, and don't forget either that I'm a mother too. I'll give you a record by Botellita de Jerez. And what else? Lefty thought a bit. Whatever you want. Can I tell you something? Go ahead. Before I forget, leave me some money to pay the bills, otherwise they're going to cut off the utilities, since you aren't going to go complain after all. I ought to take better care of my things, right? While you're learning, I'll go to Coppel and take a look at the washing machines and I'll let you know which I like, but that isn't what I want to tell you about: I nearly hooked up with Armando from Botellita. No, really? so? Uh-uh, Lefty, he was a lech, he had a girl on every corner. And he's ugly as could be. What do you mean ugly? no, Armando is attractive and very affectionate, like I tell you, I nearly stayed with him. Was that before or after Buki?

After, I was still a hot ticket then, now I wouldn't even catch Keith Richards' eye. She went off chuckling, a moment later the stereo was blasting the Stones, "Let It Bleed".

The landline rang. Trudis answered. Yes, just a moment, señor; Lefty, Commander Briseño is on the line. Edgar, I need to speak with you, let's meet at the Five Salads next to Citicinemas in half an hour, and don't turn on your cellphone. He hung up. What's this about? what bug bit him? and on a Sunday, what did we leave unfinished? As soon as Zelda's replacement shows up, I'll take her to a gunfight so she can see what's what and then she'll be happy to pay for the beers. What happened to Edith? Maybe she wants me to miss her? Well, I do, his body confessed, ever since we woke up. Me, too.

During the trip over he thought about his cases: with the murderer dead, the Gámez one was closed; the Machado Torres handbag case was going straight to oblivion, especially since the mother did not want to press charges. He concluded that everything was going fine, even the previous afternoon's adventure turned out to be routine, for sure the Commander was busy cooking then and didn't even notice. Maybe he wants to talk about Edith and her defect? He would find out soon enough. Ah, but I never gave Quiroz his envelope, that could be enough to get me in trouble. How long has it been since he last wanted to meet outside of Headquarters? Like eighty years. He took the Musala Bridge across the Tamazula

River and arrived. I'm going to look for Edith under every stone, and may it turn out however God wishes.

The Commander was voraciously devouring a green salad. Order something. I already had breakfast, maybe a beer. There isn't any. What kind of a place is this that they don't serve beer? A salad place, so people can die healthy. That's not for me. They fell silent. Did you see the news on yesterday's gunfight? The word is out, he mumbled and nodded, but I only saw a bit, yellow journalism gets me down. Especially when you're the star, right? They stared intently at each other. I'm worth shit, Lefty thought. Well, I saw the video and the news clip. The video? You're in it, twice, the first time talking on the telephone, wearing a Federal Police cap, and then talking with a doctor, both times your face is circled; and on the news clip you can see very clearly your Jetta driving down the sidewalk. He was not about to deny it, neither was he going to admit he had made a mistake, or that he played an important part in Samantha Valdés's escape. According to Murphy's law things happen because they happen and that's all, nobody was going to break him that easily. So he waited for the word from the Commander, who continued chewing as if he'd said nothing.

You are going to vanish; the Federales must be in your house by now and there is a warrant out for your arrest, your photograph is on national television every few minutes; if they see you they'll take you prisoner or they'll make you disappear, either of those options would be convenient for me, but I chose this instead, since like every good chef I'm sentimental; if anything happens call me at home, you can say you're calling from the butcher's or the supermarket, I get that sort of call every day; I was going to lend you my car but I can see you've already taken precautions. Thank you, Commander, you are more of a man than I thought you were. And you are a piece of junk, Edgar; Pineda always told me that, but I never believed him, you are an embarrassment. He continued chewing, sipped some orange juice, a damned narco-cop who deserves the gallows, he smacked his lips. You know what else? you're off the Force, do you hear me? off; I'll order them to pay your severance according to the law even though you don't deserve it; so, vanish; when you find your way out of this mess, that is if you do, stop by to pick up your cheque; if it occurs to you to go pick it up sooner, you'd save me the trouble of responding regarding your whereabouts, but you won't do that and neither will your accomplices allow you to; so get lost, you're taking up my oxygen.

Mendieta gave him a final look and stood up in silence. Now what? The Walmart parking lot was nearby and he went there to try to relax. What is going on? Was he afraid? No. Would he go on vacation? No, again. Should he join the Pacific Cartel once and for all, put himself under Samantha Valdés's orders, and let the fur fly? They would protect him, for sure. Did Samantha have as much power as the Meneses?

No, since she got detained, while the other señora pulled the doctor out of an Army interrogation so he could see to her son. He went into the supermarket, bought a bottle of Buchanan's and four C.D.s, he put Led Zeppelin on low and tried again to relax. He thought of Zelda, Angelita, efficient Gori, Ortega and Montaño. Even if every so often he hated being a badge, he knew he could not be anything else, and for years he had been part of a team of investigators who were also his friends. What about Sánchez? No, he shouldn't seek out his old partner and mentor, no point getting him into a mess he doesn't deserve, he was the one who had taught Lefty to live amid the shit without getting it smeared all over him. He knew he did not have many options, maybe only one was a sure thing. He turned on the cellphone and it began to ring continually, he was going to call Edith, but a call from Jason came through. Son, don't call me until I tell you. Then he heard: All your debts are coming due, you decrepit old bastard, and you are going to pay the price. The line went dead. Fucking kid, as Captain Hinojosa says, is that how it is between us? could it be the whisky? His voice sounded strange, sort of effeminate; some days are genuine nightmares and this is one of them. He dialled Edith, but she did not pick up, then Jason and got only static, twice more with the same result. Maybe Jason was out drinking, but at this time of day? A call came in from Angelita and six unknown numbers, for sure they were searching for him, so he turned off the

Nokia. Where is Edith? He wrapped the phone in the super-market bag and buried it in a flowerbed among the cacti to avoid being tempted by whomever. Then he listened to Led Zeppelin's "When the Levee Breaks" a second time to muster his strength. A number of people carrying gift-wrapped presents walked by, but he did not notice. I'm at a fucking dead end, but they won't catch me, fuck their mothers; who's after me, the goons or Trucks and his uglies? The Commander mentioned the uglies, who are dogged as hell. He reflected, some orders do not get carried out right away. Was that Jason's voice? Suppose it was a blackmailer? They're everywhere. An hour later he made up his mind, above all because it was the easiest option. And he would not complain, every life is an apple and the serpent had just given him his.

A man who kills should know how to do it to himself.

Twenty-Three

What is the difference between chasing after a bad guy and knowing you are the one being chased? How do you hide when you know they have you cornered? Well, what I'm going to do is put myself where they can practically touch me, I'll become their shadow. Why would I go over to Samantha? She already said why, the drug world is full of decent people; sure it is, and I'm Little Red Riding Hood, a very happy little girl. Maybe I can get out of this without her help, why not?

He went to Montaño's tryst house, but spotted an S.U.V. with no plates parked fifty metres away, two guys sitting in it, and he drove on by. They're sharper than hunger. At a gas station he filled up, paid from the envelope with Quiroz's cash. If they're watching Montaño's spot, it means they've staked out every place I might turn to, do you think he knows about it? Most likely, they'll push my friends around to find out if they've seen me, just like the Commander said; so I'd better look for help someplace else. It's Sunday, want to watch T.V.? Well, buddy, you're fucked.

He parked behind several cars, sixty metres from the building where Edith lived. Things looked quiet, one guy came out to walk his dog, a lady came back from the super in a taxi, several children were licking ice-cream cones. He smoked a cigarette. Where am I going to stay? Don't even think about going home. I'm sure Zelda would know where, that woman is so resourceful, and does she ever know how to find crucial information where you'd least suspect; but she's on her honeymoon so she won't be back for a while. I'm going to have to figure this mess out on my own, they must be watching the hotels too. Suddenly he spotted Edith Santos coming out carrying a large bouquet in a vase, and a few metres behind her a thin man in street clothes, his hair in a crew cut. The woman stood waiting, she looked exhausted, a taxi pulled up and she climbed aboard. The man got into a black car parked near Lefty, driven by a guy who could have been his double, and they followed her. No kidding, they've pulled out all the stops, as if I were Samantha Valdés; shit, I forgot: Mama's flowers, Edith's got her mother's.

Humaya Gardens Cemetery. There were so many cars he had to leave the Volvo three hundred metres from the gate. Those bastards have no reason to be here. He was carrying a lavish bouquet of red gladiolas and hiding his face behind it. He let himself be carried along in the crowd of hundreds, all weighed down by dahlias, roses, chrysanthemums, garlands made of crêpe paper and real blooms, candles, bags of food and soft drinks. By the tombs of the narcos there were norteño groups, local bands, trios, soloists, even a rock group imported from Phoenix, Arizona. People were drinking beer, tequila, and Buchanan's, and had to shout to be heard. His mother's tomb was clean, but unadorned. We're a bunch of barbarians, Mama, forgive us, and you, Papa, take care of her, she was a good woman; these flowers are from Enrique and me; I remember you liked to take gladiolas to the cemetery, the truth is I couldn't find any that were prettier or any other colour; Mama, if you could give me a hand with the trouble I'm in, I would really appreciate it; don't be mad, I'm not sure why I did it, you know better than anyone, ever since I was a kid I get these inexplicable urges to do something for somebody, that's all it is; do you remember when I gave away my new coat to that boy who was destitute and you didn't know whether to scold me or congratulate me? well, it was something like that. A man came over to charge him for cleaning the gravestone. That'll be fifty pesos; over by that blue tomb, next to the manzanita tree, there's a woman who wants you to drop by. Mendieta turned, but only saw the crowd. He paid, placed the gladiolas in two granite vases, and made his way through the throng to the tomb the man had indicated. Trudis was there, wiping the sweat from her face with a Kleenex, which she threw to the ground, then she walked off towards the gate. What's this about? Lefty spotted two agents in the crowd, following her. Oh boy, he picked up the Kleenex. He spread it out: 246. He looked around and only saw lots of people moving about, it even felt like they were pushing against him. He put the tissue in his pocket. 246, am I supposed to go to Coppel and pay that for her washing machine? yikes, Trudis, you're a tough nut when it comes to codes. Oh, of course, it's the number of a tomb. Let's see, we're at 531, they go down that way, it must be in the narco section.

He found Ignacio Daut drinking Tecates at his mother's grave, which featured a small grey-tiled monument of the Virgin of Guadalupe. What's happening, my man Lefty, catch this fish, he tossed him a Tecate Original. The tomb was adorned with a variety of flowers and lit candles. My buddies just left and my sister is coming later on, have a seat. I thought you'd already gone back. Without bringing flowers to my chief? how could you think such a thing, she put up with my wild ways and never complained; Trudis told me they're occupying your place, so you can hide out in mine if you have nowhere else to crash, you'll be safe there. Thank you, Flea my man. Stay as long as you like, there's no food in the fridge, but it's full of beer; I'm leaving in four hours and there's no way around it, my man Lefty, sometimes you lose and other times you just stop winning. Somebody kicked the fucking hornets' nest, Flea buddy. According to Trudis you've got the Army and the Federales stepping on your heels, that's no small thing, eh? Yeah, we're going to play tag, everything should be like this in life, right? why die from stress when you can die peacefully from a bullet. Divine truth, Lefty, that's why I came back, so they'd find me, but it didn't happen. Well, you aren't going to die from stress either. That's for sure, when I feel it coming on I put away a couple of tequilas and a beer, works like a charm. You are a wise man, fucking Flea. Well, got to get going, too bad you can't take me to the airport in your ship, it's classy. I can lend it to you. Not even if I were nuts, if they've got a pic they could snatch me before I get to Bachigualato. Are you sure the Long boy won't try something? Well, I didn't hide the fact that I was here waiting for them, we'll find out soon enough if he follows me to Los Angeles; but like I said last night, I didn't see any spurs on the bro and in my opinion he'll turn tail, that is, unless Hyena gives him a push and lends a hand, that'd be another story. He won't, Hyena Wong has a lot of respect for a person of calibre, you should hear him fuck with me about calling me the Cat years ago. I remember, Lefty, I knew about that too. It's true I escaped by a miracle. Just like cats who get seven lives, people say. Fucking Flea, now it's you who's going to be the cat. Well, my man Lefty, the conflab is fantabulous, but I've got a plane to catch. I'll take you partway. I've got my own ship, follow me to my house so you can stay there, and don't forget that in some dealings your enemies are a sign of your worth. I'll send you the corrido as soon as I get it written. Get the Tigres del Norte to do it, please. Nothing less.

While following the Flea, he recapped the situation: I buried my cellphone and I don't even know the number for my landline; they're on my tail and I'm not safe with my friends; no-one in the world knows the Flea except for Trudis, Long and the Hyena; Edith is being watched just like Montaño, and for sure Ortega too. What should I do? No doubt I made a mistake and I'll have to pay the price, nobody is going to forgive me, not even Zelda who loves me so, and there's no guarantee they'll play by the rules. What's more, I don't want to ask the Pacific Cartel for protection; maybe later on I'll change my mind, but for now that's where I stand. For sure they expect me to leave the city, but I won't, a city is what shelters you and Culiacán won't betray me. I've got to call Jason, why did he talk to me like that? that's really something, he knows how to do voices, I didn't know that about him, and Enrique; maybe I should go see Dr Parra. I'll find some way to contact Edith. Since I'm guilty, I don't think anyone would want to hide me, it's a serious crime too, the good thing is that the Flea couldn't care less; that's why he killed Pockmark. I heard he got warned not to do it, that the bro was a tough bone to chew, but he didn't care, he found him at a restaurant and served him his supper. Maybe what happened to his sister didn't keep him awake at night either, what he really wanted was a worthy enemy, like he says. The strange thing is that he disappeared right away and seventeen years later he rolls into town ready to hang up his sneakers; what's that about, eh? And now he's headed back to his family. Do I really have to pay the price for the crime I committed?

Is there a single Mexican who doesn't owe something to the justice system? Raise your hand. What I am absolutely sure of is that nothing is more useful than a good scapegoat. That call from Jason was not normal; these days blackmailers are really creative.

Daut's house was a one-storey bungalow, very much like Lefty's. Yellow, with two ficus trees out front, three bedrooms and a dining/living room, but no garage. It was neat; his mother, who owned it, had died four years before and Trudis, who lived next door, cleaned there once a week. She could easily slip by the stakeout because when they built the houses twenty-five years ago they put in a side gate between the two properties, and the guys watching her only paid attention to her trips outside.

I hadn't remembered that: you and Trudis are neighbours. Trudis and I are many things, including some we aren't. Mendieta thought for a second, Daut was trying to tell him something, but not straight out. That too? Absolutely, her kid is mine. He was dumbstruck, so the father wasn't Buki, no kidding, that Trudis is a bag of tricks; of course, I had no way of knowing that. He decided not to mention it, although he liked the idea of the boy being the son of a famous singer better than the son of a bro who came back to die.

They ate steaks and drank beer. He recognised Trudis's cooking right away; would the son know the Flea was his father? So you have a good relationship with the Pacific people. I won't deny that we've helped each other out, but I'm a long way from being with them. They lit up. It's strange. You think so? You even changed cars. Mendieta smiled acidly, understood there was no point continuing that conversation. Which is going to be my bedroom? The one on the right, leave the one at the front of the house alone in case the neighbours get curious, some have said hello, but others I've seen snooping, let's hope the uglies watching Trudis don't notice; well, I'm on my way, my sister will pick up the car at the airport, we'll be seeing each other.

An unfamiliar house is like the nest of the phoenix.

It was night when Trudis knocked on the door of the bedroom, where there was a bed, a television and a window onto the patio. Lefty, you are so inconsiderate, I've never in my life gone through such a horrible experience, I nearly had a heart attack. What happened? Well, nothing, after you went out I went to Coppel, I know which washing machine I want, it won't cost you much at all; when I got back there was a black Hummer parked nearby, but that was it. As soon as I opened the gate they grabbed me: Where is that shit of a policeman Edgar Mendieta? they said they were going to arrest me, that I'd better not resist, and there I was all flustered, they pushed me aside and went into the house. Lefty, they made an awful mess, they broke things, pulled out your clothes, threw your books on the floor. I was speechless, I couldn't say a word, but little by little I calmed down; the first thing I did was break free of the big oaf who had me in his grip: You know what, let go of me, don't make like you're so tough, I am a decent woman. Hey, guys, do you think this old hag is a decent woman? one of the other bastards mocked me; forgive me, but he was close enough, so I gave him a good kick in the balls. Don't you disrespect me, you idiot, you must have a mother and today is her day. You should have seen him, he turned green, bent over, and fell into the easy chair. Now, let me go, I told the big oaf, and he took his hands off me right away. It was obvious that you were in some deep doo-doo, so I told them you had gone out early to Headquarters and I didn't know anything else. You'd better be telling us the truth, you fucking old hag, the guy I'd kicked barked at me. What I'm telling you is as true as what I just did to you, Papa. Where do you live? So I told them. You can go, we're staying here to wait for that guy, who should never have been born, who's going to spend the rest of his whore of a life in prison. Well, tell me where, so I can take him his dinner on Sunday. Get lost. As soon as I got home, I saw a strange car in the street, for years the same people park here, so it was easy to know they were there, letting me go was a ploy to catch you; then I told Ignacio and since you were going to the cemetery we came up with the idea of waiting for you and it worked, though you almost didn't show up, eh? Thank you, Trudis, tomorrow drop in on them and see if you can get into the house. What! you want those bastards to rape me? No, God no, just try to take the place back, maybe another two kicks in the balls will get us somewhere.

They smiled. Laughter is more powerful than reality, isn't it?

Trudis, I've got to go into hiding, I've got to fool them best I can.

So, do you think the cartel people might help you?

That'd be like going from Islamabad to Islamaworse, I don't think they'll let me join up, I'm too old.

Another reason why you should sleep here. Tomorrow will be another day.

When you're being chased, every day is the same day, do you know how to drive?

Of course.

Perfect. Take my car. If the uglies put a tail on you and you can't lose them, in an hour I'll expect you back here. If they don't follow you, take a turn around the block and park it on the next street over, I'll get there over the roofs.

What about the Jetta?

It's in the shop, it really needs a tune-up.

Let's see if such a luxury car doesn't give me hives; by the way, Susana Luján wants to talk to you, her mother told me it's urgent, she said she called you at home and a strange voice asked her to leave a message and her phone number: it's those badges.

Susana? He felt a shudder. Fucking woman, she's off her

rocker if she thinks she can catch me in her net again.

Trudis waited for a comment that did not come, from his expression she understood Lefty was hurting and she departed.

No-one followed her.

Twenty minutes later Lefty was driving about with no clear idea of where to go.

In the city, Mother's Day continued.

Twenty-Four

Peace and quiet in the hospital. The uproar of the day before was now utter calm. Jiménez could feel the effects of the long tense night of work. The nearly ten hours he spent operating on young Meneses left him exhausted and with a painful backache. In the parking lot he got into his car and drove slowly away. A Ford without license plates or any insignia slipped in behind him like a girl's sigh. Unaware, he took Juárez towards Aquiles Serdán. When he got as far as the black market in dollars a minivan let him pass, but then blocked his pursuers, who tried to wave it aside and then got out to see what was up. Before they could say a word the minivan took off at a good clip. Turning the corner at Serdán, the doctor saw Max signalling him from a Tundra driven by Hyena. Jiménez understood he was to follow and, although he was not pleased by their way of asking, he trailed them to Mariana Kelly's apartment.

Samantha was awake.

Are you by any chance crazy? It seems I'm a fugitive now, doctor, how do I look? You should not have run away, you put your life in grave danger; God must have intervened

167

because so far nothing seems seriously off kilter, let's hope there aren't any complications because here we don't have what we'd need to save you should the case arise. I am not going to die, doctor, I can assure you of that; help me get better, I can only stay in this place for a couple of days maybe, my house in Colinas has been occupied and here I have too many neighbours. You are recovering well, I think I could see you every three days, but don't send anyone for me, it's too risky, I'll come on my own; take your medicine just as I prescribed it and that should help, but you have to take care of yourself and follow my instructions; tell them to change your sheets every day and stick to a liquid diet: no tamales, roast beef, or sauces; you shouldn't get up to go to the toilet either. Send me a nurse, there must be one who can be trusted. In two hours you'll have one, but you'll need more than one, I'll send three to work in shifts. That doesn't matter, as long as they take care of me. Don't worry, they do their jobs well and they're very discreet. And don't you worry about coming here, we've got you covered.

Before leaving, he spelled out to Garcés exactly what the patient should be fed and the sort of respect the nurses were due.

Samantha called for Max. Increase the protection for the doctor, you never know when the devil might turn up. He's surrounded by Army goons. It doesn't matter, tell Chacaleña to keep her eyes open and if she needs support give it to her, tell her to keep you up to date; is there anything on Charface or the Elf, you said they were on their way here? We're assuming the Elf was cut down at the hospital; our people in the D.F. say he was there the other afternoon, a buddy who does jobs for them here bought a cellphone from an Army guy and it might be his. Are you sure? They're looking into it, they found part of the famous list on it. Good, right now one enemy fewer counts for a lot, what about Charface? Nobody knows about that one, the night of the escape he disappeared from his house in Mexico City. Keep your eyes peeled, he could be nosing around here, he's got a reputation for being obsessive and I don't want him to give me a fright; now I'm certain the attack on me was ordered from the D.F.; dig into it, whoever it was will pay dearly, but we shouldn't act yet; I want us to have everything figured out before we strike the first blow. Señora, I hope you will forgive me for not sending an advance team, maybe all this could have been avoided. Don't blame yourself, there are things that can't be fixed; but they won't break me, I know it pains them that a woman runs the Pacific Cartel, but they're going to have to suck it up; stay alert, Charface could be closing in, what happened to Lefty Mendieta? We haven't been able to locate him, the goons are stepping on his heels and Trucks Obregón identified his voice; a clip of him is on television every day. He won't ask us for help, so find him and give him a hand, at least get him to a safe house for a few days while we negotiate, what does our lawyer say? It's going fine, the only thing left to be agreed is how much we are going to pay. Tell him to hurry; anything new on Monge? Nothing, they arrested him and took him to Mexico City, he hasn't been put on the media. And he won't be, bring Hyena in.

Wong, what makes you think Frank Monge would turn against us? His ambition, he wants to be the big cheese and he's not satisfied with what he's got. But Tijuana is paradise. Pardon me, señora, not like Mexicali, and he thinks Tijuana is too small for him. How can you be so sure? A young guy who worked for him told me so, the son of Señor Long. Is that boy grown up already? Grown up and full of piss and vinegar. You don't say, well, don't let him do anything outrageous. The only thing we'll allow is to avenge his father's death. That's proper. And a tradition. The lady capo thought for a few moments. Thank you for coming, Wong, give my best to your cousin. My cousin sends his best wishes to you, señora, and he asks you to take care so you'll get better quickly. Samantha closed her eyes and demanded: Max, where's the pistol I asked you for? Silence. Forgive me, señora, I didn't think it was necessary, we are 100 per cent around you. Give it to me now and don't argue. Of course; he placed a small Smith & Wesson under her pillow, then he invited Hyena to step outside.

That guy Monge, we ought to cut off his balls, Max, he's a fucking son of a fucking whore. Oh, we will, Hyena, you'll see; do you think he had something to do with the attack? It's likely. Then we have to find out who is behind him, that's what's key, alone he wouldn't be capable of pulling off anything that big; all we know is it was led by an Army officer who just got plugged. The badge could look into that, and you've seen he's loyal to La Jefa. The fact is not even our hawks can find him; I hope he seeks us out at some point, but he's a proud bastard. A good sign, a bastard with so much luck might let some of it rub off on us, don't forget he used to be called the Cat; Max, make me happy with an ounce of that stuff so I can cope with my sadness. Isn't it kind of early? Nope, you think this shit keeps office hours? it comes when the Chamuco gets so close you can see his hoofs, no joke. His hoofs and his horns. Absolutely.

Devil, we have to find Lefty Mendieta, the goons and the uglies are on his tail, we can't let them catch him. Should I call him? How are you going to call him, idiot? he doesn't even turn on his cell, just find him; his house is staked out, but he managed to get away; probably the señora who works for him knows something. Señora, I have been forbidden to speak to that woman, she was the love of my father-in-law's life and in the family they want her dead. Devil, stop farting around with that shit, find out about Lefty and don't pay attention to anything else, he must be going around in that white Volvo we had here. It's armoured. But he doesn't know that. Boss, could I take a few minutes to buy something

171

for my old lady and my mother-in-law for Mother's Day? Of course, mothers are sacred, and when you're there you can let them know you saw Mendieta's housekeeper, what's her name? O.K., Trudis, maybe I'll bring her a gift. Get going, while we're farting around Lefty might be getting fucked. God forbid.

Twenty-Five

In Mendieta's house the telephone rang. Two Federal Police agents, who were in the living room smoking, looked at it, as did Trudis, who wasn't sure if she should answer. One of the two motioned her to go ahead. She walked over without losing her cool, the other agent adjusted the grey device that would record the conversation. Hello. Good morning, Trudis, how are you? Fine, a little chilly. Last night a strange voice answered, he said they were painting the house, is Edgar so crazy he wants the house painted at night? three times I called, and every time, I got the same answer. It's going to be lovely, you'll see. Put Edgar on. He's not here, señor. He's not at Headquarters either and his cellphone just rings and rings, do you know where he is? No idea. Well, tell him that Susana is looking for him, that it's urgent. I'll tell him as soon as he turns up. Is he drinking too much? Same as always. I hope no-one has put a bullet between his eyebrow and his ear. God forbid, I don't want to even imagine something like that happened, he went out yesterday morning and he hasn't shown any sign of life since, but——. Ah, caramba, call the bar, El Quijote, see if he slept there, it's like his second house, isn't it? Don't say that, poor Lefty, he's a decent man. Well, tell him to call Susana or me, don't forget.

She hung up and looked at the interlopers. I don't mind you being here, but this is how I make my living, so let me do my work, somebody has to clean up the mess. The agents smiled, evidently they let her come into the house thinking they could catch the policeman sooner. The man with the recorder, the more cautious of the two, said: Last night that man called three times, is he a relative of Mendieta's? He's an uncle, he lives in the United States. I know that from his phone number, same story with the woman who called five times, but from another city. He turned to the tall one, who was the boss: The fugitive could be seeking refuge in the United States. I don't think so, we're dealing with an alcoholic, we ought to be watching the bars and liquor stores, the border's too far. Right, because if we were to stake out every corner store not even a hundred battalions would be enough. The uncle mentioned El Quijote. The tall one thought about it, went out to the garage and made a call on his cellphone, then he ordered two subordinates who were having a cigarette to go there.

And you, make us some coffee while we're thinking about what we'll allow you to do. All we drink here is Nescafé. Well, nothing would be worse.

A guard at the door said a señora was looking for Trudis. Go, and don't let your tongue wag, you fucking hag, that kick you gave me yesterday still hurts. In the garage: Doña Mary, how are you? why this miracle? Fine, thank you, is Edgar in? No, señora, he's at work, as you can see he never tires of catching crooks. The visitor did not smile and did not dare dig any deeper. Susana called again, she says she calls him and he doesn't answer, and that last night someone else picked up here at the house, she says she has to speak with him urgently. Very well, Doña Mary, I'll give him your message. So what's the story with these guys? her curiosity got the better of her. They're looking for Lefty too. Holy Mary, Mother of God.

That morning at the party hall, Edith Santos was directing two young men who were hanging bouquets of paper flowers on the walls. Then they set up the tables, wiped them down and spread tablecloths. Pick up the pace because the wedding is tonight, she was wearing jeans and a sleeveless blouse. Where are the nameplates? they should say Denna and Paolo, put away any that don't say that, those will be for another wedding.

She inspected a floral arrangement, then walked into the bathroom, spraying air freshener. Sitting in a chair by the main door, the agent assigned to her kept watch without much enthusiasm. She pulled out her cellphone and checked her messages. Very early she had called Angelita three times, until she understood from her evasiveness that the line was tapped. Minutes later the secretary had sent her the number of Zelda's hotel, she dialled, but no-one answered. She hoped Zelda would forgive her for interrupting at such a special moment; now, half an hour later she tried again. Answer, God, please answer, it rang five times. What do you expect when your telephone rings on your honeymoon? That is exactly what Rodo said to stop his wife from rushing to pick up the receiver. Tell them to fuck their mothers. Hello. I won't even ask how you are. Who's speaking? Edith Santos. Hey, Edith, how's it going? Very busy, you know, when somebody decides to get married everyone else does too, no matter what day of the week; do you remember Denna? that beautiful girl who worked in artsy things. If I didn't put her in the clink I don't remember her. Of course not, but she's getting married today and she's got us running off our feet. So what's up? Do you know the telephone of the woman who works for Edgar? Call the boss himself. I'd rather not, I want to surprise him, but I need the señora's help. Well, call the boss's house, she's always there during the day. Give me her home telephone, and make it quick or your Rodo is going to kill me. Sheesh, now you put me on the spot, girl; I don't have her number, but I know she lives near the boss and everybody knows her, her name is Trudis, I don't think she's ever left the neighbourhood in her life.

Edith walked out of the bathroom and ran straight into Mendieta, wearing a baseball cap. She stifled a scream. The detective, a bit worse for wear and stinking of alcohol, forced her to back up out of view and kissed her. Edgar, where have you been? Around, what about you? they're keeping you on a short leash I can see. I'm frightened, they asked me things about you I know nothing about, how did you know I'd be here? Something you told me, a wedding at the same hall where Zelda's was, and on a Monday. Yes, it's unusual, how did you get in? Through the service entrance, I helped carry a carton of beer; listen, I have no place to stay, is there anything you can do? She looked at him mischievously. Of course. We can't go together to your place or to a hotel. I know, she took some keys out of her bag. These are to my mother's house, she has a garage, stick your car in there and wait for me, she gave him the address; I'll be there in an hour, prepare a nice hors d'oeuvre. Does anyone live there? No-one since Mama died, it's got a For Sale sign; where did you spend the night? In the car, in the parking lot at the General Hospital. Go out after me, I'll distract the guard. He better not be ogling her, protested his body. Is it true that I was on T.V.? Television is something I never watch, I've got other hobbies.

An hour later they were kissing passionately and it was Edith who undressed Lefty, all the while nibbling at him everywhere. He took nearly every piece of clothing off her, leaving only a pink thong with black polka dots, which he then pulled aside to lick her moist labia. They took their time and their eyes went out of focus for the duration. Mendieta kissed, licked and sucked her pink nipples, explored her perfect behind and could not figure out how she managed to bend over and take his penis into her mouth and gently slurp at it. Aahh. And there they were, erasing oceans and tidal pools. Three minutes, and then it was time to penetrate her and for her body to shudder in a spasmodic orgasm, while Lefty, easy, easy, held back. Delight. A few seconds went by and she continued pulsing and suddenly he knew he was coming, aagh, again, aagh, and he could not contain himself any longer, and in he went all the way feeling that he was emptying out and knowing that this woman was the one he had never dreamed of, the only one with whom he had ever managed to achieve such control of his manhood.

They fell asleep.

Minutes later, in a living room with blank walls, after a snack that seemed more like a meal, Lefty answered her questions: I helped Samantha Valdés escape, I made a call to the officer in charge of the Federales and they figured out who I was, they're occupying my house; no, I'm off the Force, at least that's what the Commander told me; don't say anything to him, his phones are tapped, let him and his wife continue cooking in peace; I'm not sure, I suppose I'll have to talk to them; that's right, only I don't remember their numbers, not even my brother Enrique's, I want to warn him not to call me at home; no, let her have a quiet honeymoon; I'd like to make a few calls on your cell, the problem with these gadgets is you never memorise a single fucking number.

Why did you agree to help her? you're a good man, honest, an experienced policeman. I thought about that last night, do you remember the money I lost? You mentioned that. That cash was to buy some time from the Federales and facilitate the escape; since I didn't feel up to asking her for more, I figured I would get around it my own way and I failed. I'm so sorry. Even now I have no clue where I could have left that bag of cash. For sure it got stolen; but she escaped, didn't she? It seems she did. So you didn't fail. You couldn't say it came off perfectly, since I've got half the Federal Police force after my bones; would you go see Trudis? Where does she live? He gave her directions. The agents following you can have a chat with their friends. No-one followed me, I went out the service door like you. They smiled. Let's hope it doesn't affect your work. We're all done, and this afternoon I'm going to the Mass as if nothing were amiss. It's crazy to get married on a Monday. He's a producer and on Wednesday he has a meeting in London with Paul McCartney, he's going to bring him to Culiacán. That's fucking great, if it's for that, they can get married in the airplane if they like. I'd fix it up to look beautiful and you could come with me. Well, meanwhile, be careful; get Trudis to tell you what's going on in my house, and if Enrique called, get her to give you his number and Jason's too; listen, the other night I didn't find you at your apartment, I was knocking for a long—. Ah, since you didn't turn up I went to bed, and when I'm asleep not even a dozen cherry bombs will wake me. You are something else. They kissed.

At that very moment, someone was calling Lefty's cellphone.

Twenty-Six

Samantha was on the telephone with Minerva. Forgive me for not calling yesterday, Mama, I slept like an idiot; it's part of the treatment, the doctor says. You'll have to pardon me for not knowing how to fool my minders so I could come see you without being followed, there are about ten of them. Do they look really scary? Scary? daughter, they spend the whole day swatting flies. Mama, I sent you flowers, I didn't know what else to give you, you have everything. If you just get better that would be present enough, did you send something to the doctor's wife? In fact I didn't. Well, you are slow, girl, send a nice gift to the wife of the man who saved your life, and if he has a mother get one for her too. You're right, the doctor will be here soon, we'll get the particulars.

An hour later Jiménez walked in. To his surprise he found her animated, she was healing faster out of the hospital than in; so was Max, his wound had scabbed over. Señora, if you continue taking good care of yourself, soon you'll be able to sit up and eventually you'll be able to get out of bed for a bit. That'd be great, before my back sprouts feet; I can't wait to go to the bathroom, this commode is torture. Hang in there,

181

you'll be able to get rid of it soon enough; we were giving you something to help you sleep, but you won't need it anymore; try to rest and move as little as possible; try to stay calm, your business matters can wait, right now you have to focus on you. Do you think? by the way, has Captain Bonilla been bothering you? Not at all, someone reined him in. So I was told, is the Meneses boy better? It's very slow, I'm not convinced he's going to make it. The poor mother. Yes, she hasn't left his room, and now that you ask, the one who is very insistent is Obregón, the head of the Federales, he's always interrogating me, I think he's obsessed with that man who came for me the other day, I didn't know he was a policeman. He's a strange man, I haven't managed to persuade him to work for me, he just gives me a hand now and again. I thought he was one of your people. Well, that's not the case and I don't understand why he makes me beg. Well, don't forget my instructions, I'll be back in three days. Thank you, doctor; before you go, give me your address and that of your mother. With all due respect, it would be better if they did not know, I hope you understand. Not really, but if that's how you want it, I won't object.

Max came in. Señora, we've got the house in La Campiña, just as you wanted: small, discreet, with a garden, and across from a park so you won't have any neighbours looking in. Take me there tomorrow with all this stuff, she pointed to the I.V. and the oxygen tank. Do you need make-up or anything? Please, vanity can wait. Attorney Osuna called, he says Monge has gone into the Witness Protection Programme. The ungrateful bastard, we pull him out of the mud and he repays me with this. Tell us what to do. We'll wait, is there anything on Charface? The earth swallowed him up; the other one we haven't found is Lefty Mendieta, the Federales are occupying his house, they've staked out the home of the woman he was so tight with at Toledo's wedding, and his friends' houses too. Light a fire under that, Max, the bastard deserves our help. Well, yeah, but he's not letting us.

Señora, you have talked enough, the nurse broke in, you have to rest. Max got to his feet. The lady capo smiled, she liked being taken care of by a firm hand. The chief bodyguard left the room thinking about Charface and he felt an icy sensation in the pit of his stomach. That asshole is too close for comfort, God, that son of his fucking mother better not catch me unprepared, one little slip would do it. In the living room Devil and Chopper were watching "Fast and Furious 4" on the television. Boys, there's a bastard they call Charface who plans to whack the señora and any of us he comes across, we know he's short besides being lethal; we think he runs a network of assassins for the government and word has it he's coming around; so open your fucking eyes. Sounds like every child's friend. What about Lefty? Yeah, we're also on the lookout for him or the Volvo. Maybe they put him down? We'd know about it, bodies sprout wings and fly all over the place. The uglies are still in his house and they're watching the lady with the ass too. Trudis wouldn't let me near when I approached her, she said she didn't know a thing. If he comes into view the hawks will let us know, although it wouldn't be a bad idea to go see her again. Boss, Chopper is worried about his miss. Hang on, when this blows over we'll give you a few days off, you can go get lost in Altata, they say the board-walk there is spectacular.

On Diego Valadés Boulevard a car alarm went off. Garcés peeked out the window. At that moment everything was suspect. What are you waiting for? He was talking to Devil. Get going, asshole.

Twenty-Seven

Edith arrived back at her mother's house accompanied by Devil Urquídez, since when she dropped in on Trudis he was there on his third attempt to locate the detective. My man Lefty, what a pleasure to see you, you even seem younger. Don't tell me you're looking for me. Chief Garcés sent me on that very mission. Aha, so what's up? how's the big boss? She's coming out of it, but we're worried about you. Edith was standing at the fugitive's side. Well, I'm not, and he hugged the woman; Devil buddy, things couldn't be better, tell Max not to worry. What do I tell the señora? Same thing; I'll find a way out, you'll see. I don't doubt it, I know Attorney Osuna is negotiating with the uglies, we'll give the word when the danger is past. Tell the señora that won't be necessary, she should focus on getting better and we can talk then. Do me a favour, give me your number here and stay put for half an hour, maybe the chief wants to speak with you. If that's the case, I'll be here. Devil hesitated a moment, eyeing the blank walls, then walked out.

As soon as he left, Edith kissed Edgar passionately, My love, and his body swelled with happiness. She told him his house was still occupied and gave him the telephone numbers he had asked for. Three minutes later they were rolling naked in the hay and every verb meant kisses and kisses meant sounds and sounds meant movements and vapours that fogged the windows and cleaved the world before decamping to visit the bedrooms of people who are lonely. Make me come, mister tough guy, she demanded, and her voice rang out as if she were addressing a world conference in Geneva; again the waters parted, he took her calmly, unchaining the doors so she could break free and leave nothing behind but her genitals and a few stifled whimpers that never escaped her throat.

They ate camarones rancheros and drank beer. She began to apply her make-up because she had to arrive at the church ahead of the bride and groom; Lefty called Jason twice and heard only incomprehensible sounds that meant nothing to him. What's up with that boy? answer, dammit, it's your father. A third try obtained the same results. Then he dialled Enrique, who answered on the first ring. Bro, where the fuck have you been hiding, it's easier to reach the president of the United States. Say hello first, buddy, I've told you before, you're turning into an old curmudgeon. I'm not in the mood, we've been calling you like crazy, Susana and I, and who knows where you've been hiding. Susana and you? When was the last time you called Jason? A minute ago and I think his telephone is broken, all I heard was noise. Well, he's been missing for three days, his mother is desperate, they found his car in the school parking lot, his friends don't know anything. Don't fuck with me. Susana's afraid to report the disappearance to the police, she thinks it's like accepting the worst, she called her mother who went to find you and she talked with Trudis. Do you know any more? Just that. Give me Susana's number. You don't have it? Just give me the fucker, bro, my balls are already shrunk; at that moment he remembered the words he had heard before burying his cellphone: "All your debts are coming due, you decrepit old bastard." Was Jason kidding around or had he got caught up in some awful mess? He felt his mouth grow dry, sour: the taste of fear; fucking mother, I knew something wasn't right. Listen, don't call my house, I'm in some deep shit and the Federal Police are occupying it. I talked to them, they told me they were painting it; this morning Trudis answered, she seemed really strange so I couldn't tell her about Jason. Don't call this number either; wait until I call you. Is the shit that deep? More or less, don't call me at Headquarters either, every line is tapped. If you're in danger, come over here. I will not, I'm not going to leave with the snake still rattling. Wait, don't you care about Jason? Of course I do, but we've got to find out if he didn't go off with some chick, you know what boys are like. Let's hope that's the case.

Susana? it's Edgar. Oh, Edgar, I'm so glad you called, Jason has disappeared, Friday he went to school like every day, but he didn't come home to sleep; sometimes he does that, but he always lets me know, I thought that was what it was, that he forgot to call; he left his car in the school parking lot, I brought it home today, there was no sign of struggle; Edgar, she sobbed, I'm a mess, most of his teachers are retired policemen and all the ones I've talked to think it's a kidnapping, but no-one has called; I fear the worst, Jason is a good boy, but Los Angeles is a rough city. What do his friends say? They don't remember him being worried, they didn't see him with anybody new, they didn't notice; I checked the hospitals, too, and the jails, and he's nowhere; Chuck Beck, his best friend, went to the morgue and he's not there either, Edgar, what are we going to do? could you come? He thought for two seconds. Yes. Come right away, there must be a flight here, tell me when you're coming in and I'll pick you up at the airport. Does he have a lot of friends? He's shy, but he goes out with a few on the weekends. What does Chuck Beck say about it? They were supposed to get together that night, he's just as surprised. Go to the school right now and when you're with the director call me; actually, I don't have a cellphone and I can't answer at home, I'll go out and buy one and I'll call you, it should take me about as long as it takes you to get to the school; you should go to the police. Is something wrong at home, Edgar? They're painting and it smells horrible. Because a really rude man answered. Yeah, painters are the worst. O.K., I'll expect your call.

When he hung up Edith was facing him. What's happened? you look really worried. Did Trudis tell you Susana Luján was looking for me? Yes, but I didn't think it was important. Well, it is, she wanted to tell me my son has disappeared. He looked at her angrily, strode around the room. Sons of fucking bitches. Forgive me, Edgar, if I can help, just ask. Get me another cellphone, I need to make several calls. Of course, but I need to know you forgive me, I'm an idiot, but understand, I'm a woman and I love you. I forgive you, now get me a telephone, maybe we should go buy one together. No need, I'll give you this one, I have several. Perfect. Edgar, I've got to go, I'll be back as soon as I can, if I take a while it'll be because I haven't been able to shake off my minders; if that happens come to the party and go in the same way as before. It's a plan, if you don't come I'll find you. She gave him a quick kiss: I love you.

Knock, knock, knock.

They looked at each other anxiously, then turned towards the door.

Hide, I'll see who it is.

It was Devil and Max Garcés.

It's your friends, she announced coming into the bedroom. She hugged him, Edgar, it won't happen again, I promise. It's alright, don't feel bad, he wondered if that's what her divorces were about. Edith departed with a catch in her throat and her eyes moist, had she made a serious mistake?

She would find out soon enough. The visitors sat in the easy chairs and lit up.

La Jefa gave me orders to do whatever is necessary to safeguard your life. Fucking Max, what a mess you got me into. Everything can be fixed, Lefty Mendieta, in a couple of days all will be back to normal, have patience. You must be magicians. When it's a question of our people, we give our all, and that's what we consider you, besides, we need your help. Forget it, Max, I don't plan on lifting a finger for you or anybody around you, look how I've ended up, asshole, running like a fucking rabbit, and if that weren't enough I just talked to Los Angeles, do you know what's happened? my son's disappeared, some sonofabitch kidnapped my boy and I'm way over here like a limp dick. A quick intake of air, his face a mask of rage and desperation. When did it happen? Three days ago, that's what his mother just told me. Well, we're in this with you, Lefty Mendieta, Samantha Valdés does not forget a favour, especially one like what you did, and if Samantha Valdés doesn't forget, neither do her people; what a flying fart of a mess, do you want to go to Los Angeles? Of course I do, I'm not going to let them make mincemeat of Jason. It's a deal, we have people there who can help you. Well, if one of your bros can find out what's going on, it'd be better than going to the police; his mother doesn't have any money, but it could be some asshole she spurned, she's really beautiful, maybe the fucking dick wanted to give her a heart attack. I remember what a looker she was, do you want to take this lady with you? No, but don't leave her on her own, the police are watching her too, so don't do anything stupid. Fine, you stay right here, I'll set it up so you can go as soon as possible, are you still with the Ministerial Police? Get this, I've been fired. Aren't they touchy. There's a warrant out for my arrest, which means they could seize me on any public transport, you'll have to send me by car. If they've managed to clean off the windows, you'll go in our plane. They smiled. Max, I said something to you about the buddy who pickled that guy who had us in his sights outside the hospital, remember? How could I not? His name is Ignacio Daut and people call him the Flea, he told him the story. I'd like young Long to forget about him. I'll speak with Hyena, rest assured he won't have any more trouble. Complicit silence. How is she doing? Much better, that woman is made of steel; listen, I know this isn't the right time, but as soon as you get out of this we'd like you to think seriously of joining the team, for sure you know that's what the señora wants. There's no fixing you, fucking Max, for now the priority is Jason, and I want those fucking Federales out of my house. My man Lefty, Devil piped in, do you know why these walls are empty? The three men looked up, saw the marks indicating that paintings had hung there not long ago. No idea. I'm going to tell you something and I'm going to ask you to listen as if you were listening to the rain fall: Señora Edith is a gambler;

my mother-in-law also likes to play, sometimes I go pick her up at one casino or another and several times I've seen Edith there, deep into it. Mendieta paid close attention to the young man. So what's wrong with that? All gamblers sell whatever they can; she might have auctioned off the paintings so she could continue playing. Lefty recalled that her apartment had the same look. Well, I don't see what's so serious about it. Of course it isn't serious, my man Lefty, but you lost fifty thousand pesos; yesterday I took my mother-in-law her present, Edith came up in conversation, she told me she'd seen her betting big time the day we pulled out the señora. He imagined her: pale, unkempt, excited, risking everything she had left. A cigarette fell to the floor.

He dialled Susana: he told her he would see the director soon himself and she should not go to the police; that he would be in touch.

On the way to El Salado airfield he made another call. How is the wedding going? Terrific, it's ten past five, when are you coming to the hall? About eight, tell me something, did you take the money I lost so you could gamble? Silence. Sobs. Forgive me, Edgar, forgive me, I'll pay back every penny. He hung up and threw the telephone into the gutter. Fucking life.

The cartel's plane as far as Tijuana, where a car, two women and a baby were waiting. They crossed the most-frequently crossed border in the world and three hours later he was resting in a room at the Sunset Marquis Hotel in West Hollywood, which the cartel had booked. The next day Mendieta learned it was the rockers' favourite when he saw Steven Tyler and Joe Perry of Aerosmith, right down to the flip-flops, getting into a limousine.

God makes them and they remake themselves. He smiled.

Twenty-Eight

They did it at the hospital entrance. Jiménez, who had just arrived, saw Hyena Wong signalling him to get in. The doctor shook his head and walked on to his office. It was growing dark. There were seven of them placed strategically behind parked cars. Devil and Chopper were smoking as they waited. The soldiers, cool and collected. Trucks Obregón and his people looked on uneasily. Someone wants to speak with you, Obregón, so come with me, Hyena ordered him. For a moment the officer did not know how to respond. Do I know you? Hyena's eyes drilled him. Of course, I was your sister's boyfriend for a couple of months. Obregón did not find the answer the least bit funny; he decided to follow him and also not to agree to anything they proposed, but he wanted to know who he was dealing with; nobody could pay enough to buy him and no way was he going to be intimidated by that shitty cartel. I'll be right back, he told his second-in-command, and don't worry, I know how to deal with mad dogs. They walked to a black Hummer on the corner, Max Garcés was waiting in the back seat. The corrido "El gallo de San Juan" by Carlos y José was playing. I'm going to get right to the nub, Max announced. Hyena took the officer's two pistols and sat him down beside Max; the car eased out into the street, Devil and Chopper's followed. Leave Mendieta alone, and his family and his co-workers. Trucks smiled sarcastically. Forget it, that bastard is going to prison for what he did, he's fucking corrupt. You'll get fifty thousand dollars. Even if you give me five hundred thousand, there is no saving that cop, and if you want to know we've already located him at his girlfriend's house and we're on our way to nab him right now. Well, if you want to know he's not there anymore. Trucks stiffened: Let's finish, you can't count on me for this. Trucks, if you don't accept you'll be today's corpse. I couldn't give a shit, if my life helps end this plague, I'll give it. I didn't think you were such an idiot. You people don't own the country and you don't own us. But you sure as hell took ten thousand dollars from the Gulf people, and among other things you let them bring through eighty-three Central Americans, right, asshole? you think we don't know what kind of a sonofabitch you are? Silence. If you kill me, the Federales will be all over you. We already reached an agreement at the top, and they told us we should take this up with you directly, that you were bent on sticking it out at the hospital, even though you know La Jefa won't be coming back even to pick up the change. Another silence. Make it a hundred thousand, remember my commander has to eat too. Fifty is what you're worth, you figure out how to deal with the others; he picked up a black bag from the floor, handed it to him, and ordered the driver: Leave him near the hospital. Trucks looked at the bag, at Max, and said nothing. Across from the zoo, Max and the Hyena shifted to the young gunslingers' car.

At that moment Attorney Osuna was shaking hands and saying goodbye to Zurita, the federal prosecutor for Sinaloa, with whom he had just reached an agreement. They were smiling. On the floor, hidden by the large desk, lay a silver-plated briefcase that had a new owner.

Also at that moment, beside a tree on Valadés Parkway, stood Charface, dressed as a doctor and carrying a doctor's satchel, contemplating the building where Mariana Kelly had her apartment.

There are watches that never stop.

Twenty-Nine

It was after midnight when he met up with Susana Luján at the hotel bar, and he did his best to ward off memories of the pain she had caused him. The past is past, he kept telling himself. She looked haggard, but her body was still as attractive as ever, in fact perfect. A tight dress and yes, there was her behind: firm and snub. So lovely, in her case the years really did not go by. Fucking dame, she's better than ever, noted his body, remembering nothing but pleasure. Take it easy, eh, body? this thing with Jason is serious, let's not think about anything else, and neither do I want you interrupting me. Does it ever piss me off when you act like an idiot; Lefty, when are you going to understand that you're human and you need to act on everything that implies? Yeah, but you understand me, I'm trying to dodge another fucking punch, I'm not made of wood; besides, I'm with Edith now. Don't be a dummy, what commitment do you have with her? none, so if Susana is horny, you two can cook the stew, don't make such a big deal of it. Not in your dreams, what happened wounded me to my fucking core. I don't like whiners. And don't forget Jason, that's why we're here. Susana smiled her

197

naturally flirtatious smile and asked for a tequila. I want to celebrate seeing you, Edgar, and I want to relax, all this about Jason has my soul hanging by a thread. What did I tell you? and here you are being so cautious. Hold on, I've got to find out about my son.

I'm surprised how much he likes the career he's chosen, he takes it very seriously. Does he have enough money? Plenty, that card you gave him works miracles, and he's thrifty, he's happy you don't control his spending. If he learns to manage that himself he'll turn out right; you say he doesn't have a girlfriend? He goes out with an array of them, but he's never said anything was serious. Have you ever found a strange substance in his pockets? Never, he's still as straight as when he was an athlete; as a matter of fact, I don't know if he told you, he's going to run the mile at a police academies' meet. He did tell me, does he ever hide when he answers his telephone? Nope, he's pretty open and he almost always comes right home from school. I want to speak with his best friend. Do you want him to come here? No, I want to see where he lives and how he lives. I figured that, so I told him you'd look him up at the school. I'd rather do it right now, I hope it isn't too late, does he live alone? With two friends, that's what kids do; one of these days Jason will do the same and, no, don't worry, those boys barely sleep; can I go with you? Not into his house, take me there and if you like you can wait for me nearby, is it dangerous around there? Not where he lives, it's a safe neighbourhood, though given what happened to Jason who can say? Have you received any unusual calls? No. Have any strangers approached you on some stupid pretext? No, again. Someone called me from Jason's cellphone, they told me I was going to pay for all my sins and they hung up. My God. It seemed like a joke, then I thought about it and I realised the voice was strange, a bit effeminate. Jason would never say that to you, he respects and admires you too much.

They made the trip in her Toyota. Lefty thought about the moment long ago when they conceived a child and their more recent nights in Culiacán. Fucking life, there's nothing original about it, it's the same thing over and over until you're sick of it, because of course Susana had her lovely legs in full view up to mid-thigh, as sensuous as they had been twenty years before. Enough, fucking Lefty, don't be a faggot, she's sending you signals and your penis is a G.P.S., hop to it and don't be intimidated. The night was cool and the city was all lit up; despite the hour, the traffic was heavy.

The friend: Chuck Beck, white skin, blue eyes, a metre eighty, muscular, blond. When he opened the door, a hamburger was dripping ketchup from one hand. Hi, I'm Edgar Mendieta, Jason's dad. Beck smiled. Hola, Señor Mendieta, come in, he said in not half-bad Spanish, and he stepped aside for the detective, who still felt strange introducing himself that way. A map of Los Angeles was on the wall between posters of Magic Johnson and Kobe Bryant; on a table in the centre of the room, open books, a sugar Day-of-the-Dead skull, and the remains of a meal; and to complete the dorm-room atmosphere, an open laptop, clothes hanging from chairs, and crumpled paper on the floorboards. Katy Perry's "Dark Horse" on low. Sorry, I don't know why, but we can't seem to keep the place clean. Mendieta smiled, spied a pistol in pieces on the computer screen. Doing your homework? Uh-huh, I'm trying to learn about the weapon we'll use on the force, any news about Jason? Your question shows you know about it and you've got a theory. Your son looks up to you, he told me he saw you in a gunfight that left enough bodies to open a cemetery. He told you that? More or less, and it was his mother who called to tell me she was worried about him being missing. He put the hamburger on a plate and drank from the Miller beside the laptop. Edgar took everything in. We left school on Friday, we'd agreed to meet up later on, I watched him walk off towards the parking lot, and that's the end of the story; he didn't show up that night. Didn't you think something was wrong? Your son is like that, sometimes he decides to stay home or pick up some new girl; he also likes to visit crime scenes, to see the place, feel out the area ringed by yellow tape, imagine what might have happened; what seemed really strange was that he left his car in the parking lot, you might say he and his car are sort of symbiotic. I suppose. This morning his mother got it towed to her house. What time was it when you saw him walk away? Two o'clock, a little after, that's when we break free of those sinister walls. It was Friday, was there a party you were going to? Like ten of them. Any dispute with some vindictive guy? Not that I know of, what we do is walk around, talk and drink a bit. A bit? Well, sometimes too much, but we don't make trouble, we behave ourselves. How many close friends does Jason have? Probably just me; he's a nice guy, but sort of domineering and a lot of the bros don't like that. What about the teachers? No problem with them, he always does his work. So, what's your theory? No, I wish; and have I ever thought about it, I tried to remember if he's had any conflicts with anybody, but he hasn't. Silence. There is something I can't understand, if he's so successful with girls, why doesn't he have a girlfriend? Does that seem strange to you? it isn't, this city is full of girls, they hang around with us for a while and we have a good time, who needs a girlfriend? none of them has been chasing after him, at least not to the point of kidnapping him if that's what you're thinking, but I suppose maybe one wanted to spend a few days with him on the sly. Did he tell you he was planning a trip or anything like that? No, like I said we were going to meet up at ten. Are your teachers former police officers? Most of them, the one who's famous is Wolverine, he used to be a detective with the Los Angeles police. Why doesn't Jason get along with him? Who said that? he's Wolverine's favourite, Jason asks him about everything;

201

in fact Jason's the only one who calls him by his real name, Mr Jackman.

Mendieta figured this kid was maybe a bit hyperactive, but not malicious; no doubt a good friend to his son. Are your roommates in? They're staying with their girls, that's common too. O.K., get back to your homework. Chuck pointed at the screen, do you want to see the real thing? Why not? He went to his room and returned with a Beretta 90-Two wrapped up in a piece of flannel. Look at this beauty. Lefty picked up the gun and examined it, it was slate-grey and very light. Marvellous, he said, and he returned it to its owner. I'll lend it to you, right now you might need it more than me. Mendieta looked at the young man. Are you sure? Absolutely. In Mexico there are three things you never lend: your wife, your horse, and your gun. Here they say the same thing, but a detective of your calibre can't go around unarmed. It occurred to him he did not have a permit to carry a gun in this country, but he decided not to mention it. What did you find at the morgue? Nothing, I went everywhere and zero; don't bother looking there, he's alive, I'm sure of it. Mendieta handed him a card from the hotel: If you remember anything else that might be of help, please call me.

He left the apartment worried and without any clues, fully aware that he would have to find his way in an unfamiliar city. While waiting, Susana had taken advantage to do some shopping at the local supermarket. Lefty told her a few things about his chat with Beck and he asked her to let him off at the Marquis. I wanted to cook you something at home so you'd have a good supper. Absolutely, we're hungry, his body enthused, but the man recalled the drunken nights that nearly killed him thanks to her, the tears that came unbidden, and he declined the invitation. It's late, I need to meditate on this stuff, do you know Professor Jackman? Of course, Jason admires him nearly as much as he does you. He felt something sharp jab him inside. Another bastard who must be in love with her, I hope he doesn't get prickly, because the fur is going to fly. I'd like to meet him. If you like, I can take you, his class is at seven in the morning; as a matter of fact, he called today to ask about Jason, I told him about what happened because I think Jason really likes him. Hmmm. Mendieta watched the flow of people coming and going; it was obvious he was in one of the largest cities in the United States.

Edgar, she said sweetly when Lefty opened the door to get out, forgive me. Silence, the detective put his foot on the ground. Let's focus on Jason, his friend doesn't seem to have any idea what happened. Forgive me, I was afraid I'd mess up, I'm really foolish about these things, I've spent my life running away, do you remember when I said, I don't want sex, I want love? well, I think the only person who ever truly loved me was you, and I ruined it. She looked at him, heartbroken. I was the one who was a jerk. No! Listen, Susana,

I'll call you in the morning, I want to see Jason's Camaro, we can look the teacher up later on. He closed the door and went into the hotel. My God, the only reason you aren't more of an idiot is because you aren't any older. A girl blocked his way, waving a small notebook. Can you give me your autograph? Of course, he wrote Jim Morrison. Oh, my God. No shit, Lefty thought. At the elevator, as he waited, a man sidled up to him. People call me Crazy Mouse, you must be the Cat; he was old, thin, he looked like that dancing comic Resortes. Max Garcés sent me. Mendieta looked at him and pointed towards the bar, which at that hour had only three customers.

They sat in a corner, ordered Coronas and Don Julio. He heard the powerful voice of Janis singing "Maybe", the volume low. My son disappeared, I'd like you to help me find him. Uh, sure, finding lost sons is my specialty, he smiled. Though he was put off by that response, Lefty told him the story and handed him a photograph of Jason. He was going to say he wanted him alive, but he refrained; why play innocent, he knew how unpredictable the end result of a disappearance was. Are you kidding, brother? No, God forbid, why would I? You've given me a picture of yourself. Well, he looks more like me than he should, but that's him. Uh, this sucks, eh? another thing: don't go see that guy Jackman, uh, he's a bastard, he hates all Hispanics, let me tell you, he put the screws on a lot of the bros on the East Side, we know all about him. That's happy news. Uh, they call you Lefty too, don't they? and you were part of the operation to get La Jefa out of the hospital, right? My job was to close the door. Fucking great, I know about it, uh, Señor Garcés was very clear. He drank his second tequila in one swallow, then his beer, and he stood up. Don't leave the hotel, my people, uh, will work on this tonight; tomorrow I'll drop by to pick you up at ten; uh, don't go to the police either, if there's a way out of this, we'll find it.

He called Susana early. He agreed to let her pick him up to go see Jason's car. The woman was wearing dark glasses and a flowery scarf on her head. Delicate perfume. Lefty, as always, in black. Neither had slept much, thanks to their son's plight and their conflicted feelings about each other. She told him the sunglasses were an early present from Jason for Mexican Mother's Day and he had promised to give her another present for the American one. Did you take flowers to your mother's grave? Red gladiolas, eight dozen. You know, she liked me, she always smiled at me, she had a lovely smile. Mendieta nodded while distracting himself with the hubbub on the streets.

It was a yellow Camaro S.S., 2002, convertible. People say a son is an investment, not an expense; by the way, Enrique is coming tomorrow, he's dying to see you. That's great, how far away is Oakland? Six hours by car, would you like a Nescafé? If there's no way around it, who brought the car from school?

A tow-truck, there's a second key, but I didn't find it until the other night; listen, I've got Colombian coffee too, wouldn't you rather have that? Sure, did you look inside? You know, I couldn't bring myself to, Jason always insists that when there's a crime it's better not to touch anything, you've got to leave it to the experts and that's what you are, how about some eggs with machaca? it's machaca from Culiacán my mother sends, or I could make you an American breakfast: six fried eggs, bacon, hot cakes and maple syrup. Machaca's fine. Despite Susana's efforts, Lefty, seeing her in tight jeans and sleeveless blouse, refused to let down his guard. Would you bring me the key? Take it from the table, and while you're doing that I'll make breakfast.

It smelled of air freshener and everything seemed normal, no flyers from a hotel or some other destination where he might be. In the glove compartment, only the registration and the service booklet, up to date. I can see he takes care of it like the girl of his dreams. Inside the car he sat still and drank in every detail once more. Jason, you're something else, my son, what good taste you have. He concentrated on the smell, but nothing called to him, the aroma of peach air freshener was overpowering. Let's see: Jason, come with us, we want to have a word with you. Who are you? We're every child's friend and if you don't keep quiet we're going to fuck you, understand? now give me that cell, I'm going to call your fucking father, that shit of a badge who's finally going to pay for all he's done, but I'm going to disguise my voice, I'll be a dear little old woman. I don't have his number. You sure do, we know you two talk all the time. Don't mess with my father. Of course we'll mess with him, don't think he's so clean-cut, he's a bum, corrupt. He lives far away. What, isn't the world smaller nowadays? let's find out. What do you want? Nothing, we're just kidnapping you. And they took him away, but where? how many were they? how did they know about him? what are they really after? Susana waved at him that breakfast was served. Obviously, it has to do with me, since whoever called was direct as could be: All your debts are coming due, you decrepit old bastard. I've never arrested a gringo, would a Mexican come all the way here to give Jason a hard time? The offence must have been truly big for him to take such a risk, who? why? what for? He felt his stomach burning.

He tried to relax. Jason did not have a girlfriend we might suspect, or any acquaintance who would want to hurt him like that. They lived in a peaceful neighbourhood of Latinos who owned their own businesses. Has anything like this ever happened? Never, I tell you he's a good kid, always behaves himself. Have you two run into any Mexicans who have a relative I might have arrested? Not that I know of. One question had Mendieta's tongue on fire and he did not wait any longer. Forgive me, the last thing I want to do is pry into your private life, but could one of your admirers have a grudge against Jason? Of course not, besides, since we came back from Culiacán I haven't been going out with anybody, I haven't met anybody, and I'm not interested in anybody. So this business is about me, I told you I got that call where they threatened me; wow, is this machaca ever good, could you call Enrique?

How's it going, good-for-nothing? Hey, are you over here already? Yup, and I want you to think about who around here I might have hurt, or maybe a family member of some asshole I tossed in the clink. How about saying hello first? You're right, I'm getting to be like you. Are you O.K.? A bit overwhelmed, but determined to find the kid. Good, right now I'm at work, but tomorrow I'll be there first thing, and I haven't heard of anyone who wants to get back at you. Come to the Marquis in West Hollywood, just off Sunset Boulevard. The rock stars love that place. I got taken for Jimmy Page and I had to give eighty-three autographs. My fucking bro. See you tomorrow.

They had breakfast at Susana's kitchen counter. Call me a taxi, would you? they're expecting me at the hotel at ten. Edgar, you haven't finished your breakfast, let me at least feed you, don't be spiteful. Susana, I have to be there at ten and that's all there is to it. Alright, just don't forget that I'm his mother and I took care of him for eighteen years. Why would I forget that? It's something else, Lefty, he heard his body saying, she wants some caressing, don't leave her high and dry, a lot of women kill themselves over less. Don't mess with me. Edgar, I understand your attitude, but it doesn't seem fair, do you think it's been easy for me? maybe I haven't been the best mother I could have been, but it was no cakewalk working, having my son, raising him, and keeping hundreds of horny jerks at bay; you ought to know, and in case you don't, let me tell you how it is: every fucking man wants to go to bed with me, and not only now, they were after me even back when I was living in Culiacán; it's true, I don't deny it, with you it was different, you might say I seduced you, but you were the only one: you were so gentle it made me want to protect you, teach you things, spoil you; so many times I've tried to get them to take me seriously, and what have I got to show for it? nothing, no-one sees me as a respectable woman; when we talked about living together a year and a half ago, I was happy, but then I got scared, in fact terrified that it wouldn't work, and then all three of us would end up worse off; so I'm asking for some understanding, if I want to treat you well it's because you are the father of my son and because you are the only man in my life who has never tried to hurt me; that's why, let me make it clear, if I treat you well it's not because I want to get something going with you, I don't think about that because I already ruined what might have been. She took a deep breath, her jaw was set, her gaze hard, and she was not going to shed a tear. I understand, but excuse me, I have to go to the hotel now, please. Fine, I'll take you. Fucking Lefty, are you ever worth shit, asshole.

In the Toyota, Susana turned up the radio: Buki's heart-rending voice, "No hay nada más difícil que vivir sin tí," and Lefty could not utter a word.

Thirty

Edith Santos was sitting in the Casino Royale, drinking beer and betting. Her face was etched with excitement and doubt. Beside her, men and women were paying close attention to the greyhounds racing on an enormous screen. Three who had placed bets got to their feet, shook their fists, and urged on their favourites with penetrating whispers. The dogs reached the finish line, Edith hung her head: she had lost yet again. Her first thought was that she was the one who had lost, now she was certain it was the dogs' fault. Those useless beasts. That night she gambled away what remained of Lefty's cash. She wanted to win so she could pay him back, don't think that was not the case, she wanted to do right by Edgar, who had gone off who knows where. Wagging tongues say I'm a man-eater who leaves her lovers bankrupt, but if that were the case, why do they miss me? That detective is a good boy, but even so I couldn't resist taking his money. She got up and walked resolutely to a small office that housed a bank branch. A pleasant young man greeted her.

Any new paintings, Señora Santos? We haven't made a thing from the ones you brought before, but as you know, for us the customer comes first and we'll make every sacrifice to serve you.

Somewhere I've got a Toledo and two Picassos, but I want to hang on to them as keepsakes.

The Picassos could be worth our while, as long as the price is reasonable, that's up to you, maybe we can recuperate some of what we've invested; I can send someone for them right now.

No, I want to sell my house.

She took several documents out of her handbag and handed them to the banker, who's eyes were shining.

Perfect, Señora Santos, I'll give you five thousand dollars so you can keep playing, while we send someone to make an assessment.

Edith nodded, signed a receipt, gave him the keys and the address of her mother's house. Then she took the money and went back out. Her hair was mussed, but her expression now glowed with life. Devil Urquídez, who was waiting for his mother-in-law beside the washrooms, watched her and felt pity.

Meanwhile, the tall police officer was giving Trudis a slap that instead of scaring her made her mad, and she sent a wad of spit at him that barely made it beyond her lips. Where's that badge, you stupid hag? Tied by the hands and feet, she only spouted curses. She knew nothing about Lefty or his family or anything else. You fucking faggots, aren't you the tough guys beating up a woman, untie me and then we'll see who's who, and she tried to spit at them again. You must know something, piss-panties. Pissed is your fucking mother, and like Bob Dylan said, the answer is blowing in the wind, assholes. Who's that guy?

The officer's cellphone rang. He listened attentively. Understood sir, got it, right away sir. Then he turned to his buddies. Friends, pick up your junk, this rice is cooked; then to Trudis: You got lucky, you fucking witch. She felt her soul return to her body. In five minutes they disconnected the equipment, packed up everything they had, and left without another word. Hey, at least untie me, the woman called, but no, out they went and they did not even close the door.

Charface, impassive. He watched Dr Jiménez depart, observed the movements of the guards, two young men, usually, and a fat guy, who by his age and attitude must be the boss. A señora who for sure was her mother. A Chinese guy who maybe was the cook. It'll be easy. As the Elf liked to say, the coincidence is a given.

The city's streets were all keyed up, police and criminals on the move, expecting something to happen. They did not know who would give the order, but someone should and then for sure, on to killing each other as God wishes. In the meantime, they just exchanged glances and greetings, convinced that never in their lives had they been so close to hell.

Thirty-One

Third floor. His room was comfortable, wide bed, forty-inch television screen, a view of the street, which was steep, tree-lined, and without much traffic. At ten o'clock he was in the lobby for his appointment with Crazy Mouse. Fucking Max, couldn't he find a loonier bastard than that guy? A rock band arrived, utterly wasted, they had been recording all night. He sat down in a green easy chair, then in a blue one, he stood for a while, walked around, but nobody came. He waited about forty minutes. I wonder how Jason's doing, who knows what hell he's going through and here I am like an idiot. Who did I hurt so much that he does this to take revenge? In the more than twenty years I've been a badge, I must have stepped on a fuck-weight of toes. He went to reception to see if any of them spoke Spanish: none. "Somebody called me? Room 327," he dared to ask. A girl who looked like Brooke Shields took five minutes to understand and answered no. He stood at the entrance not knowing where to go. What's the story? No point waiting for that crazy bastard, so what if he didn't show, it won't stop me, but where do I go next? Do I take a taxi to Susana's, wait for Enrique, look for the Flea, go back to Chuck Beck, go to the police academy? This is no crossroads, it's a fucking dog's breakfast, or maybe a very long straightaway to nowhere. And it's not like I want to play tourist at Universal Studios.

He decided to call Susana. No way around it, she was his only contact, maybe she knows the Flea. He could also ask her to introduce him to Jackman, who Beck said knows more about the students than the director.

Señor Mendieta. Who should cross his path just then, but Chuck Beck, accompanied by a beauty. I called you this morning, but you didn't answer, how are you? Kind of worried. I bet, this is Cindy Ford, the girl most interested in becoming part of your family. Really? Pleased to meet you, Señor Mendieta, she said in high-school Spanish. She was blonde, with penetrating green eyes. Is there someplace nearby where we can get a cup of coffee? On Sunset Boulevard they found a Starbucks.

Your son is really great, even if he never wants to go out with me. You're so pretty, he probably feels intimidated; I bet you get plenty of invitations. There's something to that, but the only guy I dream about is Jason, and in case you don't know, he won't let anyone catch him, he's gone out with so many we've lost count. Maybe we should take that up some other time, you have something to tell me, don't you? Whether it'll make a difference, I'm not sure. When was the last time you saw him? That's the point, I saw him on Friday, outside

215

the school, when he was walking to his car; Mendieta's brain turned over: that was the day he disappeared. So? A gorgeous girl was waiting for him, a redhead with long curly hair; they kissed and went off together. On foot, in Jason's car, in hers? Walking, holding hands; as you might imagine, I was crushed, I got into my car and sat there for a few minutes thinking, Why can't I get that boy out of my mind? he hasn't even asked me out for an ice cream, maybe he just doesn't like me; then I left. Did you see which way they went? No, the parking lot has four exits. Chuck piped in: According to Murillo, the man who guards the lot, Jason's car didn't move until his mother had it towed. That girl, what colour was she? White. Was it the first time you'd seen them together? Yes. So he's not kidnapped, he thought, he just went off for a few days to relax, and he felt a little more at ease. But why hasn't he called Susana? why did they threaten me from his telephone? Was she carrying a purse, a laptop bag, a sports bag, anything? Nothing, she looked strong, a good body. What do you mean a good body? A big behind, big boobs, in shape. Do you think she was a gringa? Most likely. Beck, does Jason go for a particular type of girl? We call him the ambulance because he'll pick up anyone. The times you've been out with him, did you ever see that redhead? Never, I remember a few girls, but none as pretty as Cindy says this one was. Señorita Ford, how was she dressed? Very sexy, really tight hot pants and a red blouse, showing off her damned ass and tits. Dressed for the beach, Lefty reflected, but after spotting two young ones entering the café, he figured girls here dress like that wherever. How far away were you when you saw them? Maybe twenty yards. Did Jason look excited? That's something I couldn't tell, but the kiss was long and passionate. Did you notice any brand on her clothes, any tattoos on her arms? No, I just felt really bad. Chuck, are you sure there's nothing familiar about that girl? The truth is no, your son gets as many girls as he likes and he hardly ever talks about them. The conversation moved on to a few school-related things that gave Lefty nothing to go on. Neither of them had ever seen him train.

He excused himself and returned to the hotel to call Susana. In the lobby a man in grey was waiting for him.

Only one? There were three. The others were stationed by the entrance and by the door to the restaurant. Lefty needed a cold beer, but they intercepted him. Señor Edgar Mendieta, come with me, someone needs to speak with you about an important matter. Voice soft, but forceful. With whom do I have the pleasure? Agent Jeter of the F.B.I., no more questions. What can I do for you? He took Lefty by the arm. Walk, you'll talk somewhere else. Mendieta broke free. Don't you grab me, I'm no bum off the street, I am a citizen of Mexico and I entered this country legally. Don't resist. The other agents came over. These gentlemen could subdue you in a second if needed. The detective thought about how there are sons of bitches everywhere. Face like ice. Could we have a drink first? on my tab. No, Jeter grabbed his arm and squeezed, the detective relented and allowed them to lead him out. Fucking mother of all fucks, no doubt within two hours I'll be kicked out of the United States, left in some godforsaken hole at the border. So, if in Mexico City Charface had him on a list of Samantha's friends, what list was he on here? A few metres uphill from the hotel entrance, Jeter opened the back door of a grey car; Lefty got in, thinking he would have to work double-time to get back as soon as he could, if Jason was kidnapped he had to lead the search; maybe if he had accepted Susana's invitation to sleep at her house he would not be in this mess, but that would have been riskier, even if she says she has no claim on him. Who has the better body, Susana or Edith? Edith has a bigger ass, but Susana is perfect. Aha! his body reacted, cut the stupid shit: the better one is the one who's closer.

Win Morrison, an F.B.I. agent he had once helped out on a case in Culiacán, was sitting in the back seat barely managing a smile.[*] You come to Los Angeles and you don't drop by to say hello, Señor Mendieta? Hey, Win, what a surprise, true, I didn't look you up, but I guess I let you find me; as you must know, letting yourself be found is a form of looking. Aren't you the philosopher today, Señor Mendieta, did they

* In the second book of the series, *The Acid Test*

frighten you? No way, though I'll admit I pictured myself in Matamoros, as far away as could be. Did you feel a bit like a migrant? Yeah, and the first thing that came to mind was that as soon as I got sent back, I'd look for some way to return; I would ask how you found me, but that would be an insult. So don't do it, and first let me tell you I know why you're here. Well, misfortune makes the world go round. Like I said, aren't you philosophical today. Better you call me phenomenal, which is what I'd rather be. They were alone, Jeter had pulled back to some nearby vegetation. Your son is a good kid, very sharp, and he's got good instincts, he's promising. Don't tell me you're monitoring him. Of course not, why would you think that, in this country nobody gets monitored. Lefty smiled, studied her expression and saw nothing untoward; maybe she said that to make it come true. Do you have any news for me? Sorry, I'm afraid not, Señor Mendieta. He decided to tell her the only thing he knew. One of his classmates saw him with a white girl, very pretty, with curly red hair; it makes me think he might be off having a good time. That would be normal. What isn't normal is that he told no-one, not even his best friend or his mother, and the day I called him a voice threatened me. Tell me about that voice. They said I was going to have lots of regrets, and that I was a decrepit old bastard, the tone was pretty nasty. Man or woman? It was strange, it seemed more like a woman. Young? That I couldn't say, the call wasn't coming in clear and for sure the voice was put on. Have you got the cellphone? No, I buried it. She looked at him doubtfully. So they wouldn't trace you? Something like that. Then it's true you recently got into a lot of trouble and you're still a friend of the narcos? Who told you that? You're a friend of the worst of them all, that poisonous woman who's so elusive. You must be repeating the official line, because word has it the narcos have solid agreements with the D.E.A. Are you trying to tell me she isn't a malicious pusher and a notorious criminal? No, all I'm saying is someone opens the door for her and rolls out the red carpet. Silence. They watched Steven Tyler get out of a limousine, protected by a pair of sultry beauties who followed him into the lobby. Win, thank you in advance, whatever you can do for me will be for my son, who is indeed a promising young man. The woman looked at him for a moment. I'll put everything at your service if you help me arrest Samantha Valdés. Shall we sign a contract? because of course you don't trust my word. If that's what you want. Let me think about it, I confess I was happy to see you, happy that you're part of an organisation that's so efficient you found me before I'd even spent a full day here. A few hours ago a criminal we had on file got killed; in his pocket we found a piece of paper with your name and the hotel. Mendieta smiled. This is a strange day, how can I find you? No, I'll find you; as you must know, you are not allowed to work in the United States. Of course, except for washing dishes, mowing the lawn, or harvesting lettuce; if I were a doctor my degree would be useless too. We'll give you forty-eight hours to find your son; if you don't find him, I want us to speak seriously about what I just suggested, how sick is she? If your people in Culiacán haven't given you that information, fire them, you're wasting your money; on the other hand, I appreciate your consideration, he tried to open the door, but it would not budge until Win deactivated the lock. Two days only, don't forget, Señor Mendieta. Win, truly, it's a pleasure seeing you again. She flashed her half-smile, Lefty got out and slammed the door. So they killed Crazy Mouse, would that have to do with Jason or with me? Christ, I barely met him, but now he's part of the package. Guess I'd better tell Max his man was out in the first inning, and now where do I look?

An hour later at the Amarone restaurant he met up with Susana Luján, who arrived carrying a bag from Macy's; he told her about his conversation with the young people and about the redhead. Jason never mentioned her, Cindy yes, that she was chasing after him, but he said he wouldn't go out with a woman he didn't like in the least; he's cold that way, like his father. Like me? where do you get that? She smiled and sipped her wine. Lefty, this woman is happy to see us, let's give her what she wants, there are still a lot of embers in those ashes. You two are alike, Edgar, and not only physically, both of you prefer it when we women take the initiative. She was eating *ravioli di ricotta e spinaci* and he was having a *bistecca di manzo* and thinking that he was such a fucking Culichi, set in his ways, since instead of sharing a bottle of Barolo Costa di Bussia he was drinking a Corona. Poor Jason, he has a tough life ahead of him. Don't exaggerate, she smiled coyly; they drank. Come on, Lefty, she still remembers the last night she spent with you. I bought you a pair of black pants and two T-shirts, I hope they're your size, if not we can exchange them. You shouldn't have gone to the trouble. It's nothing. Mendieta sliced off a piece of fragrant meat and decided to return to the topic of their son. Do you know Ignacio Daut? No. He's from Sinaloa, he's got a tortilla factory here, they call him the Flea. Oh, of course, the Flea, he used to supply me when we had the taco place, I didn't know his real name, I probably have him in my contacts. Call him, please, but first get me an appointment with Jackman.

Flea buddy, I think we're going to see each other sooner than we planned. What's up, my man Lefty, did you wriggle free already? Practically, I'm here and I'd like to see you. You're in Los Angeles? Absolutely. You're something else, when did you arrive? Yesterday. Great, where are you staying? At the Sunset Marquis, could you come over? We'll be eyeing each other in an hour. It's one-thirty, suppose we meet up at five? Whenever you want, listen, where are you going to take me? Uh, I don't understand. When I was in Culiacán I went to a fortune-teller, the bro told me my troubles would end, and end happily, when a close friend takes me on a trip. What's your fortune-teller's name? He called himself Polo, they whacked him more or less when I looked you up. No shit.

Another wine and another beer were served. Nicola di Bari was softly singing "Chitarra suona più piano".

Thirty-Two

Doña Mary was surprised to see Lefty's door wide open, a rare sight, especially in mid-afternoon. A few minutes before, she had watched the Federales depart and, curious, she stepped inside. She tiptoed through the living room and the eat-in kitchen, both in shambles. Silence. Is anyone home? From Mendieta's bedroom, Trudis recognised her voice and called out. The señora approached the door cautiously. Holy Mary, Mother of God, Trudis; she attempted to free her, unsuccessfully. My God, look at you, girl, she got a knife from the kitchen and even so it took her several minutes to cut the grey duct tape from her ankles, wrists and waist, where they had bound her to the chair. Look at what those wretches did to you. Thank you, Doña Mary, Trudis managed to mumble. She got Trudis onto the bed, cleaned off her face with a moist towel, made her drink water. I'm going for the doctor.

Two blocks away lived a physician nicknamed the Relative, who wanted to become a forensic doctor, but Lefty discouraged him. He was a favourite son of the Col Pop.

What happened to you, Doña Trudis, did you pick a fight with Samson? That's it, Relative, but I didn't manage to cut off his hair. He checked her blood pressure, gave her an anti-inflammatory, sent Doña Mary to buy an I.V. because she was seriously dehydrated, prescribed hot soup and complete rest. You have to stay in bed for at least an entire day, Doña Trudis, you've got several bruises, but those will go away soon enough; didn't Edgar defend you? He just crossed his arms, can you believe it? That's something I'll take up with him when I see him; well, I'll leave these samples with you and if you need anything give me a call; tell Edgar to introduce me to his friend the forensic doctor, I still want to see if I might specialise in that. I'll tell him, thank you, Relative, God bless you. Anything else I can do for you? If the stereo still works, put on a C.D., there should be one by Janis around somewhere if those Neanderthals didn't break it. What Neanderthals? The ones I dreamed up, she smiled painfully. I get it, a mess like this couldn't have come from anything else.

Two minutes later "Piece of My Heart" was blasting out. Trudis's only thought was that the best things in life are things you've already lived through, and whatever is to come will be worth nothing but shit, and she fell asleep.

She awoke an hour later. Her son, a boy with long, fairly thick hair, was patting her cheek. Even though you're looking very pretty, I didn't want to take your picture without your consent, he held up his cellphone. Don't even think it, I can feel how swollen my face is, and it hurts. Joe Cocker's "You Can Leave Your Hat On" filled the room. But you look great,

Mama, he brought the phone closer. I said No. They smiled, the boy did not move, he giggled mischievously. Later on you can tell me what happened, should I take you to the hospital? No way, by the time they see to me I'll be dead, they have no respect for patients. I mean a private hospital. And with what eyes, my divine one-eye? With the thousand dollars Don Ignacio gave me, he asked me not to tell you, we can spend it on making you better. That Flea will always be a generous man, but no, my son, I'm not that bad off. Doña Mary, who had cleaned things up, came in with a new I.V. bottle and a plate of meatballs. Relative said you should eat, I brought you this and some fish with rice. Oh, Doña, you shouldn't have. It's nothing, today I do it for you, tomorrow you do it for me. Trudis drank some water. Would you like Nescafé? No, water's better, only my boss likes that garbage; Doña Mary, please call Susana, tell her to tell Lefty those vermin who were messing with us are gone; do you know what the problem is over there? She hasn't told me, but it must have something to do with Jason, she wouldn't contact him otherwise. Call her from here if you like. I'd better do it from home, I've got the number there, don't think I know it, even though I've spent years dialling it. Thank you, Doña Mary, may God keep you well for many years. You too, Trudis, now eat, you're looking skinny. God forbid.

Edith, convinced that she would never see Lefty again, arrived at the casino prepared to gamble away whatever remained of her mother's house. She knew full well that she would only stop gambling when she died. She watched the officer tailing her talking on his telephone, then she saw him get into his black car and disappear. What's that about? But it cheered her up. At the entrance she ran into Devil Urquídez, though she did not recognize him. In her head there was only one party and it was not the wedding coming up the following Friday.

Thirty-Three

The Flea arrived right on time. In the hotel restaurant they ordered beers. What's up, my man Lefty, what brings you to Los Angeles? the day before yesterday we said goodbye in Culichi and you're here already. I came so they could knock me off, my man Flea. Don't mess with me, fucking Lefty, that's nothing to joke about, you know what a bitch it was to escape the Grim Reaper's clutches. I'm going to tell you, but first I want to know if you're willing to risk your life. You know I am, no fucking matter what it's about or how it turns out. My son Jason disappeared last Friday and I'm here to find him. Wow, you've got a kid? With Susana Luján, do you remember her? Of course, what a beauty she was and I bet she's still kicking the can; so Lefty, you're the one who won the lottery? the toughest dudes were drooling over that babe. Well, they got fucked by my old bones; listen I called you from her cell, she knows you by sight because you used to supply her with tortillas; as a matter of fact she had to close her taco shop because twenty-two people got poisoned by your shitty worm-ridden stuff. What? stop fucking with me. Don't try to rope me into your troubles, take it up with her. I don't believe it, my tortillas always pass the health inspection, and what's more they've got a reputation for being especially hygienic. Don't get stuck on that, what counts now is Jason, and I'm going to tell you the whole story.

While they rode in the Flea's Honda pickup towards the Hollywood Café, where Lefty was to meet with Wolverine, he summarised the stories of Crazy Mouse and the redhead. This sounds really heavy, my man Lefty, and that bro you're going to see, who is he? He's an instructor at my son's school, his name is Jackman. That guy? he's a real asshole, Lefty, a dude who's got it in for all Latinos, I thought he'd got killed. Nope, it seems he's a very good teacher and he gets along well with Jason. I'm going to be right there in case it gets hairy. Listen, what was it you were saying about Polo, the fortune-teller? Right, I had that problem, so when I got to Culichi I went to see the buddy, he was recommended by my sister; he told me I was going to get off, I didn't believe him, I'd heard really awful things about Pockmark Long's son, disfiguring bodies and shit like that; then after seeing him I knew he wasn't such a big deal, he's missing the essential element, vengeance is no piece of cake, Lefty, don't try to tell me it is; anyhow, the guy also gave me a long fucking spiel about a good buddy who would invite me on a trip and I should know what to do; well, here you are, and I'm with you to the final consequences, then we can go get drunk. Agreed. Did they catch the dude who brought Polo down? He wouldn't give himself up, he met us with a hail of bullets, and then he committed suicide. Typical.

It was a place filled with old artefacts from the movies and photographs of famous people on the walls. Wolverine was waiting with a cup of coffee in front of him. Señor Jackman? Pleased to meet you, Señor Mendieta, your son truly really admires you, unusual as that is. You speak Spanish well. For twenty-five years I walked a beat and in the streets you hear so much Spanish only people who don't want to learn manage not to. I hear you were really tough on Hispanics. Only on the crooks, it must be the same with you. More or less, the telephone threat crossed his mind; well, I wanted to see you about Jason, his mother thinks he might have been kidnapped. Did you call the police? Not yet. In the United States that's the first thing you do, Señor Mendieta; you should notify the Los Angeles Police Department. Will do, meanwhile, did you see Jason with any strangers last Friday? Are you interrogating me? you can't do that, even if you are a good policeman, you're not allowed to undertake an investigation in this country, it doesn't matter that the victim is your son, who, by the way, is a great kid. Mendieta opened his mouth, felt a flood of irritation, the sort that ruins your day. Are you serious? Of course, that's what institutions are for and the L.A.P.D. is one of the best, let me remind you: you are not allowed to work here. Mendieta's guts twisted, he understood why Jackman had the reputation he had, and he decided to cut the conversation short before he ended up punching the guy. Why would Jason look up to this jerk? but he wasn't about to depart without goading him, who does this asshole think he is, that he's so special, that he lives in a perfect country? Let me congratulate the Los Angeles police and you for how well you upheld the law in the O.J. Jackson case, you know, that guy accused of killing his grandmother? Señor, you're in no position to judge the L.A.P.D., they did their job. Of course, the way they did with Rodney Queen, were you in on that? Señor Mendieta, what do you know about it? that comment is irrelevant; contact the police about the disappearance of your son and then go shopping like everybody else, buy yourself some new clothes and some chocolates. Clothes, here? why would I do that? you think maybe I'll find Levi's not made in China? What are you bragging about? we both know Mexico is the most corrupt country in the world and the police there are hardly clean. Sure, but if your son was kidnapped and you asked us for help, we wouldn't tell you to go to hell; and this is a kid who likes you and trusts you and believes in what you teach, he got to his feet and walked towards the door. Jackman's voice held him up: Maybe one of Jason's friends knows something. He turned, the retired policeman pointed to the chair where he had been seated.

Will you go to the police? No. They remained quiet for a moment, Jackman sipped his coffee, Mendieta asked for a double espresso. He's attracted to strange people, like Beck for instance, his best friend, who's like an overgrown child; that one loves playing with guns, if he doesn't wise up in time he'll be the first in his class to go down; pause during which Mendieta felt the Beretta against his coccyx. There's a handicapped guy who runs a liquor store, he also works as an extra when a director needs somebody fearless in a wheelchair; look for him in Santa Monica, near U.C.L.A., the place is called Philip Marlowe, for sure you've heard of him. Do you know his name? No, people say he's Egyptian, they call him Bionic Chair. Thank you for that; he was about to apologise, but he refrained; I was told that the last day he went to school, he was seen in the parking lot with a redhead. My class is from seven to nine and I've given you a tip; now don't forget to go to the police. Mendieta nodded and left by the door he came in.

Forty-three minutes later they found the place. It was well-lit and well-stocked, but they did not see anyone in a wheelchair. Is Bionic Chair around? A young man with circles under his black eyes stared at him suspiciously. Who's asking? Jason Mendieta's father. The kid smiled. I thought you were Jason years later. Are you the man? That's my father, he left fifteen minutes ago. Call him, tell him I need to see him, it's urgent. The Flea asked for a six-pack of Miller. The young man handed his telephone to Lefty, who moved far enough away so that no-one would hear him. I need to speak with you. I'm just getting home and I'm bushed. It's about Jason, he's disappeared, missing for four days. Oh, my God. Silence. Come here, I'll wait for you in my car in the street, it's nearby. The young man took Flea's money and gave him the address.

They arrived in ten minutes. They found him parked in front of a splendid white house. Mendieta got in beside him. Good evening, then he got right to the point: I know that you and Jason are friends and perhaps you can help us get to the bottom of this. Whatever I can do, I consider it an obligation because he's close to us; the same black eyes as his son, thin but muscular. When was the last time you saw him? Friday, he came in with his buddy for a bottle and they stayed for a while chatting. Did he mention any worries, or that he was planning to leave the city? Not exactly, usually he asks me about my work as an extra; I haven't always been in a wheelchair, just since the time I fell while we were shooting a scene in "Titanic", I haven't been able to walk since then; Jason thinks the studio was responsible, that their lack of security was a crime; he didn't say he was leaving the city, we couldn't talk long because Chuck was in a hurry, that kid is always anxious. How did you meet my son? Naguib and he went to high school together, they were both athletes and they became friends; and, as you can see, he still drops by. So he wasn't worried. Correct, and he really admires you, he's told me a few hair-raising things about your work in Mexico, you're one of those policemen who aren't afraid to take risks. Mendieta understood that Bionic Chair would not be able to tell him much, he tried to pinpoint why; his quick conclusion, the man was an incorrigible chatterbox. Once I was a double for DiCaprio and he turned out to be too tall ...

O.K., sir, excuse me, what is your name? Jack Mahfuz. I thought you would have an Egyptian name like your son. Well, Jack isn't my real name, but it brings me at least a generation closer to this country. Have you noticed if Jason prefers a certain type of girl? Mexicans, he's drawn to beautiful Mexicans, who look like Salma Hayek or that Colombian Sofía Vergara, although that day he said something, I hope I didn't hear wrong, he said at last he was going to discover the mystery of redheads. He said that? More or less. Anything else? where was he going to do that? with whom? he felt his adrenaline pumping. That's all, because right then Chuck came in and took him by the arm, I tell you, that kid is in a big hurry to live his life and in a policeman that can be fatal. Have you ever seen Jason with a redhead? Never, and I don't think it means much, they've got a reputation for being hot and horny, but I don't know if it's true. Señor Mahfuz, your help has been invaluable, thank you. You're welcome, come by the store and we'll have a drink, I don't drink, but you do, we'll drink to that. Lefty opened the car door. For sure, take care. Find Jason quickly.

At the wheel, the Flea had drunk three of the beers

and was listening to Luis Pérez Meza's "Corrido de Heraclio Bernal". Fucking Flea, won't they give you a ticket for drinking in the car? Only if they catch me, what's up, everything alright? No progress, the only new bit is that Jason was curious about the mystery of redheads and so he went off with one, any idea what that mystery might be? You can frisk me, I stick with the local goods. Uh-huh. Now what? Let me off at the hotel, we'll see each other tomorrow. Go ahead, have one. Let's see what we've got: Jason meets a redhead and they become friends; Friday they meet up, most likely he made a date with her or she went looking for him; then, under the pretext of revealing her mysteries, she takes him to the beach or the mountains or the desert, maybe to Las Vegas or they just head off. They could be in a motel along any highway or in Yosemite; he called me from somewhere, suppose they're still in Los Angeles? The fact is that this day's over and I'm at a dead end.

He went up to his room. On the desk was a letter-sized manila envelope with his name on it. He picked it up, weighed it in his hand, saw it was a bit bulky, and opened it. He pulled out something round wrapped in gauze. A piece of a finger. Black. Ugh, Lefty felt a blow in the pit of his stomach. Shit, he froze, trembling. The telephone began to ring. He put the amputated finger on the desk and pulled a small card from the envelope. The telephone. "All your debts are coming due, you decrepit old bastard," the red letters were very clear but crooked. His hand picked up the receiver. Yes. Edgar, it's Susana, I called to give you a message and to see if you need anything, I just spoke with the Flea and he told me you were at the hotel. Can you come? Of course, are you alright? No, someone just sent me a finger that might be Jason's. *Oh my God.*

Thirty-Four

Susana came into the room and stared at the manila envelope. Show me. Lefty pulled out the lump of gauze and unwrapped it. The woman brought one hand to her mouth and resisted a sudden urge to sob, she sat on the bed. Is it his? That's what we're going to find out, do you want to see the message they sent? She nodded and picked up the card. That's Jason's handwriting, his penmanship is so awful I'd recognise it anywhere. Are you serious? Lefty contemplated the message. Oh yes, he writes with his feet. A few moments went by in silence. Can we go to Chuck's place? Hang on, I'll call him. No answer, this late he's probably making the rounds of the bars, he does that. Leave him a message, tell him I need to speak with him urgently, that we need him to find us a lab to test the finger, the school must have that sort of connection. I hope so. You know what? let's go to his place, he's probably asleep or maybe he'll turn up any minute. My mother called on behalf of Trudis, she says the trouble is over, the people who were in your house went away all of a sudden, she says they mistreated Trudis, but the Relative took care of her, she's going to spend the night with her. That Trudis is

237

a treasure, I've still got to get her her Mother's Day present. She gets along really well with Jason. You could say they love each other. My mother told me she had to clean up, those people trashed the place. Thank her for me; maybe I ought to buy a telephone. Use mine.

On the way, they talked: She met Jack Mahfuz and his son when Jason was in high school; Jackman is like that, the kids think he's a mutant, that's why they call him Wolverine; she did not know about her son's interest in redheads, what's more, she had never seen him with one nor had he mentioned anyone with red hair.

They knocked. First politely, then not so politely. Mendieta stood where he could be seen through the peephole. Susana phoned Chuck and they banged on the door again. It opened, there he was, drunk and with Cindy hanging off him. Hi. Sorry to bother you. They smelled of sex. Come in, no problem. Just a couple of questions, Chuck; the computer, which maybe he only used as a lamp, still had the gun on the screen. We learned that Jason wanted to discover the mystery of redheads and from what Cindy said he found one, so what's the mystery? No idea, I never knew they had one. Did he talk to you about that? Never, like I told you, with women he goes his own way. Lefty looked at Cindy, who put on a pretty-girl face. From what I can see, so do you. They smiled. Susana remained silent, scrutinising the mess. Another thing, we've received what might be Jason's finger, do you know where we can get it tested to see if it is? Their mouths fell open. Uh-oh. A finger? What savages, what's the ransom they're asking? Nothing, or at least they haven't said yet. Beck was wide-eyed. At this time of night it's impossible, but I'll find a lab tomorrow, we'll find out who can do it; you know it takes a while. That doesn't matter. What finger is it? Cindy's eyes were also wide. It must be the middle finger, he turned to Susana, does he have any scars? No. O.K., as soon as you have something let me know.

At the hotel. Can I stay with you? I don't feel well.

They went to bed with their clothes on, his body understood that it was better to wait and it hung on in silence, not moving a muscle. Susana fell asleep immediately, while Lefty drowsed. What a fucking bitch life is, why would they butcher Jason? The poor kid, so full of dreams; don't act like an idiot, it's about me, but who? why? how do they have such reach? Police work has a way of stepping on people's toes, rarely do we end up on good terms with everyone. It's like people get used to having criminals in their family and they think they're decent, when really they're a deadly plague. These guys can't be just anybody, kidnapping is a serious crime and whoever dreams it up and pulls it off has to be not only a real bastard, but angry as hell. And then to do it to a kid who lives so far away from me and with whom I haven't had much of a relationship ever, except for last year when he went to Culiacán. They killed Crazy Mouse, could that be about me too? The

Flea I don't worry about, he knows how to protect himself and he just wriggled out of a major league mess; the one who didn't get out was his fortune-teller, the poor bastard, well at least he had a good time with Irene. And what's the story with Win anyway? she turns up and gives me forty-eight hours to find Jason, what a jerk. I've got to protect Enrique and Susana; doesn't she smell good, when did she start using that perfume? He pulled a blanket up over her and hugged her timidly. She snuggled against him without waking.

Lefty? how are you? you're never going to die, God bless the mother who bore you. Susana told me they gave you quite a caressing. It was nothing, another stripe on the tiger, I'm all better, Marco and I stayed over in your house. Ah, Marco, how is your son? Even more handsome than his father. That's great, how bad is the damage? Moderate, you'll see when you get home, because you are coming back, right? Well, the gringos want to hire me, so I'm considering it. Don't be unpatriotic, come back as soon as you can. I'll think it over, what else has happened back there? Last night that boy who used to be with the police, Devil, came over, we gave him Susana's number, he said he wanted to speak with you, that he'd call today. Perfect, has anyone from Headquarters been looking for me? Yes, last night Angelita called very worried, I assured her you were fine, also Señor Ortega and Dr Montaño, and just a minute or two ago someone who said he was the Camel and another who called himself Terminator, how is Jason? Better than you and me together; he wanted to ask if the Commander had called, but he held off; any strange calls? None. Threats? Nothing, those guys are gone, I hope for good, what are you doing in Los Angeles, if I might ask? watch out you don't get hitched over there. Trudis, please. Better you come home, remember we haven't paid the utilities, they're going to cut them off, and what about my present? Take it easy, as soon as I convince the gringos that I only came to shoot a movie I'll be back. I'll be jumping for joy. Well, if anything happens call this number and Susana will give me the message.

They were having breakfast when Max Garcés called. How are the English classes going? All F's, have you heard about Crazy Mouse? Yes, but it has nothing to do with you, it was a personal matter. Are you sure? Absolutely, those jerks don't understand they have to be careful how they live, every time something happens to them it endangers the group; the fact is the F.B.I. picked him up and the shitstorm is growing; however, nothing to do with your problem. The dude was losing his memory or what? Well, I did just find out he forgot important things. They found a paper with my name and hotel in his pocket. Aha, no shit, who did? The F.B.I., an agent I once met in Culiacán told me that and gave me forty-eight hours to find my son. What a pussy, instead of helping you out. That's for sure, she's only going to give me a hand if I introduce her to your boss, she wants to have a cappuccino with her. Tell her she doesn't like coffee; look we're going to change your hotel, a buddy will come pick you up, he's not so involved in the East Side as Crazy Mouse and he's not in any trouble, do you know who's behind the kidnapping? No idea, they sent us a finger and I want to find out if it's my son's. This buddy will help you, they call him Gordowsky and he always knows what to do. How do I know I can trust him? Because I'm telling you, here's one bit of information: he's the guy who keeps an eye on the señora's son, he fixed it with the school so they give him special treatment; I'll ask him to work on the finger, which must be worrying you, have they told you how much they want? Nothing, it seems the pickle is just with me, somebody's taking revenge. I see. By the way, thank you, I learned yesterday that Culiacán is heaven again. Even if you aren't with us, you are one of ours, Lefty Mendieta, and we aren't going to let you down, the señora asked me to remind you of that. How is she doing? Every day a bit better, she sat up once, for about a minute, then she got dizzy. Tell her that as soon as she's well I'll take her out to the Guayabo, did you see about Ignacio Daut? It's all settled, and Charface too, so focus on your son. Thank you, Max, and give my best to the ball-buster.

Steven Tyler made his way along one side of the restaurant, he had to catch a plane, he was late, but even so he stopped just in front of Lefty, he was wearing a black tee and jeans, but the detective saw him in his long coat and scarf singing "She Came In Through the Bathroom Window", "Golden Slumbers", "Carry That Weight" and "The End", exactly the way he did at the Paul McCartney tribute at the Kennedy Center Opera House in 2010. They smiled at each other, the rocker waved goodbye and went on his way; Mendieta savoured his coffee.

Some moments will stick with you for years to come, flash-frozen and inexplicably preserved, ain't that the case?

Thirty-Five

I'm Dr Dionisio Lima, Dr Jiménez is in the operating room so he sent me to have a look at the patient. He was dressed in white with a stethoscope around his neck, a black bag in one hand, and in the other several forms from Virgen Purísima Hospital. Hyena Wong looked him over from tip to toe. This dude is not the toad he claims to be, he thought. Hang on, he called Max over and explained. Garcés dialled Jiménez and his minder, Chacaleña, but neither answered. The doctor didn't say he was sending a replacement. Well, that's none of my business, he asked me to do him a favour and I'm doing it, that's all, if I can't see the patient, please tell him I was here as promised; he wiped the sweat from his brow. He never comes this time of day. This is when I could make it, if I'm not going to examine her, please call the nurse so I can ask how she is and if needed give her instructions. She hasn't come. So the patient is alone? She's with us. In that case, excuse me, good afternoon.

Charface walked towards the elevator. Max felt conflicted. Fucking mother, I already made one mistake, I don't want to make another, but the doctor did not tell us a thing and

244

he's not answering his cell; of course, if he's operating he can't answer; Chacaleña doesn't answer either, I wonder if he's operating on her. Hang on. Charface stopped and slowly returned, he knew the nurse would not come, she was nearby, inside his parked car with her throat slit. Come in.

In the semi-darkened room, a bouquet of yellow tulips glowed, Garcés explained to the señora and she didn't object; a fat and ugly doctor must be good. She watched him as he checked the oxygen, the I.V. bag, and wrote cautiously on the hospital forms. Her men stepped outside. How are you feeling, Señora Valdés? At the end of my rope, doctor, I can't find a way out. Are you having trouble breathing? A bit this morning, since noon I've been feeling better. Well, you don't have to worry now, you fucking hag, he covered her mouth with his left hand, you'll get all the rest you need in hell. At that moment she realised who he was, saw his moist deadly smile, the stiletto in his right hand, noted how his eyes paused on the tulips, and she fired. She had grown suspicious when he failed to remove the blood pressure cuff, and because she was wary by nature. Naturally, she had the pistol she had asked for a few days before in hand. Max and Hyena stormed in a second later and riddled him with bullets. They hadn't moved from the bedroom door, which they had left ajar.

It's Charface, the lady capo said. Get the new stew-man to take care of the body.

We need to know who's behind it, call Chacaleña, ask

her if Dr Jiménez is alright. She just called back and yes, the doctor is in the middle of an operation. Well, tell her not to let him out of her sight. Samantha closed her eyes and lay still, Max hauled the body out and Hyena mopped up the blood. In his bag, they found a small notebook with only two telephone numbers.

Thirty-Six

They had told Enrique to meet them at the restaurant in the Millennium Biltmore on Grand Avenue at Fifth downtown, and he walked into Smeraldi's at eleven with a folder in his hand. Howyadoin, you bastard. Christ, bro, you look so goddam ugly, I thought life in Gringolandia was treating you well. You're full of shit, take a good look at me, my old lady still rents me out as an escort, they hugged each other in a long embrace, then he kissed Susana on the cheek, anything new on Jason? Not much, they sent us a finger which we just sent to get tested to see if it's his. Don't fuck around with me. Just like you're hearing it, they're real sons of bitches. How much do they want? They haven't said, it seems it's someone who has a grudge against me, on the telephone they said I was going to pay the price for all I'd done. With Jason? what assholes. The finger came with more or less the same message. Could it be one person? Who knows, usually they're gangs, so far all we know about is a girl, Jason told a friend he wanted to discover the mystery of redheads and the last time he was seen he was headed off with one; that's all we have. What a pickle, listen, I didn't bring the girls or my wife because

I didn't want to frighten them. You bastard, frights are for sharing too. Really? Call them and get them over here right now. Susana smiled. Let me call Mirna, I'll tell her you're keeping something from her and for sure she'll cross her legs and go on strike. Wait until we find my nephew, stories with a happy ending are so much better. I should wish her a happy Mother's Day. Do it later, you know how nosy she is. You probably haven't had breakfast, we ate early at the other hotel, do you want something here? Hotel food is not what I'd call my favourite, but I'll make the sacrifice, remember, I work in one. You're going to like it, they say the chef is from Guamúchil and he's a good friend of Víctor de la Vega's, do you remember him? Of course, twice he helped me escape the anti-guerrilla police. By the way, you can go back to Mexico whenever you want, you won't have any trouble. That's what you think, there are people after me who don't believe in the amnesty, what's more, I'm fine here; in fact, I brought along the paperwork to sign the house over to you, he handed Lefty the folder, which featured the logo of the Oakland hotel where he worked in maintenance: Inn at Deep Creek. It's totally legal, if anything is missing, get Díaz Salazar to fix it, I called him yesterday and he said he'd do whatever you need. Lefty's mouth was hanging open. But, bro, this isn't necessary, maybe we don't have to pay a lawyer. Look, you live there and I'm not going back, every time I read the news from Mexico it gives me hives, it's a bitch watching all those politicians with their fucking smarmy grins, as if they were doing everything just right, so many senseless killings it makes me sick. Add another forty-three for the students in Guerrero. We Mexicans put up with our politicians only because we somehow manage to separate them from our own sense of shame, they're a fucking stain on the country that even acid won't remove. I like what you say, but I live there, in the thick of it, and now we've got this mess. You in the thick of it? don't make like you're innocent, I spoke with your boss and he rubbed my face in it, you being fired, you being the worst sort of cop, corrupt and colluding with the narcos. Surprised looks. He told you that? Susana stared at him, shocked. No more, no less, I told him my brother was not one of those, and I told him to fuck his mother, I only hope he's not right. Well, he is. What? You don't need to be a narco to have a relationship with them, I'm a policeman and the fact is our work coincides with them more often than anyone would find reasonable. I can't believe it. Believe it, it's not anything that makes me proud either; right now I have their support and my only motive is to get my son back; it's hard to imagine how much those bastards control; for instance, one of them brought us to this hotel and took the finger to a lab to get it tested; of course the Los Angeles police don't know about it and I hope they never find out, but who do you think does know? the F.B.I., who by the way gave me forty-eight hours to find Jason, and that runs out tomorrow morning. You are something else, bro, I can see why you don't want the house, it's not good enough for you. Enrique, I don't work for them, understand me, we just cooperate, he grabbed the folder, and I do want the house.

While Enrique, who weighed about a hundred kilos, ate eggs and bacon with toast, Lefty grew more and more uneasy. Three hours before, a strait-laced young man, dressed elegantly but discreetly, had introduced himself as Gordowsky. He brought them to the new hotel and took the envelope with the finger and the note, as well as blood samples from the two parents. He also advised him to leave the gun in the room.

He spotted Agent Jeter coming in. Aren't they quick off the mark, he thought. We've only been here two hours and they've already found us, he got to his feet. While you finish having breakfast, I'm going to do a few things appropriate to my gender. He greeted the agent cautiously and followed him to Sai Sai, a small Japanese restaurant in a corner of the hotel, where Win Morrison was drinking tea.

If I'd known you were coming I would have waited to have breakfast. I know you are a gentleman, Señor Mendieta, but you did the right thing, would you like some tea? She was dressed casually. Thank you, I don't recall ever having tea in my life. My mother was a student of Asian culture and she taught us to appreciate this infusion and to enjoy its subtle aromas. I gather tea has a rich heritage, just like coffee, and half of humanity drinks it, did you come to remind me that my time is up after today? Something like that, and also to ask you how it's going. It's a disaster, the only thing we've learned is that my son wanted to discover the mystery of redheads, remember they saw him with one. What mystery? No-one knows for sure, have you brought me any news? Well, I know you didn't go to the police, and for that reason I haven't sought their help. I met with a retired policeman, one of my son's instructors, who said the same thing as you, that I can't work here. So you see it's not just my hangup, it's the nature of the system. Mendieta knew he was not called there for chit-chat, especially at this point; besides, the F.B.I. always knows more than they let on; they could turn the country upside down if they wanted to, that is, if the hackers don't expose them first.

He decided not to tell her about the finger and the message, since they were already in the hands of experts working for the cartel. He told me to go buy chocolates too, what do I look like? The point is you are just one more tourist here in Los Angeles, you can visit Hollywood or go to a concert, that is, unless you collaborate with us; we'll give you immunity through our Witness Protection Program; the only thing you have to do is point out Samantha Valdés's movements; from Mexico City we received information that you are one of her people; I know you are a man with a certain degree of honesty and that you would be a magnificent informant for the F.B.I.; and as I told you, our entire anti-kidnapping department would take up the case of your son. She poured herself some tea and scrutinised the detective's face, her eyes were cold. Why don't we rescue my son first and talk later? They stared at each other for a few seconds. That isn't how we work, we'll only help if you commit to us. And I'd sign a contract, you already told me. Win sipped again, Lefty stared out the window, on the sidewalk two men in grey ignored three homeless people asking them for money for breakfast. Shit, what do I do? he thought it over, one of the things that life had taught him was never to betray anyone, every single person he knew who had squealed was lying six feet under; besides, getting involved with the Americans was no walk in the park, as he knew quite well; on the other hand, his son was in grave danger, if the finger turned out to be his, for sure his scruples would crumble, but until then . . . Win, where I'm from there was once a politician who said the only thing he lacked was the ability to give birth, and that's the case with me; the fact is I have to think it over, give me another two days. Of course not, you have until tomorrow at ten, her manner changed slightly; Jeter will pick you up, why did you change hotels? that other one is very nice, the atmosphere's excellent and it has stupendous food. She stood up, left five dollars on the table, and walked out. Damn her clever response.

Lefty's mind was a blank, then he asked himself: why is it

so hard for me to say yes? don't fuck around, Jason's life is in danger and here I am standing by my stupid scruples. Could it be because the gringos always give me the heebie-jeebies? Several times I swore I would never have anything to do with them, ever. It might be, because what the fuck do I owe Samantha that is worth the life of my son? Nothing, the fucking broad; besides the fact that she insulted me in a particularly ugly way, she put me in a horribly embarrassing situation where not only did I lose my job, but I turned up on a fucking list that links me to her, even though it's not true. Fucking Chilangos, they write whatever names come into their heads, what am I doing on that list? Thanks to Belascoarán at least I found out in time. I'm going to say yes, get those bastards looking for my son and I bet they find him in a few hours. He hurried out of the restaurant by an exit to the street, but neither Win Morrison nor her bodyguards could be seen. Fucking mother, another day wasted, he looked at the big buildings of the financial district, at the homeless people gathered in Pershing Square, and he went back into the hotel. Gordowsky was waiting for him in the lobby. Shall we sit down for a minute? He pointed to a couple of easy chairs.

Señor Mendieta, they are working on your specimen now, by tomorrow noon they will have preliminary results, obviously this sort of thing takes time, but we will have a general idea; I already called Señor Garcés, he asked me to hurry things along, but it cannot happen any faster; the handwriting expert is in Hawaii, he arrives tonight, and he will give us his analysis tomorrow; I do not know how to tell you this, but you should take it easy if you can. Of course, go buy clothes or chocolates. I don't know your tastes, but if that is what you want there are brand-name stores all around us, and if you like dressing up, three blocks down Broadway there is a place that sells outfits from the movies very inexpensively; no reason you should know but I bought this suit there, Al Pacino wore it in "The Godfather Part III". Thank you, I'll expect you tomorrow. Here is a cellphone number if you need to reach me.

He found Susana and his brother still at the table in the restaurant, their faces ashen. He sat down and waited for them to speak. Edgar, they called from Jason's telephone, they said tomorrow they'll send us an ear. Call them back! She dialled and handed him the telephone. Whoever you are, let's fix this once and for all. The response was a long, loud smooch.

Thirty-Seven

After walking around the buffet twice without even giving it a glance, he sat down. I forgot all about that, I got loud kisses over the telephone two or three times, just like now, no words, but I didn't link it to anything; the threats came later on. They sent me those smooches too. Why didn't you tell me? Who knows, I didn't think it was important. Lefty figured maybe she got them every day from her boyfriends and he felt a twinge of jealousy; he kept that to himself, he had thought his were from Edith. What a pair of idiots we are, he said out loud, and now we better hurry or they're going to mutilate Jason again; we'll get the preliminary results of the lab test on the finger tomorrow. My balls know more science than that fancy-pants you just stepped out with, if this woman will excuse me. You're right, he's from the F.B.I., then he turned to Susana: Dial this number for me, would you? Enrique looked at his brother and felt a certain pride: fucking snot-nose, and I thought he wasn't going to make anything of himself. This is Edgar Mendieta. Yes? Can we trace the origin of a call made cellphone to cellphone a few hours ago? Let me look into it and I'll call you back at this number. I'm going to the ladies' room, Susana said, and she headed off. The years don't go by for my sister-in-law, tell me it ain't so, bro. What sister-in-law? Flickering smiles. Don't make like an idiot, it's obvious more embers are burning between you two than in fucking Ceboruco Volcano. Don't mess with me, asshole, show a bit more respect. There's something going on. Well, yeah, a son in trouble. What's up with the F.B.I.? They don't want me looking for Jason. Christ, you're walking between the horse's hooves. They tell me to go to the police, but I don't think there's time, besides, the kidnappers want to get at me. Spiteful assholes. Do I ever hope that finger is not my son's. Suppose it is? Who knows, I'm already freaked. The idea of going to the police is not crazy, bro, here isn't like Mexico. I know, they shoot a different calibre bullet and they play judge and jury before anyone gets to court, I've got a buddy in Ferguson, Missouri, he wasn't surprised when they killed that young black man. I'm serious, here the police investigate cases and make arrests, and we citizens feel safe. Mendieta realised just how integrated into American society his brother had become, and decided not to argue. I'll think about it. Let Susana do it, she's an American citizen, I bet when she thinks of policemen she only thinks of you and that's Jason's fault for admiring you so much. I'll ask her. If you like I'll go with her. Perfect, as soon as she comes back we'll tell her, so what about that folder? Well, what do you want? this would take care of the family's interests. You're a bastard, does Mirna agree you should give it to me? She's the one who got the papers drawn up before I even asked her to, you'll see. Susana returned, lightly made up. They suggested the next step, she said she would do whatever Edgar thought was right, and off the two of them went.

Lefty wandered down a hallway filled with old photographs of Oscar ceremonies. He went into the Gallery bar and asked for a Macallan with one ice cube; he could not rein in his anxiety. Who kidnapped Jason? Who would force me to deal with some past event that way? Hyena Wong must know where the guys who used to call me the Cat ended up, maybe one of them still wants to knock me off; but why didn't they do something in Culiacán? Another attack, burn down the house, or riddle it with bullets like they did before. It couldn't be the Federales, they aren't like that, besides it doesn't fit the picture, this happened at the same time I was getting into trouble with them. It's someone more determined, more subtle, more vindictive. It's not the narcos, Max Garcés would have told me, who would want to do such a thing? Let's see: lately we haven't put so many people in the slammer, they all got condemned by divine justice and executed right then and there by their victims; Rudy's friend is right: punishment catches up to the guilty party no matter how fast he runs. Would that young guy who sent Gori into a tailspin a couple of years ago dare? It could be, he was a champion in extreme martial arts and he loved insulting us; would Zelda be back at work yet? I need somebody to find out if he's still in Culiacán. But not her, I should leave her be, a honeymoon is sacred and more so if one of them is having a birthday. That guy travelled all over, I'll ask Robles to look into it; if I give the task to the Camel and Terminator they'll try to arrest him and I wouldn't want to be in their shoes, he'll give them the beating of their lives. Who else? I can't think of anyone; it wasn't that long ago that I learned I had a son; before that, I didn't even imagine he existed. None of the adversaries I can think of knew about him and even if they did, they wouldn't think of doing anything like this. Eventually pain grows old and there comes a time when prisoners just want to regain their freedom, they lose interest in revenge, although their descendants can get prickly, like young Long, who was going after the Flea. Why would Win give me only until ten o'clock? that makes twenty-two hours. I've got to ask that Flea bastard, he knows a lot of people in Sinaloa, maybe even the one who thinks I owe him something; and Max too – if he hadn't sent me that absent-minded rodent I wouldn't have the F.B.I. all over me.

When he ordered his second drink, he noticed that an old man, his long hair held back by a bandana folded across his forehead, was playing the guitar and singing "Always on My Mind", accompanied by a piano-player; he could have been Willie Nelson. When he began paying attention to the musicians, a brawny young man approached him holding a police badge and a set of handcuffs; he was dressed like a cowboy, same as his partner standing next to him, who must have weighed a hundred and ten kilos and it was pure muscle. Edgar Mendieta? He went out to the bakery. Passport and visa, please; the detective obeyed. This visa is expired. It can't be, they checked it at the border, maybe you need glasses; the policeman put both documents in his pocket. I am placing you under arrest, charged with entering the country illegally, under an expired visa, and with working without authorisation, investigating a kidnapping even though you are not a member of any police force in the United States; you have the right to a lawyer and . . . Lefty opened his mouth, tossed the whisky in the man's face and tried to hit him with his chair, but the big guy grabbed him. Hold it right there, buddy! The other wiped his face with a napkin, slapped the cuffs on the troublemaker, and hustled him out. There was an exit directly onto Grand Avenue, which they chose not to use. The singer carried on as if nothing had occurred, now doing "She Is Gone".

Thirty-Eight

Sitting up in a La-Z-Boy, Samantha was still connected to the I.V., an oxygen tank was by her side in case of emergency. A nurse put something into her I.V. solution, took her blood pressure and temperature, and left the room. Minerva was knitting and keeping a close eye on her. Max came in. Yes, Señora? Has Wong called? Not yet. Call him, I want to know exactly where he is.

The honourable Secretary, despite his age, is on his way to eat sushi, perhaps to relive the days long ago when he was Mexico's ambassador to Japan. He likes a restaurant called Haruki in Mexico City's Colonia Juárez. He will have to climb stairs, but the food will be well worth the effort. As many as six security guards accompany him almost round the clock.

That was what Samantha Valdés related after reading the note she had been handed, and that was where Hyena Wong stood, awaiting the right moment. La Jefa did not want to attract attention, but the Hyena could not care less; what made him effective was precisely his lack of scruples. With him were his six most daring henchmen. Their job: to mount a gun battle as tumultuous as the attempt on the life of the lady capo of the Pacific Cartel. Let those bastards hear it loud and clear.

Hamburgo Street is narrow, usually with little traffic. The grey Mercedes came to a halt in front of the restaurant door. Three bodyguards got out of a black car and took up positions around the doorway, they waved their guns to tell a couple on the sidewalk to move across the street, a fourth went upstairs to see that everything was as it should be and to let the staff know the Secretary was on his way up. The other two covered the street.

Hyena Wong came out of a small grocery store twelve metres from the doorway and put three slugs in the Secretary as he got out of his car. He collapsed, dead. At the same moment six A.K.-47s opened fire from several directions, riddling the bodyguards with bullets and putting dozens of dents in both vehicles. Amid four passers-by running for their lives and a few others rooted to the spot, Hyena Wong and his men departed, betraying no sign of haste. Then the assassin's cellphone began to vibrate.

That very night, Frank Monge committed suicide in Guadalajara.

Thirty-Nine

They led him out through the lobby. When my wife comes back, please tell her that I've been arrested, Lefty asked a bellhop who could have been Cuba Gooding Jr and who gave him a scornful once-over: Goddamned Latino sonofabitch, I'm not your message boy. The ones in charge of the parking lot showed more interest: Look at this guy, maybe they caught him with his hands in the cookie jar. What do you think?

After eight hours locked up with three head-bandaged cellmates who had lost it at a Lakers game, they took him to a white room where Susana Luján was waiting with a man in a dark suit. What happened? What do you think, I was sitting in the bar and they grabbed me, where's Enrique? He's outside. Señor Mendieta, I'm Jack Robinson, your lawyer, we'll clear this up as soon as we can. Could it be right now? Sorry, I'm afraid not. We found out about the fine, Susana said, but they won't let you out today. But why? what did I do? they accused me of entering the country illegally, but that's not true, they took away my passport and visa, claiming the visa's expired, and that's not true either, there's no fucking justification. Those documents are in their possession, Señor Mendieta, and no matter how hard we tried it was impossible to convince them of your innocence; tomorrow you'll be brought before a judge and they'll fine you several hundred dollars for resisting arrest. Señor Robinson, I have a serious problem to deal with and the last thing I need is to be behind bars. I understand, but the system is inflexible; we've submitted our request and we expect them to let you out sometime tomorrow. In other words, it's not a sure thing. The violation is not serious, but it will depend on the judge and when we get to present our case. Don't frighten me. Let's just hope the party that accused you shows up. Huh? Mendieta's eyes were wide. There is a charged lodged by someone named Jackman, a former policeman. What a sonofabitch, rage rose from his heart to his head and he was on the point of over-turning the table. Relax, everything will be alright; try not to pick any fights. I'm sorry, Edgar, truly, I never expected the teacher to do anything like that; oh, your friend called, he says yes it can be done, he didn't tell me what, and he'll give you the numbers, he asked me for Jason's; Chuck called too, he's ready to do whatever you need. Can Enrique come in? No, they only allowed us, and only because Señor Robinson convinced them that I had to be here. Am I hoping my older brother could protect me? he said to himself, Parra would love that one, and he cried out: I can't fucking believe it, it's incredible that this stuff happens in the most powerful country in the world, they waste their time jailing a jerk like me; so that lunatic turned me in, now I understand why his students call him Wolverine, fucking turd of a mutant; alright, how did it go with you two? Fine, they took down our story and sent it off to the right people. Susana, do me a favour, call Trudis, tell her to look up Officer Robles at Headquarters and ask him to find the whereabouts of the young guy that had Gori all depressed back in December year before last, and how long he's been wherever he is; and tell her not to let on the information is for me. Why not your partner? She's on her honeymoon.

He did not sleep.

He had time to reflect on the dilemma bedevilling him. He was a policeman who was somewhat involved in corruption, it's true, but he wasn't a fink; how could he rescue Jason quickly without accepting Win Morrison's deal? The cartel had kept its word, they brought him to Los Angeles, paid for his hotels, supplied him with advisers, one who had a memory like a sieve, they fixed my troubles in Culiacán, they took care of Charface, who had me on his list. Fucking list, even Win has it; this arrest doesn't make any sense, the reasoning is so stupid, just because some fucking grouch wants me to do things his way they pick me up in a bar where some asshole is singing heart-throb tunes? It's fucked up, and I'm not going to forgive him, how did they know about my new hotel? are they watching me that closely? If that finger turns out to be Jason's, Wolverine is going to have to deal with me, the faggot; and if it isn't, he still will, what made him want to fuck up my life? Too bad I wasted that whisky, when you get arrested like that you've got to down your drink right away. What's the story with Edith? what a bitch, eh? She took the fifty grand just like that, did she really believe she was going to double it? Well, yeah, that's what gamblers are like, in their imagination they're always winners. How many paintings do you suppose she's sold? The poor woman, and she came off as being so great; maybe she spent her husbands' money and that's why they're so down in the dumps; well, I can't deny her good points. You agree with me? The interruption came from his body, who was never perturbed by life's problems. Yes, indeedy.

Counting the minutes requires techniques that only those condemned to die appreciate.

At 4.48 they led him once more to the room where he had met with Susana and Robinson. Jeter was waiting there, seated and fresh from the shower, wearing his traditional grey suit. He smelled of aftershave. Good morning Señor Mendieta, he said with a certain familiarity, did they wake you up? Do I look like I slept? Don't be angry, I'm here to take you to your hotel, Special Agent Morrison does not want you to miss your appointment, he handed over the passport and visa. Lefty looked him in the eye. Just like that? We are the F.B.I., Señor Mendieta, in America we're the eye that never sleeps;

you'll have time for a nap, he got to his feet. Lefty did too, he had many questions, but all he could think was: Just like in the movies. Do you know why she said ten and not twelve? It's her teatime, so is nine at night.

Susana, asleep in the bed, woke up when he opened the door to the room and turned on the light. Edgar, you startled me, what happened? Well, I'm about to sell my soul to the devil. Are you serious? We'll soon find out, but I don't suppose it's like selling a kidney. He thought of asking what she was doing there, but it seemed silly. How come you're free? don't tell me you broke out. Strange things are happening to me, he sank into one of the easy chairs, her clothes were spread over the other, closer to the bed. This country seems sort of like what you see on T.V. or in the movies, but I can't explain it. What counts is that you're here, have you eaten anything? there's a sandwich on the table. I had a hamburger and a Coke, the F.B.I. agent that sprung me took me to the In and Out. Silence. Come, lie down, you look tired. Remember what I always say, blockhead, his body piped up. Don't get dramatic. Mendieta closed his eyes, he did not want to puzzle it out or remember or think anything at all, he went over to the bed. Take off those clothes, they must be full of germs, she held back the sheet. Lefty did not resist and once he felt her warm body by his side he had an enormous erection. As always, she took the initiative and conducted him to an orgasm worthy of a sailor. They fell asleep.

At eight o'clock they were awakened by a call from Enrique, who was surprised to hear his brother's voice. What? how did you manage that, you bastard? The president found out about it and he ordered my immediate release. That's great, so what happens now? We continue looking for Jason. You didn't have to sign anything? Nothing, I'm free, no charges pending, they gave me back my visa and passport. You are a heavy, fucking Edgar, I didn't think you had so much clout. Well, now you know, I just don't like to flaunt it. You're an incorrigible bastard; listen, if there is anything I can do, all you need to do is ask, I'm staying in this hotel. Thank you, brother; he was going to say that any help would have to come without so much respect for the country's institutions, but he decided not to mention it, the important thing was to rescue his son. For now, I'm going down to the restaurant for some coffee. I'll see you there in twenty minutes.

Under the shower. As soon as I can I'm going to find Wolverine and we'll see who comes out on top; fucking crock of shit, what does he get out of this? nothing, for sure; I'm wondering about the guy who beat up Gori, but what I have is a redhead, what could link the two of them? The guy comes to Los Angeles, shows off a stack of bills. Hello, my love, would you do something for me? because you are the one; taking advantage of the boy's interest in redheads the girl turns the trick and hands him over, then the vengeful bastard calls me, putting on a faggot's voice, he sends me and Susana loud kisses. Where is he holding him? how did he get Susana's number? where is the redhead if she was only the lure? or is she the kidnapper's partner? why would she want to do me harm? Forget it, I'm going to take Win's offer, in two hours that bastard and that babe will have the biggest posse in the world on their tails. Samantha Valdés, I'm sorry, we won't have coffee at the Miró anymore, nor will you mess up my life, you fucking hag, if you thought I betrayed you the other time, you won't be surprised now, you goddamned shitty poison-pusher, fuck you.

Before entering the restaurant, he phoned Gordowsky. How's it coming? Bad news, Señor Mendieta, the finger is your son's. Don't shit me, are you sure? As far as lab tests can prove anything, there is no mistake. I'm fucked. He moved the telephone away from his ear, Susana guessed and let out a sob, she clung to Lefty, who went back to the call. Sorry. No problem, regarding card with the message, you told me it was your son's handwriting. That's right. The analyst tells me it's acrylic ink, written with a very fine drawing pen that's practically new. Hang on, he turned to Susana, does Jason take art classes? He never has. Into the cell: Any other news? For now that's it, is there anything I can do for you? Tell Max Garcés I need to speak with him urgently, tell him to call me right now, he realised he did not have any way to reach him. How come I don't have his number? since I'm in with them up to my ears.

On the television they were announcing that a high official of the Mexican government had been assassinated leaving a restaurant; his bodyguards were also killed. They showed a panoramic view of Mexico City and a couple of shots of Hamburgo Street.

Neither Lefty nor Susana paid any attention. Pale and worried, they barely reacted to Enrique's charm. Are you sure you want to have breakfast here? there's a Le Pain Quotidien around the corner that's fucking great.

Forty

Mendieta was nervous. They might leave the kid with no ears, sheesh, I've got to find him, no matter how. Enrique and Susana saw his troubled expression and did not dare say a thing, both got up and went to the salad bar. Lefty was still drinking coffee when Susana's telephone rang, he sprang to his feet, startling Susana, and grabbed the cell just ahead of her. The detective pushed the answer button: Mendieta. I know it's you, idiot, you are going to pay for all your misdeeds and in a little while you'll get an ear from your heir; a long, loud smooch. The same put-on voice, closer to a woman's than to a man's. Do I think it's a woman because of the redhead? it could be, sometimes you hear what you want to hear. Wait, I'm ready to hand myself over, you can quarter me if you feel like it, but don't you touch Jason. It hurts, doesn't it? now you know what it feels like, asshole, another smooch. Please— the line went dead.

He stood stock-still, as if he were struck dumb by the radiant marine-themed mural on the back wall of the restaurant. He thought: Fucking mother; let's see, what have I got? nothing, I need to think, who is it? is it the redhead? how did

I affect her? where is she calling from? what time will Jeter turn up? He turned to Susana, whose eyes were wide, Enrique was holding a plate filled with fruit, but he had not missed a beat. Please, call back the man who just gave us the report.

Yes, Señor Mendieta. Have we got anything on the telephone calls? Not yet, forgive me if I don't say more, but I should respect procedure; as soon as I have something I'll call.

Susana brought him a mushroom omelette that he did not touch, he just drank coffee. Enrique chewed slowly, at a loss for what to say, obviously he could not kid around as usual. Trudis told me you were a lousy eater, that all you'd have was coffee, and now I'm seeing it with my own eyes. Ever since he was a kid, he had no appetite, Mama thought he had worms, do you remember? Mendieta smiled. I took her red gladiolas from both of us. She must have been pleased; even though there were only two of us, she called us the Three Musketeers. Did she make a fuss when you joined the police force? Never, she never spoke against it. And in her letters she never said she didn't like it. She was easygoing. My mama too, only now she's really scared because of what happened at your house. Listen, those Mexican cops are bastards. And really vulgar. Don't tell me you were expecting hugs. The edge was beginning to come off their nerves when Susana's telephone rang. Max, Lefty thought, but it was Trudis.

How are you, Lefty? Fine, but so it goes, what's new? Robles just called, he tells me the man you asked about has been in

271

Australia for a year and four months, he got married there and has a child. How did he find that out? He asked his family and at an auto parts store. Thank you, Trudis, how are your bruises treating you? If you want to see them you'd better hurry, Doña Mary hasn't let me down, she's always looking in on me; listen, don't worry about the utilities, Marco lent us something, when you get back you can settle up. I'll do that, please thank him for me, anything else? Well, no, the dogs died. What? Don't get mad, it's a joke, when you come back I'll explain; Señor Ortega came to ask for you, so did Dr Montaño, and he examined me and told me I've got the blood pressure of a fifteen-year-old; Gori and Angelita call every day. Thank you, Trudis, if you hear anything, call this number. What number? you can't see it on this telephone, you've got to buy one with a screen. This is Susana's cellphone. So you've got company, eh? that makes me happy. He hung up. Why does everyone think they know who's your perfect match? more importantly, how many people have faced what Jason's going through? a very pretty girl picks him up from school and kidnaps him. He turned to his companions: Are there redheads in Australia? A shitload, even kangaroos have red hair. Is the one that bewitched Jason Australian? Good question, he tasted the omelette, no salt? Trudis told me not to give you salt. Fucking Edgar, you can't complain, not the way they baby you. Susana and Enrique started chatting about the things people of a certain age need to do to stay healthy.

Mendieta considered the matter of Australian redheads and it seemed ridiculous, how could that guy, whose name he did not recall, be so organised as to kidnap Jason just to give me a heart attack. He's in the butt end of the world, it's just not logical. But criminals don't think logically, especially crazy ones like kidnappers. Could that bastard have come all the way to Los Angeles with a redhead to lay a trap for my son? How did he know Jason was interested in the mystery of redheads? I've got to talk to the Flea, I want to know more about the future Leopoldo Gámez predicted for him. Could the girl have dyed her hair? no, I don't think so, Jason would have to be pretty stupid to want to discover a mystery on the wrong body. It's true, there must be something in their faces and the ones who dye their hair don't have it; I've never met a redhead. Fucking Jason, what the hell were you looking for, my son? women are all the same. The telephone brought him back.

It's the man with the report. Yes. Señor Mendieta, we have something else on the card, do you remember the message? "All your debts are coming due, you decrepit old bastard." That's right, I mentioned that it was written in acrylic ink, with a German art pen; according to the technician, it's one that's very popular in the United States. Lefty tried hard to control his thoughts, which were already heading down dark alleyways: Easy now, listen first. And the most interesting bit is that the T in "debts" is thicker than the rest, and so are the E in "are", the C in "decrepit" and the A in "bastard"; the expert thinks it might be a code, do you follow me? Absolutely, thank you; so is there some city in the United States you or the technician think it refers to? None comes to mind. A good investigator always distrusts such findings, coincidences like that tend to make the smartest guys look ridiculous; so Lefty took it without much excitement, his feet feeling like lead; T, E, C and A could be a brand of beer, but also a place, and Jason might be there. Good on Jason to send a message. What news? Susana upset, and Enrique biting his nails. Jason might be in Tecate. He did not want to feel rushed, he would let the machinery that sees all comb through that city, where he had never been; good thing Max didn't call, that will help me burn my bridges, fucking narcos, they make me sick.

It was 9.30 according to the cellphone, in half an hour he would agree to Win Morrison's deal and they could follow up on that lead. He saw Jeter and two agents, one in a suit, the other dressed like a cowboy, occupy the booth by the entrance. Are those your buddies? The white one looks like a kid. No way they could hide the fact they're the fuzz. They're from the F.B.I. Are they really your friends? And the other sure ain't a scientist. They're more like business partners, and if you want to know, in a few minutes we'll reach an agreement to find Jason. That's great, they're on top of everything. So it seems; Susana, would you call Chuck Beck for me?

Señor Mendieta, where have you been, we have to take the finger to the lab, they've promised to have the results in a week. Don't worry about that, Chuck, it doesn't matter anymore. Did my friend turn up? Not yet, put my mind at ease: do you know if Jason knows anyone who studies painting or has a place for painting? Not that I know of, we hang around with a bunch of partiers, none of them studies art or anything like that; most of us are going to be detectives, F.B.I. agents, or spies in Europe, we all like action. Do you know if he has friends in Tecate? Sorry, but isn't that a brand of beer? It's also a city near Tijuana. Oh, I don't think so, he never mentioned it or travelled there that I know about. Any girlfriends who are painters? Nope. Is Cindy there? No, would you like me to find her? Yes, I would appreciate that, tell her to call us. How is my big piece behaving? Couldn't be better, thank you for entrusting it to me. He hung up, the Beretta was in his hotel room. Over his T-shirt he had on a thin black sweater, which Susana had brought him to wear in jail, but they would not let her bring it in.

The telephone. From Mexico, she whispered.

Fucking Max, why does he call me if I don't need him? He thought about not answering, no, he wanted to lay everything on the table, after all, they had risen to the occasion, but suppose it's the gambler? He put himself on high alert. Fucking Edith, didn't you turn out to be a bitch. At their booth, the F.B.I. agents were watching and drinking coffee.

Mendieta here. Lefty Mendieta, what a pleasure to hear your voice, how is it going? He was listening to the friendly and animated voice of no less than the head of the Pacific Cartel. Samantha, he stumbled a bit, how goes the recovery? Bit by bit, it's slower than I'd like, but I'm getting along, for the first time I'm sitting up in a chair without getting dizzy. So you can go the bathroom now? Don't talk to me about that ordeal, it'll be the first thing I do after this call. Did Max tell you about Agent Morrison? We know who she is, she's a hardliner, no-one has been able to make her ease off, and she's obsessed with me. Mendieta again felt his mind churning, not knowing which way to go, and since he was about to meet with Morrison he decided to give it to her straight. If I tell them where they can find you, they'll help me find my son. Yes, and they'll also give you some shiny coloured beads; I hate to have to tell you this so directly, especially now that I know you a bit more, but don't be an idiot, Lefty Mendieta, do you really think they're going to keep their end of the bargain? the United States is a paradise for us and I don't need to tell you why; besides you don't even know where I am or where I'll be next week; we've stuck by you because I owe you a lot, but if that woman convinces you to turn your back on me you're going to be worth shit, is that clear? You sound like your old self. Now tell me if you are going to stay with us, or if you're going to act like those fucking politicians who spend every day raffling off another part of the country for peanuts, what worthless bums, how I would love to do away with them; take your stand now, Lefty Mendieta, either you're with God or with the Devil. They sent me a finger. And it's your son's, I know. And soon they're going to send me an ear. O.K., if you think those hypocrites are more faithful to you than we are, go right ahead; and I have to tell you one more thing before letting you go: although it might not seem that way, nobody is obliged to stay with us; tell that fucking hag I'll have coffee with her if she can catch me, and I'll be here waiting for her if she has the balls to come and find me. Lefty's mind was still spinning, new doubts accosted him, and he had to acknowledge he was facing a hard reality, a long straightaway that had nothing to do with coincidences or ideals. I'm fucked, he thought, what the hell should I do? should I go with the gringos, or is it better to stick with the devil I know than the angel I might meet? He realised his instincts felt more comfortable with the devil he knew and he decided to chance it: Would you have coffee with me? There was a long pause before Samantha Valdés responded. Are you sure? you know how I hate dealing with scaredy-cats. How about when I get back to Culiacán? It's a date, Lefty Mendieta, and if you want to know, I'm lying down again, I'm exhausted and the way things look we'll just be drinking fucking water. You should take better care of yourself, now put Max on, please. You are a bastard.

How's it going with Gordowsky? So far, he hasn't forgotten

a thing, Max, I have to go to Tecate and I'd like to request some support. Hyena Wong went last night to Mexicali, I'll send him to you. Not a bad idea, but that's not all I need, could you get me a video of the people who've crossed the border at Tijuana and Tecate over the last ten days? Enter Mexico by way of Tijuana, take the Otay crossing, then look for the first Oxxo store you see, a buddy will be waiting there with the videos. Thank you, Max. Good luck.

Susana, could you lend me your telephone? Of course, I've got another right here; and it's the first in your contacts if you need to reach me. Got it, now please call the Flea for me, is there any place nearby where I might meet up with him? The Last Bookstore is a ten-minute walk away. The man answered. What's up, Flea buddy, how are you? Lefty, where the fuck have you been hiding, you bastard? you changed hotels and you never told me. Demi Moore insisted we keep everything private. You should have told me, I'd have brought Pamela along and we could have made it a foursome. Listen, near the Hotel Biltmore Millennium, there's a bookstore, The Last Bookstore, let's meet there in half an hour, can you? Give me the address, we're not out in the countryside. Fifth, close to the corner of Spring, downtown. No need to say more. The detective realised it was ten o'clock. Enrique and Susana, I need you to take Cindy Ford to Tijuana, go through Otay, pull in at the first Oxxo you see and, if I'm not there, wait for me; ask Chuck how to find her. Enrique took down Chuck's number and the Flea's. These guys got you out of the clink? he pointed towards the entrance. That's right, now I'm going to meet their boss about Jason. Mendieta turned towards the agents, who got to their feet.

From the ceiling speakers, "Jumping at the Woodside" by Count Basie and his orchestra.

Forty-One

Win was drinking tea in Sai Sai at the very same table. Mendieta took a seat, tried to clear his mind, but it was useless. Two people were having breakfast. A black folder lay next to the small pot of tea. Would you like some, Señor Mendieta? although you've already told me you prefer coffee. Thank you, Win, do they make a good cup of tea here? There are a couple of better places, but this one suits me fine. They gave each other the eye and didn't try to hide it. So, have you thought about it? First, I love your sense of time, it has been twenty-two hours since you laid down your ultimatum. Time demands coherence, Señor Mendieta, and in this profession coherence is fundamental, or do you actually believe in coincidences? She poured, Lefty observed Jeter having a few words with a homeless man outside the restaurant. What is the plan to rescue my son? You have to tell me first if you will collaborate with us, we've shown you we are not indifferent to your problems. I'll promise to work with you to rescue my son and get you nearer to Samantha Valdés, the rest is none of my business. We are an institution and it will be the institution's specialists, not Win Morrison, who will search for your son. A short pause. Where is Samantha Valdés? No idea, as soon as we find my son and I get back to Culiacán I'll set about finding her, she'll be delighted to see you. I need some guarantee you won't try to game me. Like what? You have an American brother, suppose he stays with us until you tell us where Valdés is? You mean he'd be arrested? You might interpret it that way. Excellent idea, but first let's rescue my son. Win looked at him as if she were in love. Mendieta held her gaze without blinking. Fucking dame, you can see what a bitch she is, just like the redhead; good thing they aren't on the same team, together they could destroy the world before you could say Amen. Can I accompany your people? You'll stay in the hotel, we'll let you know of any news; just to be sure, Win opened the folder and pushed a few postcard-sized photographs towards him. Jason, impossible to deny it was his son. Lefty looked at the pictures and knew he was about to break, he looked up at the ceiling until he recovered his composure. Fuck their fucking mothers.

Jeter came in. Señor Mendieta, I will be your contact, try not to leave the hotel. It doesn't seem right that you want to keep me out of this, he's my son and I'm a policeman, he gave Win a pleading look. It's better for you to stay in your room, trust us, the woman got to her feet, she had not gained a gram since he first met her, she placed a five-dollar bill on the table for her tea, picked up the folder, and said goodbye. Jeter followed her, dodging the passers-by immersed in their own lives. The detective, looking crestfallen, watched them get into a car and drive off. He walked slowly back to the hotel lobby, went up to his room to get the Beretta, came down. Then, moving quickly in case they had put a tail on him, he went directly to the Grand Avenue exit and slipped out. What would Dr Parra make of all this if I told him the story? For sure, he'd say I was totally recovered, the fucking nut. Fucking Crazy Mouse, if those bastards hadn't put the screws on you they wouldn't have found me. This had better work out.

Where are we headed, my man Lefty? They hid the pistol in a special compartment inside the driver's seat. They were on Figueroa Avenue. Feast your eyes on those babes, two young women in miniskirts were walking provocatively down the sidewalk; sheesh, and me I can't get it up. Take it easy, fucking Flea, nobody wants to hear about your sorrows; if you can make it with Pamela, why wouldn't you be able to do it with either of those two? and to answer your question, we're going to Tijuana, do you know how to go by way of Otay? It's my favourite route. Tell me again what Leopoldo Gámez told you. You're funny, fucking Lefty, you seize on every little thing that might hint at what's up with your kid. My balls insist, you'd do the same; listen, your son Marco is just like you, there was trouble at my house and he lent me money from what you left him. Nothing unusual in the fact that our kids resemble us, my man Lefty. And like in the

Joan Manuel Serrat song, that's the first thing that gratifies us. Indeedy, too bad it happens only a few times. It's a good thing, maybe life will turn out better for them than it did for us. They took the San Bernardino Freeway to Interstate 10, and then the 5 that goes right down to San Diego.

They were passing the exit for Laguna Beach when the telephone rang. Yes. Hello, hello, boss? how are you? Agent Toledo, what a pleasure to hear from you, how's it all going? Really well, we got back yesterday and I reported in today, Angelita told me all about the fortune-teller's case and what happened at the Virgen Purísima, what are you doing in Los Angeles? because no-one has been able to tell me, not even Trudis, and she always knows everything, she was the one who gave me Señora Susana's number. He could not lie to her. Jason's been kidnapped, do you remember him? Of course, your good-looking clone, made any progress? Not much, we're still empty-handed. Are they asking for a lot of money? They don't want money, it's someone who's taking revenge on me for something I did. Oooh, yikes, do you want me to help? you know I wouldn't mind leaving Rodo on his own for a few days, I've made a deal with him, and the Commander's no problem because I'm still on leave this week, remember? you signed my letter. Are you at Headquarters? Yup, I don't know how to hang around the house, besides I don't want Rodo to get used to me being there, he might forget his promise to let me keep working with you even when I'm pregnant. Like in "Fargo". I haven't seen the damned movie, but as far as the promise is concerned I figure it's still on. Did Angelita tell you I was thrown off the Force? Yes, and also that the Commander gave her and Trudis instructions that as soon as you turn up he wants to have coffee with you at the Miró. That made Lefty happy and he had an idea: Would you like to give me a hand? That's why I'm calling. Look into the relatives of the last few cases we've worked on and give me a detailed report on their sons, daughters, wives, how they look – beauty, hair colour, skin colour, social class, where they live – and send it as soon as you can to this number. That's my boss; what are we looking for? Young red-headed women. I'll get right to it; if people here want to call you, what should I say? Nothing, tell them you don't know. O.K.

Two hours later they crossed the border.

Lefty, you know where your pistol is, I'm saying in case you need it. Let's hope not. They parked at the Oxxo next to a black pickup with tinted windows. As Mendieta got out, so did Hyena Wong from that very truck, as if synchronised. You're right on time, Cat, Max and La Jefa send you greetings. Thank you, the hitman handed him a black envelope. In case they didn't tell you, my orders are to accompany you wherever you go, all the way to hell itself. Are you alone? In those Toyotas I brought along a few apostles, he pointed to two smoke-grey pickups parked up the street and to eleven men puffing on cigarettes nearby. Plus my driver, young Long.

The Flea Daut is with me, did Max tell you about him? Yes, I'm all up to date and don't you worry. Mendieta nodded, I've got to watch this video. If you like, this rattletrap has a player. Let's wait a bit, somebody's coming and I want her to see it. Whatever you say, Cat. Twelve minutes later Enrique's S.U.V. pulled in with Susana at the wheel, she parked next to the Flea. With her were Cindy Ford and Chuck Beck. Those three are part of the team, they need to watch the video too. Susana and Cindy walked up. Buenas tardes, Enrique decided to wait for us on the other side, he'll explain why. Young Long was watching, as was the Flea, who had recognised him. Mendieta made the introductions.

The quality of the video was awful, but you could see the profile of the redhead clear as could be. Lovely. No good view of Jason, who was in the passenger seat and you could not tell if he was distraught. That's her, Cindy declared. Can you freeze the image? The girl pressed a few buttons and stopped it on the face of the young woman. You're the one who saw her, do you think her hair is dyed? It was real, a lot of redheads have freckles, but from where I was standing I didn't see any. He stared at the screen for a few minutes and the only thing he knew for sure was that Jason had very good taste. Fucking kid, I've got to find him before they cut off his ears. Susana peeked in and contemplated the image. That girl is no gringa. No? No way, I'd swear she's from Sinaloa, I know that attitude, that self-assurance, the way she's flaunting her good looks; she knows she'd hold up traffic. Mendieta, now with one mystery less, looked again. I'm worth shit.

Wong, have you got people in Tecate? That's our territory. Let's go there, it might be where they're holding my son. Susana let him know she was not about to be left behind and she promised not to get in the way. At that moment a message came in from Zelda with a long text that Lefty read, but it didn't ring any bells; all of the recent cases had relatives of both sexes, all ages, and a variety of hair colours, including ten redheads, seven female and three male. He didn't think it was worth much and he handed it to Cindy so she could study it on the way. A call came in from Jeter, which he ignored.

Forty minutes later, in a caravan that would make your hair stand on end, they drove into Tecate, a city famous for its beer and for the people who drink it.

This town brings back memories, my man Lefty; when we first slipped out of Culichi, we spent a few months here until they could get us across to the other side; a shitload of folks from Sinaloa live here and they're all tough bastards. Do you know any of the bros? Not really, it's been years since I was here, but if you like I'll look them up, it'd be easier to find those guzzlers in the cantinas than in their neighbourhoods. Well, you tell us where to start.

Meanwhile, in her office in Los Angeles, Win Morrison picked up the telephone and listened to a long, loud smooch.

Forty-Two

After making their way through six bars without success, Mendieta pulled the Flea and Hyena Wong aside. O.K., I'm looking for the red-headed babe in the video, which Flea didn't see, or maybe a dude, regular height, athletic, and a martial arts master; I'm not sure about the dude, but for the moment better not to eliminate him from the picture; first I want to find the babe, she's the one who brought Jason from Los Angeles, so let's focus on her; they sent me a message in my son's handwriting where he gave us the clue that they're holding him here in Tecate; according to the expert it was written in an acrylic ink that artists use, I think people also paint their fingernails with it; so we've got at least two possibilities: that the babe or the dude, or one of the kidnappers if it's more than one, took along some artwork to fend off boredom while keeping an eye on the prisoner – by the way, they haven't even talked about money, just revenge for something I did to someone, I have no idea who; the other possibility is they're holding him somewhere where people paint. The detective paused, looked at his interlocutors. Well, no kidding, that's a bitch, it means nothing to me, Daut mumbled. Among the bros you knew, did any of them make art? they might be friends. Forget it, all my buddies were lushes. What about you, Wong? Well, I never heard of anyone like that, the bros I know are in the same line of work as me, and the less anybody knows about them the better. Which means you have no idea where they hang out. That's it, Cat buddy. Right, I remember when everybody started calling you that. He was famous, this badge, nobody could explain how he managed to come out alive when his car got blown to bits. The fact is he's tougher than he is pretty. My son might lose an ear or maybe both, that is if they haven't already cut them off, so start remembering, please. They grew quiet; to give the silence some fragrance, they lit up. Let's find an art store. Here? no, I don't think there is anything like that, you can see what kind of town this is. Still, let's do it. I'll send two dudes out to see if there is one and we'll drop in.

Do either of you know anyone in Tijuana? Hyena shook his head. The Flea piped up: I once had a buddy there, we called him Shakes, but they took him down, cut the poor bastard's balls off, really ugly. The detective gave his friend a look that said he did not find that at all funny. The guy used to buy paintings. What kind, the landscapes they sell in the street, or something else? What would I know, but he spent a load of dough on it; Lefty, if I remember right, your squeeze knows the detective who investigated the case of the Shakes, it was a woman. No shit. I'm telling you because asking won't cost a thing. No coincidences, please; nevertheless, he beckoned Susana over.

I'm really not sure, I've got a neighbour who teaches at U.C.L.A., she was a customer at my taco place; one night she brought along one of her girlfriends, who turned out to be the detective in San Diego who solved the case of a guy who got castrated; that's the sort of thing you don't forget. Once when I brought you tortillas you told me about that woman; of course, I didn't tell you the dead guy was my buddy. Does she live in Tijuana? My neighbour said San Diego, do you want me to call her? because I've got her number. The detective's? No, my neighbour's of course, what are you thinking? Tell me Susana, is it true you closed your hole-in-the-wall because of my tortillas? No, who told you that? Call her, please, Lefty intervened, giving the Flea a pinch.

She went to the S.U.V. for her telephone and called. The sun glinted off her shades.

Her name is Madame Garza, her office is in La Jolla and here are her numbers. Mendieta dialled. Madame Garza? Can you explain the decibels of this May sun? that's what's setting the country on fire, all the grass is burning and it's a disaster. Lefty was startled, but after a few seconds he recovered. Madame Garza, I was told that you are the dancer who invented reguetón and that lately you have been wearing a hat. Señor, in May the cordilleras change their names. I am Detective Edgar Mendieta, from Sinaloa. Oh, Sinaloa, a true ship of dreams with no national anthem. I want to hear about the boyfriend you have in Tecate. Tell me, colleague, what can I do for you? Again Mendieta was knocked off balance, but he reacted in time. Thank you, Madame Garza, I'm in Tecate on a case. Was he castrated? that's my specialty. Kidnapped, and he wrote a message in acrylic ink and I can't stop thinking that either the kidnappers are artists or they have him someplace where there's paint. Picasso used to kidnap women and Modigliani would set them free; I've seen little jars of acrylic ink, artists use them as missiles when the ink's used up. I was told your castrated victim used to buy paintings. He was no collector, but yes he did. Are there painters in Tecate? About fifteen hundred. Give me the name of one, please. Kidnappers often mutilate their victims as a matter of course, has yours been castrated? Jesus, I hope not, all they've sent us so far is a finger. That's a form of castration! you'll need reinforcements. Stupendous, while we wait for them, how about giving me the name of a painter in Tecate. Look up Álvaro Blancarte, he loves the colour grey and he conjures up an intimate and turbulent universe; Heriberto Yépez once said he's an artist who knows how to see himself in his own shadow; Álvaro turns his hallucinations into symbols of human association, he knows everybody. Do you know his address? Once upon a time I was near there, but my body lost its waterline and everything turned to scum, like an ejaculation before orgasm. Thank you, colleague. His companions, who sensed something was up, were on edge. Let's go find Blancarte, Detective Garza doesn't know his address or she didn't want to give it to me, the name was all she let on. I think I knew that bro, Hyena said, if I'm not remembering wrong, he's a Culichi; sure, he was a badass. Madame Garza says he's a painter. I don't believe it, let's ask, maybe he's a gymnast or he teaches fencing. They must know him in one of the cantinas. The boys who went to look for an art store were back. The only place they sell art stuff is at the community centre, three blocks down on the right.

While they drove towards the spot, Mendieta could not stop thinking about his aversion to coincidences; they count insofar as they cheer you up and give you the sensation that you're onto something, but that's all.

The cellphone rang. It was Zelda. What did you find? In a minute I'll send it all in a text: that guy who got Gori down, remember him? he's in Australia, Robles told me you asked about him, I managed to reach him, he's married and he's got an auto parts store in Adelaide, he said he owes you, if you ever go there, he'll take you out to eat because we were crucial in helping him realise he was leading a life of crap. You don't say, we rehabilitated someone? So it seems. No-one will believe it, what else? The text will spell it all out, if you need me to dig deeper on any of them I'm sending along my cellphone number. Thank you, Zelda, you're amazing, you know how to be indispensable.

Look for him at his studio, he calls it the Snatch. A young man explained how to get to Colonia Aldrete. Cat, just to reassure you, these bastards who are with us, wherever they put their eyes they put their bullets, you won't need to ask for reinforcements like badges usually do, but if things get busy a few of our hawks could reach us in twelve minutes, according to the directions they gave us at the community centre. Don't say another word, just tell them that a dead son is only good for crying over. Off they went.

The Snatch was a squat one-storey building, painted blue with a white door, nothing unusual about it. No-one around, only a minivan parked in the street. The gunslingers took up positions behind their vehicles. Lefty, the Hyena and the Flea, guns in hand, walked up to the door. Susana got out of the S.U.V. and took cover behind it, Cindy and Chuck mixed in with Wong's men. Young Long, who couldn't take his eyes off the girl, whispered to her: I'll take you out for supper, wherever you like. Cindy turned to him and smiled: how about next Friday at eight in Short Order, 6333 West Third Street. In San Diego? In Los Angeles. I'll see you there. They sealed the deal with a smile.

Lefty knocked. A tall individual with a Van Dyke beard opened the door. Blancarte? Buddy, he yelled over his shoulder, somebody's here for you. Right then the Flea put the barrel on him and clarified: If you move an inch, I'll fuck you. The guy raised his hands and nodded. They stepped inside.

Two men were at a table, where there was beer, wine and some food, plus two unfinished paintings. Nobody moves, sons of fucking bitches, and keep your hands where we can see them. They obeyed, putting their hands on their chests. Which one is Blancarte? Six of Wong's hitmen spread out among the easels and large work tables of the studio, which was lined with shelves crammed with jars of paint. I'm not play-acting, assholes, anything I don't like and I'll send you all to fucking hell. Blancarte, schooled in the barrios of Culiacán, where he was known as Blackie, and later a graduate of Tijuana's slums, was not about to be unnerved by any old thing; he recognised the Culichi accent and answered: I'm Blancarte, born in Culiacán, this is Rommel and that fellow is Dr Adame, tell us what we can do for you. He looked to be enjoying eternal youth, broad back, thick moustache, a glass of wine in his right hand. Mendieta put a pistol to his forehead: Since when are you a kidnapper, you fucking son-ofabitch? The older man remained calm. I'm a painter, never in my life have I kidnapped anyone. Rommel, who had turned yellow, dropped his glass of beer, Hyena moved a step closer and took aim at him. One of your accomplices lured my son, don't act like a limp dick, you fucking bag of bones. Blancarte breathed deeply. Don't insult me, if you are a Culichi as you seem to be, let's settle this like men, I'm no kidnapper and neither are my friends. I live in Mexicali and I've seen you, Rommel mumbled, pointing to Hyena, at the Qiu Xiaolong

293

restaurant. What, is the redhead your girl? Uh-uh, I don't know any redhead, I'm just back from two months in Medellín, Colombia, where I was teaching painting. Mendieta knew there was no reason they should know about her, that he was falsely accusing them because that was how the police work. Stick in the needle to pull out the thread, his mother used to say. I know one, Dr Adame said. Like robots they all turned towards him. Where is she? She was here at the Snatch, but it looks like she took off, she said she was going to stay a few days with a friend; we came in a little while ago and she wasn't here; pal, he turned to Blancarte, I was going to tell you I lent the place to a young woman, one of my patients. They stayed here? Well, yeah, at least I found pizza rinds and empty soft drink cans in the bedroom. Where does she live? In Los Angeles, but she's Mexican. Wong, let's take him out so he can see the video. Can we lower our hands and have a drink to calm our nerves? asked Blancarte. Mendieta agreed. Thank you, homeboy, you have one too. Later.

Adame confirmed she was the girl, that her name was Francelia, and she was studying fashion design in Los Angeles. He didn't remember her last name.

You lent her this place? She's really high-strung, I like her, she mentioned she was coming with a friend and since Blancarte wasn't around . . . Did you meet the friend? No, I just gave her the keys, which by the way she hasn't returned. Was it just one friend? That I didn't find out, when she came to me she was alone, she asked if I could find her a place where they would be comfortable. When was that? Maybe ten days ago. When did they come here? No idea. Then tell me when they left. Truthfully, I don't know. Where do you have her address? At the office. Susana, who had come over to the group, wrung her hands nervously. Any news, Edgar? It looks like they were here; Flea, go with the doctor for the address and her last name, then both of you come right back. Cindy, check the names they sent me from Culiacán in the last text, he handed her the telephone, look for a Francelia; Chuck, come with me.

They went back inside Blancarte's studio, straight to the small bedroom where they found a cot, the remains of fast food, empty cans of Coca-Cola and Tecate beer. Hyena Wong remained at the door. They went over the small bathroom, the bed, the bloodstained sheet, a chair, the wastebasket where they found a pizza minus two slices, many bloody kleenexes, and a black T-shirt with the logo of the police academy, also bloodstained. Chuck behaved correctly, touching nothing and taking pictures with his telephone. Mendieta wished Ortega were there, since he's the one with a clinical eye at a crime scene, catching every detail. Is this his T-shirt? Oh yeah, it's from the school uniform. I haven't seen you in one. They won't let me wear it, I'll explain later. Given how much pizza is left, maybe they found out we were closing in and took off in a hurry. Or Blancarte turned up. Mendieta asked the

295

painter if he lived in the neighbourhood. Twenty minutes away; I got here before my friends, by myself, that's when I remembered I'd left the keys with the doctor; so I went to his place and Rommel was there; when the doctor said he didn't have them, Rommel pulled out a set and we managed to open up. Did you knock on the door? No, but I did get out of the car and walk over, I didn't hear a thing. Was there a car outside? A blue Toyota. Who turned on the lights? They looked at each other. They were already on. Why does your friend have keys? He's been dropping into my workshop for years whenever he feels like it.

The Flea and the doctor returned, handed the detective a slip of paper with the girl's address and full name: Francelia Ugarte. That last name sounds familiar, he thought. Who is it? If she's Culichi, like Susana figures, maybe I locked up one of her relatives. Cindy found the place in Zelda's message where her parents' names were listed. Then Lefty remembered: I handed her father over to Samantha Valdés so she could get even for a big affront.* And he understood: Of course, she would hate me until her dying breath, but how did she find out I was the one who nabbed her father? How did she locate Jason? How did she know he was my son? You could tie up the whole world in a handkerchief. Now, where could she have taken him? The cellphone rang, everyone

* In the third book of the series, *Name of the Dog*

296

looked at it as if it were some strange beast, they were sure it was her. But no, it was Gordowsky. Señor Mendieta. I'm so glad you called, Lefty interrupted him, I want you to go to this address, he read it out, and find out if Francelia Ugarte lives there, she's very pretty and a redhead, she might have my son with her, she drives a blue Toyota. Understood, however, I called to tell you that I have the report you asked for on the calls to your cellphone: they were all made from Los Angeles. No shit.

Forty-Three

If the kisses they sent from my son's telephone came from Los Angeles, what does that mean? Maybe they never brought him here; but there was blood, his T-shirt, scraps of food and drink, and the lights were on when these guys arrived. Maybe they're holding him somewhere else, Jason wouldn't have lied in the message, would he? It might be a gang of kidnappers. Francelia was the one who lured Jason and the one seeking revenge; who could the others be? The voices could all be hers, or were they? They didn't seem very masculine, how old is she? Suppose both of them were kidnapped? Francelia's father is dead, maybe they called her mother? He dialled Zelda. At your service, boss. You don't need to call me boss anymore. They told me, and I hope you aren't taking that seriously, you know the moment you're ready I'll tell the Commander so you two can work it out. I'll think about it, right now do me another favour, call Francelia Ugarte's mother, Francelia's the daughter of the guy who killed Mariana Kelly, she was on the list you sent, ask her if her daughter is alright, if she's received any strange calls. I'll get right on it. The instant he hung up he heard a gunshot, everyone turned towards the door, Mendieta had the Beretta 90-Two at the ready. Repressing their own curiosity, Blancarte, Adame and Rommel stayed put and drank in silence. Lefty emerged into the sunlight. Susana, her eyes wide, had one hand over her mouth. Hyena Wong and his men stood around a body on the ground. The Flea. What happened? his eyes went to young Long and spotted him next to his boss, gun in hand, wearing a satisfied look. Daut crooked a finger at Lefty, who put his ear close. No big fart, my man Lefty, my number was up, the fortune-teller said so, but I didn't want to hear it; they fucked me, no way around it, if it had been a little later I might have escaped, maybe, the good thing is that this is Mexico; make sure I'm buried in Culichi, next to my dear old lady, where we met up that day, remember? That was all. Lefty looked around him, everyone was wearing sneakers except for Hyena, who never took off his plain leather cowboy boots.

Lefty pulled Wong aside. What's the story, didn't we agree nobody'd touch the Flea? Cat, leave this business to us, if you really want to know, it's a bitch; on the one hand the kid disobeyed an order and on the other he had the right to avenge his father's death. Let me remind you that the Flea saved the Señora's life. I know, but don't you try to tell me what to do, I'm a big boy now. In his eye a blinding gleam. What I want to get through to you is that this dude was a good buddy of mine and this hurts. Well, cry for him, Cat, that's the right thing to do, but don't mess with me. Even water is no clearer than that: Well, fuck it all, we've got to get a move on, I have no idea where they could be holding my son, it could be Tijuana, Ensenada or anyplace in California, since people live everywhere. Too bad we can't get you the video of the crossing from here to there; but if you need us, we can give you a few more hours.

He turned to face the body. Poor Flea, he even seemed happy, and I promised nothing would happen to him; I'm royally fucked, peeing outside the bowl. Susana, I've got to keep looking for Jason, do you have the number of the Flea's business? She called his family, gave them the bad news, and told them about the dead man's last wishes. They would leave him at a funeral home.

Wong, can you stick around until they pick up the body? Go ahead, Cat, no worries, that much I will do for you.

While they waited in line at the border, Susana called the hotel desk. No, ma'am, no envelopes have arrived, I'll connect you so you can find out if you've had any calls. A call came in at 11.46, but there was no message. Maybe it was from Jeter. Or from Jason. She hung up and the telephone rang at once. It was Zelda. Put Chief Mendieta on, please. What have you got? Boss, I just talked to Francelia's mother and she says her daughter is fine, they speak every day, she's studying fashion design; here, take down the daughter's number.

They got through the crossing and he called the girl. It rang for twenty seconds and cut off. They were travelling in Enrique's S.U.V. after picking him up at a Starbucks. He looked nervous, but he took Chuck's place at the wheel. Is everything alright? We're making progress, Lefty responded, and he turned to Susana: Dial again, and put it on speaker. On the third try someone picked up. Francelia Ugarte, I know where you live, who you are, and what I did to you; I'm prepared to give myself up to you and you can kill me if you like, but let my son go; I understand what you must have gone through and I'm ready to pay the price, which is what you want. A long, loud smooch. She hung up. Susana sobbed. Mendieta stiffened. Fucking bitch. Do you know who you're up against? Enrique wanted to know. A nutcase. God, my poor nephew.

Fifty-eight minutes later the telephone rang. It was Win Morrison.

Señor Mendieta, where are you hiding? In the butt end of the world, Win, what's up? Didn't I ask you not to leave the hotel? where are you? Oh, I went out to buy chocolates and I found some T-shirts that will make you die of natural causes. Well, we have your son, we rescued him, we're talking to him now, and we'll drop him off at the hotel in an hour and a half. I want to speak to the kidnappers. After they talk to us they'll be at your disposal; there are two of them, a support man and the red-headed girl.

They had to wait a few minutes at the hotel entrance before a grey car pulled up and Jeter got out. He opened the back door and there was Jason: drawn, dirty, thinner, and with one finger freshly bandaged. The first thing Mendieta noticed was his eyes, a dark probing look. He was transformed, nothing was left of the dreamy, bewildered boy. They embraced. How are you, my son? Jason tried to act unperturbed: Thank you, Papa, but then he hugged Susana and broke down and sobbed. Enrique also shed a few tears. Fucking nephew. Cindy kissed his chapped lips and Chuck Beck patted him on the back. To his mother's three suggestions he answered yes: eat, shower and rest. Mendieta let him know he was going to interrogate the kidnappers and asked if he could give him any advice. Kidnappers? it was just her, if there were others, I never saw them. She mutilated you herself? He nodded: She's a bitch, and did she ever trick me ugly. You'll have to fill me in on the mystery of redheads. You think I found out? actually, yeah, I guess I did, no way around it.

Jeter was waiting. Mendieta asked him to give him half an hour with his son. The señora is impatient. Call her, tell her I masturbate too, O.K.?

In the hotel room, Susana ordered food for everyone. Lefty returned Beck's gun. It's a marvel, take good care of it; the young man smiled, then Lefty took Jason into the bathroom to hear everything.

I met her at the gym, I told you I was going to compete again, remember? A redhead doing calisthenics, everybody was looking at her. She came over to me and since she was so pretty I asked her out. It wasn't like she put a spell on me, usually I don't pay much attention to girls, but this one had something special, more than a great body and that flaming hair, I don't know. She didn't give in on the first date or the second; in fact, we only had sex when she kidnapped me, if you could call it that. She picked me up at school, I suppose Mama took the Camaro home, we bought hamburgers and went straight to Tecate; at first I thought it was strange, but I didn't ask, all I was thinking was that I was going to eat her alive and I could do that anywhere between here and hell. I never suspected she was kidnapping me, what she proposed was a day or two away from home, but my plan was to return right away, that night, that's why I never told Mama, she's really protective and she asks questions I don't feel like answering, you know: who are you going out with? what time will you be back? where are you going? She told me she had the ideal spot in Tecate; when we got there, she had the keys to that studio and in we went. I never found out how she managed to get the place, there were a lot of art supplies around, when she insisted I write the note she gave me a really fine art pen, I'm so glad you understood my message. What we were doing seemed pretty crazy, she tied up my feet and hands, she said it was to make the sex more intense, and then she told me I was kidnapped, that my father was the worst policeman there ever was in Mexico, that you arrested her father, a man about to die from cancer, and you turned him over to Samantha Valdés, who shot him without an ounce of pity. She was outside his house when you nabbed him and she watched and saw Samantha arrive; she also wants to take revenge on her. When she told me all that I thought she was playing a game, that she gets off on hyped-up emotions and felt like making up a story. Then she slapped me so hard it brought tears to my eyes, her face scared me to death, all distorted by rage, and that's when I understood she was serious, that she'd laid a trap for me. In my life I never felt so stupid. I admit it, what you say is true: a pair of tits pulls more than an ox, but it was unbelievable to live through it like that. Then she told me she wanted to do you in and that if you didn't die, the corpse would be me. Yeah, I was listening the first time she called you from my cellphone, the loud kisses she sent you, she did the same thing to Mama. After the third day she would leave me alone, sometimes for as long as five hours; she'd go out for food, I don't want to eat another pizza for the rest of my life. I tried, but the way she'd tied me I couldn't break free. She never threatened to cut off my ear. I never thought she would cut off my finger, I thought that was just bravado, but nope, she didn't hesitate. She used a hunting knife, then she put something on it to stop the bleeding, though I still bled all over the place. Yesterday she told me that today she'd set me free; I didn't believe her because the day before she was talking about killing me. I asked her if she'd got her revenge and she said it was on the way, that you were going to pay for all the harm you caused by handing over her father. She told me you were in Los Angeles, she even knew the name of this hotel. Since she took so long to come back yesterday, I thought she'd done something to you, you never spotted her prowling around? Maybe she had an accomplice here. Today we left the Snatch about one o'clock. I didn't hear her telephone ring, wait, now that you mention it, she left the room where she had me tied up and when she came back she said we were leaving, that any minute they would kill you and the same thing was going to happen to me, but someplace else; that's what she said, as if there were several of them, but like I say I never saw anyone else. We crossed the border without any problem; when we got near Los Angeles two grey cars forced her off the freeway, they took her out, handcuffed her, and put her in one car and me in the other; they were from the F.B.I. I didn't see her again, they cut off the bindings, took me to a clinic where they cleaned the wound, and gave me a tetanus shot, then Agent Morrison interrogated me, you know her. It was about a forty-minute conversation. Yes, it was just her, I never saw anybody else, but for sure, somebody must have warned her about your whereabouts before and after you went to Tecate.

You're going to be a good policeman. Not any better than you, Papa, and forgive me for summing it all up so quickly, the truth is I'm really sorry and I feel like a complete idiot. They hugged. How was the interrogation with Morrison? She wanted to know the same stuff and I told her, she seemed pretty easygoing, maybe because she knows you and she knew I was in a hurry to see you and Mama. Well, there is no trouble that doesn't blow over in the end, so try to relax; I'll see you in a little while, we're going to stay here. I'm going to take a shower, then eat something and rest. And it will be rest well deserved; listen, that idea of taking up running again is a good one; but see a doctor first and follow his advice.

Trudis called you, and so did the man with the reports and Agent Jeter, who has been waiting for you in the lobby for ten minutes, would you like to try this steak? it's fabulous. Come on, you spoiled brat, eat a little. Later, dial Trudis for me. Lefty, how are you? Fucked but happy, Jason sends you a hug. Tell him I send him a thousand; listen, a señora came by here to bring you a painting, she said it was a Picasso and that you would know why; whoa, is she ever ugly, don't tell me you've got something going with her, besides if she wants to set things right with you she sure picked a lousy way, what a tiny little painting she brought you, I could hide it in my crotch. If she turns up again give it back to her, and she has nothing to do with me, she's a friend of Zelda's; you know what? don't give it back to her, donate it to the zoo, tell them it's authentic and they should sell it to feed the animals; I'll call back soon. He hung up. Susana hugged him and looked into his eyes. Edgar. Pause. I'm serious, I'd like us to think about getting together. Lefty felt the colour drain from his face. Are you sure? Absolutely sure, they kissed fervently. He could call Gordowsky later.

The agent was waiting next to the elevator, in his usual attire.

Thank you, Jeter, I owe you a hamburger. It will be a pleasure to share a meal with you again, Señor Mendieta, only I hope this time it won't be so late at night, shall we go?

On West Fifth, a few metres from the hotel entrance, a grey car was waiting. All these shows of attention were making him nervous, what should he do? Should he turn on Samantha Valdés after she provided him with so much support and after he swore to stand by her? It was a fucking bind, could he really be that two-faced? Maybe not, but your face changes with age and betrayal pops up everywhere, even in horoscopes, and after that happens everything's worth shit; people who say revenge is best served cold must be cousins of Al Capone. Well, I'd better focus on the kidnappers, especially the redhead, who was so angry she fucked up my son and wanted to pickle me. Fucking broad, is she ever sick. Her father was a murderer and besides, I didn't kill him, all I did was find him and hand him over. It was Samantha who whacked him, they were old friends and there was some sort of bad blood between them. Parked behind the grey car was a black sedan with a driver, and they headed towards it. You'll travel in this one, the agent said. What about you? In that one, pointing at the other. Seven steps more and the door opened. Morrison was inside. Mendieta sat beside her, the car pulled out, all he could see of the driver was the brim of a grey hat. Thank you, Win, his mother is very grateful and wants to know where to send you a present. That won't be necessary, why are you Mexicans always giving gifts? all we did was do our duty. In Mexico, if you don't give gifts you don't exist; and we also like to receive them. I suppose so. Win, I know I've got a deal with you, but after interrogating the kidnappers I'd like to spend a few days with my son, I want to help him get over this, I don't want him to make a mess of his life. We'll take charge of your son, Señor Mendieta, we'll set him up with a psychiatrist or whatever he needs, you're going straight back to your country. How's that? Yes, on the night flight to Mexico City. We had agreed I would interrogate the kidnappers, I thought we were going to where you're holding them. That won't be necessary, we'll send you a report. It is so necessary, they went after my son to take revenge on me, they were very explicit on the calls and then they sent me loud kisses; of course I need to know who they are, what they're about, and who I have to watch out for in the future, my family too. I'm sorry, Señor

Mendieta, but you will go straight to the airport to take your flight to Mexico City and from there to Culiacán, Agent Jeter will accompany you. Shit on my balls, he murmured to himself, but what he said out loud was: You can't do this to me. As soon as you locate Samantha Valdés, let us know and we'll grab her, you'll be able to live in the United States if you wish, but now you have to go back to Culiacán and fulfil your end of the bargain, Jeter will tell you how to communicate with us. They looked each other in the eye. No love lost. In other words, I can't even stay to spend a couple of hours with Jason. I'm sorry. Rage coursed through his heart and flushed his face. You are a bitch, Win Morrison. None of that, Señor Mendieta, I am helping you to fulfil your end of the bargain, we did our part. You didn't even let me say goodbye to my family. Win signalled the driver, who pulled into the parking lot of a Japanese restaurant where they served the tea she liked best. Excuse me, I would invite you in, but you would miss your flight; you, get out of the car and keep watch, she ordered the driver, who turned around: it was a beautiful girl with a very tender smile. Jeter parked next to them. All four got out. At that moment the shooting started. Bullets hit bodies and cars or whistled by. Lefty threw himself to the ground, saw the driver get shot and fall flat, then he edged under the car. To his right he saw Win Morrison go down with half her head missing, he turned towards the other car and there lay Jeter's pummeled body. Shit.

Footsteps. Cowboy boots, sneakers. Twenty seconds are an eternity.

Where the driver's body lay motionless, a man kicked the chassis. Cat, come out of there, we've got to get going.

Forty-Four

Mendieta, on his feet, observed the body of the driver, who had lost her hat. She was lovely, strong, a hairnet held her coppery-red locks; he pulled it off and the long tresses fell loose and spread across the ground. No shit, he was shocked, even more than he had been by the rain of bullets that somehow missed him. This must be Francelia Ugarte, it couldn't be anybody else, what game was Win playing? Cat, get a move on, in two minutes this place will be a swarm of angry bees. A pickup drove off. Hyena, who held his A.K.-47 in full view, tugged on his arm and he let himself be pulled away after one last glance at Morrison's body, her face destroyed, a pistol in her hand. In the restaurant not even a shadow moved. They climbed into a small car and drove away utterly unhurried; at the wheel was young Long, who as it turned out had not an ounce of cowardice. Three blocks away they pulled in at a house with an enclosed parking area and got out. Next to them were two used pickups.

Gordowsky was there waiting. Get into the trucks, we're leaving right now. Wong and Long put on white chefs' outfits. Get into this, Mendieta was handed a pair of gardeners' overalls. Several sirens rang out in the distance. Let's go, Wong announced, see you later, Cat, and one truck departed in a roar. Gordowsky was wearing dirty overalls. Hurry up, Señor Mendieta, you'll be the first one they'll be looking for. The bed of the pickup was filled with gardening tools. Unnerved by the wailing police and ambulance sirens drawing near, they pulled out.

Why didn't you call me? The detective looked at his companion. Were you going to warn me about the gunfight? Of course, I was going to tell you to get down on the ground and not be surprised. I was flat on the pavement, but how could I not be surprised? this isn't Syria or anyplace like that. Well, this isn't over yet, I have to get you out of the United States lickety-split. What about my family, what's going to happen to them? Señora Susana Luján is not your wife, they'll interrogate her until they're blue in the face, they'll keep an eye on her for a few months and that'll be it; the one who might have persecuted her for years on end won't ever leave that restaurant parking lot; your son will face more or less the same treatment as his mother, he's going to be a policeman and for sure they have him down as a good prospect for the Bureau. But, not even a hug, not even chocolates? My orders are to take you to Mexico and that's what I'm going to do. He thought about Susana, he'd have to mull over her proposal about living together. They travelled on in silence until they got on Interstate 5 heading towards Palm Springs. Mendieta pondered: This could be worse than the case of the agent that got killed in Guadalajara in the '80s; I hope none of my family has problems, especially Enrique, who seems so settled in this country; was that redhead really Francelia? Gordowski, that girl who was driving, was she really the one who kidnapped my son? One and the same, she joined the F.B.I. six months ago, it seems this was her first mission; in Culiacán they'll give you all the details. The detective sat thinking. Of course, their target was Samantha; Jason and I were just the way to get to her, and even so she cut off his finger, the bitch; maybe once she learned I was the one who found her father she couldn't resist taking revenge; maybe Win told her that to inspire her. How did you find out she'd be driving and we would stop right there? Win Morrison goes to that restaurant to drink tea every day, more or less at the same time, it was unlikely she would choose some other spot, all our men had to do was wait for her; our source was Agent Jeter, with whom we have an arrangement. But he got killed. No, he's only wounded, I hope not seriously; he couldn't have got off without a scratch. I never thought the Pacific Cartel had so much power. I swear neither did I.

Dark night. On the stereo Ely Guerra singing "Júrame" with Alondra de la Parra. The detective was deep into his memories of the young Susana, and he had to admit that more than a son tied them together. What a bitch life is, you'd have to be a pretty smart fucker to figure it out.

313

*

Samantha Valdés, wearing a hospital johnny and seated comfortably, welcomed him to her mansion in Lomas de San Miguel. Mendieta thanked her and asked if the attempt on her life had been cooked up in Los Angeles. I have no idea, all I can tell you is that everyone involved paid dearly; in the United States what they want is to put me in prison, at least that was Agent Morrison's obsession, her team's too, including the redhead. Who surely died. You've got to cut the devil to pieces before he fucks with you, don't ever think the bastard is going to play by the rules; now I suppose you won't have any objection to working with us. I'd rather not take that step. Lefty was drinking whisky instead of coffee, she had not touched her glass of water. Do you want a few days to think about it? That's something I've already done, is anyone at Mariana's apartment? you know I've got to pick up the Jetta. You don't like the Volvo? It's the colour, white doesn't suit me. They smiled. I figured, is there anything I can do for you? Well, I've got a lot of questions. She looked him in the eye. You're alive, aren't you? and, though he's got a mangled finger, so is your son. The detective nodded. Why did you want to see Leopoldo Gámez? Me? where did you get that idea? she looked at him, her face a blank. Fucking women, God knows there's no beating them, aren't they all alike. They both got to their feet. Take care of yourself, Lefty Mendieta. You too.

Outside was a brand new grey Jetta with the keys in the ignition. He hesitated for four seconds, which according to confessions is the average time people hesitate before allowing themselves to be corrupted. He got in and started it up.

It was night when he finally got to his house in the Col Pop, two days after his escape from the F.B.I. Everything was clean and tidy. He poured himself a Macallan and then two more. On the table in the centre of the room was a note: "There's roast beef and tortillas on the stove, we're at the San Chelín at Ignacio's wake." He put music on the stereo: "Good Morning Starshine" by Oliver, and it was as if everything he had lived through landed square on his back. Fucking songwriter, was he ever right.

ÉLMER MENDOZA was born in Culiacán, México, in 1949. He teaches literature at Sinaloa Autonomous University and is widely regarded as the founder of "narco-lit", which explores the impact of drug trafficking in Latin America. He won the José Fuentes Mares National Literary Prize for *Janis Joplin's Lover*, and the Tusquets Prize for *Silver Bullets*.

MARK FRIED is a literary translator specialising in Latin American literature. He lives in Ottawa, Canada.

Élmer Mendoza

SILVER BULLETS

Translated from the Spanish by Mark Fried

For Detective Edgar "Lefty" Mendieta, tormented by past heartbreak and dismayed by all-pervasive corruption, the murder of lawyer Bruno Canizales represents just another day at the office in Culiacán, Mexico's capital of narco-crime.

There is no shortage of suspects in a city where it's hard to tell the gangsters from the politicians. Canizales was the son of a former government minister and the lover of a drug lord's daughter, and he nurtured a penchant for cross-dressing and edgy sex. But why did the assassin use a silver bullet? And why, six days later, did he apparently strike again?

Mendieta's hunt for the killer takes him from mansions to low-life bars, from gumshoe reporters to glamourous transsexuals. Unearthing the truth can be as dangerous as any drug.

MACLEHOSE PRESS

www.maclehosepress.com

Élmer Mendoza

THE ACID TEST

Translated from the Spanish by Mark Fried

When the mutilated body of Mayra Cabral de Melo is found in a dusty field, Detective Edgar "Lefty" Mendieta has personal reasons for bringing the culprit to justice. Mayra, a well-known stripper, had no shortage of ardent, deluded and downright dangerous admirers, and Lefty himself is haunted by the night he spent in her company.

As Mexico's drug war ramps up, Lefty's pursuit of a gallery of jealous and powerful suspects, all with a murderous glint in their eye, leads him to Samantha Valdés, the godfather's daughter, who is battling to retain her father's empire. And as the mystery deepens, the body count rises.

MACLEHOSE PRESS

www.maclehosepress.com

ALSO AVAILABLE

Élmer Mendoza

NAME OF THE DOG

Translated from the Spanish by Mark Fried

Christmas in Culiacán, and Detective Edgar "Lefty" Mendieta can't believe his luck. An old flame has returned with a teenage son he knew nothing about. Happiness seems to finally beckon for our careworn hero. The only snag is that Jason Mendieta wants to follow in his father's footsteps – even as Mexico's drug war descends a slippery slope toward chaos.

While Lefty pursues a lunatic who has taken to bumping off dentists with a heavy-calibre pistol, a secret agent infiltrates a meeting of the drug lords and hears Pacific Cartel boss Samantha Valdés implore her underlings to stay out of the war. But an audacious murder provokes Samantha to change her mind and launch a wave of grisly killings across the country.

Samantha then persuades Lefty to help her find the killer that pushed her over the edge. The truth he discovers will underline an old adage: revenge is a dish best served cold. No quiet family Christmas for our detective.

MACLEHOSE PRESS

www.maclehosepress.com